BIRTH OF A DEATH

Wally sat in the dark at the window of his room. He lit a cigarette. The flame of the lighter showed melancholy on his face.

Anne would have to go. Before she brought ruin on him, he would have to kill her. But it was a difficult assignment. She was young, healthy, and on her guard.

The moon had risen, and he could see the dark shape of the old well. If he could push Anne into it late at night and lead the search for her the next day . . . But the well had been permanently sealed, and there would be no plausible way to account for opening it.

The gun, then? He shivered. He hated the sight of blood. He couldn't face a shooting. He couldn't.

But then he had it. He knew what he must do . . .

DORIS MILES DISNEY
THAT WHICH IS CROOKED

ZEBRA BOOKS
KENSINGTON PUBLISHING CORP.

ZEBRA BOOKS

are published by

Kensington Publishing Corp.
475 Park Avenue South
New York, NY 10016

First Zebra Books printing: December, 1989

Printed in the United States of America

To Norman A. Pokorny, M.D., whose knowledge of pediatrics has carried my daughter successfully through her first four years and whose knowledge of poisons has carried me through two books.

That which is crooked
cannot be made straight:
and that which is wanting
cannot be numbered.

ECCL. 1:15

CHAPTER ONE — 1898

It was a perfect October day, warm and still and clear, with the foliage at its fullest range of color. At the depot the dust raised by the crowd started Wally Howard sneezing. His mother said, "Cover your mouth, boy," without removing her gaze from the track that wound north over the bridge and was lost from view above the Dickson pasture.

The Howards stood with the welcoming committee on the depot platform. This privileged spot was not theirs exclusively. They shared it with the families of the other three young men for whom the day had been planned.

There were seven of the Howards: the widowed Emma, her two daughters, and four of her sons. They were wearing their Sunday clothes and made a handsome group, red hair and height their outstanding characteristics. Only Emma, her married daughter Mary, and twelve-year-old Wally were small and slight and dark.

The train was late. Wally fidgeted and pulled at

9

Virginia's sleeve to attract her notice. She jerked her arm free. "Don't muss me!"

"Will Nick be different, do you think?"

Virginia, four years older than he, laughed in scorn. "Of course not, silly! He's only been gone six months."

"Still, he might be changed," Wally persisted hopefully. He wanted to find some change in his brother. The tremendous experience that Nick had undergone should leave a visible mark. It should be something to reflect credit on all of them.

Virginia did not answer.

The far-off shriek of a train whistle was heard. The crowd surged forward and the cry of "Here it comes!" burst from many throats.

Wally pressed past Virginia to stand beside their mother. Emma was not aware of him, however. She was straining forward as they all were for a first glimpse of the train as it swung around the curve. Enthusiasm swept through the crowd like a brush fire. Men roared a greeting and women wept.

Emma did not weep. Wally shot an upward glance at his mother and saw that her eyes were dry. She never gave way to any emotion easily.

He found himself remembering the only time he had seen her in tears. That was three years ago, the day his father was buried. Wally had gone into the front parlor early that morning and come upon Emma alone with her husband's body, crying bitterly. He had tiptoed out of the room; she hadn't known he was there.

Weakness invaded his legs at the memory of his

10

father's death. "Don't think of it," he commanded himself. "Not even a little bit.'

For three years he had been trying to forget the way his father died.

The train came to a stop. Beside the depot the Kinnelly fife-and-drum corps straightened its ranks. The color-bearer sprang to attention, the big new flag he bore hanging limp on its staff.

Down the steps from one of the cars came four young men in blue; the tallest of them was red-haired, grinning Nicholas Howard.

The fife-and-drum corps struck up "Hail the Conquering Hero Comes," and an obliging wisp of a breeze fluttered the flag. The train went on its way, passengers staring out the windows.

The first selectman shook hands with each of the young men in uniform. "We're proud of you, boys, very proud, and mighty glad to have you home," he said. The other members of the welcoming committee echoed the greeting and stepped back to let the young men's families hug them and kiss them. Then the parade line was formed.

It was led by the fife-and-drum corps; behind the corps marched the full complement of the G.A.R. post, the four homecoming young men of the First Connecticut Volunteers, the volunteer fire department, schoolchildren marshaled by their anxious teachers, and, finally, the carriages for the members of the welcoming committee.

This was the parade, the sum total of it.

Along Main Street it moved to "When Johnny Comes Marching Home." The sidewalks were lined with cheering spectators, the houses decorated with flags and bunting. Not since President Harrison had come to town to dedicate the Garfield oak on the green had there been such a turnout.

The Masonic Hall facing the green was the parade's objective. Here members of the Ladies Aid bustled about long trestle tables, setting out dishes of preserves and pickles, straightening napkins and silver, attending to last-minute touches to the meal. Nervously giggling and drifting about, a bevy of the town's prettiest girls waited to serve at the tables.

The crowd at the depot broke up to follow the fading sound of the music. Gradually the dust settled and the platform was once more deserted. Another war was over.

At the head table in the Masonic Hall the town officials sat with the four young men and their families. The Howards were in a row, with Wally, far down the line from his mother's eye, free to wriggle and squirm without admonishment. Even Virginia, who fancied herself as a substitute for their mother in telling Wally what to do, was two places removed from him.

The chicken was eaten and the pies were served. The rattle of crockery and silver died away as Mr. Lyman, the high-school principal, who enjoyed much local fame for his oratory, was introduced by the first selectman and got to his feet.

He cleared his throat. "Mr. Chairman, fellow members of the committee, ladies and gentlemen . . . I know you all join with me in extending to our brave young heroes a heartfelt welcome home . . ,"

Nick Howard didn't listen to a word that followed. He watched Grace Sawyer as she came from the

12

kitchen. He caught her eye and smiled, and she smiled back at him.

Mr. Lyman was fully launched. "The Spanish tyrant has been quelled," he proclaimed. "He has been taught a lesson he must never be allowed to forget. From the flower of our young manhood he has learned that the forces of freedom are greater than the yoke of foul slavery . . ."

Wally listened dreamily, letting the words roll over him and wrap him in visions of bravery. He led the attack on San Juan Hill and rode a horse more fiery than the Larcom stallion. He was Colonel Wallace Howard urging on his men, carrying them with him to glory. Far in advance of his support, he captured General Linares and saw the defense crumble under the loss of its commander. . . .

Emma Howard's thoughts were on Belle Powers, the new hired girl. Belle wasn't too bright. None of that Powers tribe was. The girl would never be able to set the biscuit to rise for supper in spite of the written instructions left for her. . . .

Emma turned her head, her eyes seeking Nicholas. He looked handsome in his uniform. His father, she remembered, had been wearing a similar one the first time she saw him. Nicholas, Sr., had been only eighteen in 1865, fighting through the last months of that earlier, bloodier war. He hadn't paid attention to her, her family new in Kinnelly, Emma herself only thirteen. But she had fallen in love with him on sight and never changed. He had not been a faithful husband; her love had glossed over many things.

Emma closed her eyes against the memory of the day that Nicholas died. It wasn't, however, one of the times when she could escape hearing the sound of Wally's screaming, the shocking, nerve-ripping screaming that wouldn't stop.

Beside her Henry whispered, "Going to sleep, Mother?" and she opened her eyes to smile and shake her head. Henry, exactly like his father, was Emma's favorite child.

The festivities did not end with the welcome-home dinner. In the evening there was a band concert on the green. The green was strung with lanterns, and away from it the street lamps were a crisscrossing necklace of lights. The outlying sections of the town had no such illumination, but farm wagons and carriages furnished them with moving globes of brightness on that deep blue October evening.

The bandstand was the focus of attention for Emma and Wally and the two daughters. The Howard young men found them seats and melted away to attend to their own concerns.

The crowd shifted and flowed into changing groups within the circle of benches that ringed the green. Its younger element isolated itself and broke up into twosomes. Darting about, small boys pursued their own games and purposes.

Wally Howard was not one of them. Seated next to his mother, he watched his contemporaries but felt no desire to mingle with them. When he had started school five years ago he had found out how rough their play was and that they didn't seem to experience the myriad fears that beset him. Only he was unmasked, the butt of ridicule. His brothers, none of his schoolmates gave thought to being hurt in a fistfight, a game of ice hockey, a football match.

14

He avoided such contests. A boy who found recreation in reading and playing with Betsy McArdle, aged ten, was safe from the broken leg Pete Farrell had sustained or from losing an eye like Sanford Blake.

So Wally remained close to his mother, whom he loved best of all, whom he tried hardest to please, and from whom he never received as much attention as he wanted.

The moon was an ice-white circle high in the sky. The earlier gentle motion of the air turned brisk and sent dry leaves skittering before it. After all, it was October, an autumn night, the season for band concerts was over, was the wind's message.

Grace Sawyer drew her jacket closer at the throat. In the covering dark Nick held her hand and let his fingers slide up under her sleeve to close around her arm.

He was walking her home from the concert. Her mother's assent had been reluctant, but today Nick Howard was a hero, one of the principals for whom the celebration had been planned. Mrs. Sawyer felt obliged to overlook the fact that before he went away to the war there had been much gossip about Nick and the kind of young women he knew.

Grace recalled bits of the gossip with a tremor of excitement. She had kept away from Nick until tonight. Tonight no girl could rebuff him, the way he looked, the way he carried off his triumphal return. But she wasn't like all the others who fell for him so easily. He should find out that not even one kiss waited for him at her door.

She had a round face and dimples. She was a charming little thing, Nick reflected, his hazel eyes taking her in from head to foot. Perhaps she didn't know how her father's orchard looked by moonlight. Tonight she'd see it with him.

He was just home from the war, wasn't he? He'd take no refusal tonight. . . .

The concert was ending. The band swung into "My Country 'Tis of Thee."

CHAPTER TWO — 1899

Even at eight o'clock in the morning the day was stifling. Alone in the kitchen, Virginia looked with distaste at the stacks of breakfast dishes piled on the sinkboard and in the sink itself. Water for washing them was coming to a boil on the range. The netting at the open window over the sink moved inward, but the air that filled it carried no refreshment.

The window faced the barn and outbuilding. Pumping cold water into the dishpan, the girl saw her brother Henry leading out big brown Nellie to hitch her to the cultivator. She looked with fresh distaste at the dishes, dried her hands, and went in search of Wally.

He was still at the partially cleared dining-room table. The shades were drawn against the heat, and Wally was reading in the dim light, eating a last piece of corn bread with *Surry of Eagle's Nest* propped open against the milk pitcher.

"Wally! Put down that book! You'll catch it from Henry. You know very well you're supposed to ride

Nellie this morning while he cultivates corn. He's got Nellie hitched up already."

Wally pushed back his chair and jumped to his feet, saying aggrievedly, "I was just going. I've got a right to finish my breakfast, haven't I?"

"Well . . ." Virginia turned mild. "I was wondering . . . you said yesterday that the sun gave you a headache. If that's the case, it crossed my mind that perhaps we could swap around. As a favor to you, Wally. You can do the dishes and help Mother and I'll ride Nellie for Henry."

Wally disliked farm work. And Henry bullied him. She saw his face brighten at the prospect of escaping a morning of his brother's society and drove a harder bargain. "But you'll have to clean the silver tea set too. Mother said it was to be done today."

He looked at the elaborately carved service on the sideboard, weighing it against the hot sun and his brother. He sighed. "All right, you go with Henry."

Virginia raced toward freedom. Tall for a girl, with shoulders whose breadth anticipated a figure ideal nearly two generations in the future, she had thick braids of red hair pinned up for the first time in this, her eighteenth summer, and a long, pale, freckled face that had, without beauty, a certain fugitive attractiveness. She paused at the door of the back kitchen to call out, "Wally and I are swapping work this morning, Mother. I'm going to ride Nellie for Henry." She was gone in a billow of swirling gingham before Emma could give or withhold consent.

Wally closed his book reluctantly. It was a story of courage and daring deeds in which he took vicar-

18

ious part. His dark eyes had an inward look as he washed and dried the dishes. Emma came in from the back kitchen and stood in the doorway. Clouds of steam from the clothes boiler on the laundry stove sent their heat into the room. She held a long stirring stick in her hands. There was some amusement in her eyes as they rested on the small, thin figure of her son.

"Well, Virginia got the best of you again, didn't she?" Emma remarked. "I suppose you didn't realize it was washday. You'll have all the beds to make and plenty of dusting too. I'm helping Belle get the clothes out."

Wally would not admit that the advantage lay with his sister. He smiled at his mother over his shoulder and said, "I don't mind. The sun's hot out there in the south lot. I'd rather be here—with you." His tone asked nothing as he voiced the preference, but his eyes hoped she would say in return that she enjoyed having him in the house with her.

What Emma did say with briskness was, "Well, get those dishes done, and when you go upstairs be sure to leave your book down here."

He made the beds; his own first, in the back room that had been cut in half two years ago to provide space for a bathroom. It was furnished with a single bed, a chiffonier that didn't match the bedstead, a straight chair, and a shelf where he kept his books. It had one window. The floor was covered with straw matting. It was the least desirable room in the house, but Wally accepted it as what he should expect. He was the youngest and his elders came first. Someday, however, when the others were married, he'd have a large corner chamber, perhaps the one across the hall from his mother, and have a desk in it, an easy chair, and many other comforts.

Barefooted, as he always was after school let out, wearing overalls and a shirt from last summer that proved his small frame had grown a trifle, since it was tight on him, Wally went last of all to his mother's room. Belle's attic quarters were no concern of his. She must find time to make her own bed or it would go unmade.

He hesitated at the door. He never wanted to enter the room. Nicholas Howard, Sr., had died here before the eyes of his youngest child. Blood had spattered about him, a torn fragment of flesh had hung from his face. The gun that killed him still lay in a drawer of the highboy. Even four years later the thought of the gun, the roar it had made going off, was enough to turn Wally sick.

He stood at the threshold and sucked in his breath. Then he marched across the floor to the bed and began to make it, keeping his eyes away from the spot near the windows where his father had fallen. It was only when Emma was here with him that her presence could exorcise to some extent the image of the towering, redheaded father.

His laughter had had a booming note. He had had no nerves, no imagination. When Wally was five he had thrown him into the river to teach him to swim and shouted with mirth over his son's frenzied terror. He himself had been hardy and fearless. His form of attention to his children had been to roughhouse with them. Wally had admired and hated and been afraid of him; and finally death had become his ally and removed the formidable parent forever.

That was the second time death had been an ally to Wally. The first time had been nine years ago, when he was four and still his mother's baby, receiving the extra attention that is the baby's due. A sister had been born then, and overnight everything changed for Wally. He was told that he was a big boy now; his mother was occupied with the newcomer. . . . He still retained a vague memory of the little Louise. She had cried a lot and had had a fuzz of dark hair and solemn dark eyes very like his own. He was told he must love his baby sister, and he made an extravagant show of affection for her when his mother was present. In secret he resented her and prayed that she would go away; then that she would die. People died and were put in the ground. When that happened to them they couldn't come back to trouble you again.

When Louise was seven months old she died.

More clearly than the baby herself, Wally could remember the guilt and remorse he had felt. He had wished she would die and she had died. He had wished away her life.

At her funeral he had been the one who cried hardest of all; and, approaching five, he had thought his first long thoughts about death; the finality with which it removed an obstacle.

He went downstairs to dust the back parlor, the dining room, and the sitting room. A door from the sitting room led out to the porch. When the dusting was done Wally went out through it and broke off clusters of rhododendron from the bush at the corner of the house. He arranged the flowers in a cut-glass vase and carried it out to the kitchen to put water in it.

The scent of coffee filled the room. At ten-thirty the last piece of washing had been hung out to dry, the white pieces spread on the grass. Mrs. McArdle, who lived near by, was seated at the kitchen table with Emma and Belle over coffee and soda biscuits.

"Well, Wally," their neighbor said heartily, "what a nice bouquet you've got there. You certainly are a good hand at fixing flowers; better than my girls, I must say."

The boy's narrow, oval face flushed, His brothers laughed at him because he liked to cut flowers and arrange them about the house. He mumbled that he was glad she liked them and took the vase into the dining room, where he set it on the sideboard beside the silver service. He carried the silver service back to the kitchen with him and got out cloths and polish.

"You want a cup of coffee?" Belle asked.

"Yes." Wally drew a chair up to the table eagerly. His mother split a biscuit, piled jelly on it, and handed it to him.

This he enjoyed: sitting at the table with the women and listening to their talk while he sipped the delicious coffee, yellow with cream. The sun had moved past the windows and a faint breeze touched his face.

He only half listened to the story about someone's last illness. He sat beside his mother and he was happy. For the moment all the problems of adjustment to the outer world and to the other members

22

of the family could be dismissed. Ned, Douglas's setter, dozed at his feet. The hunting season was far off, and the rest of the year the dog's fidelity to Wally was a source of pleasure to him.

Mrs. McArdle came to the end of her tale. "It's a terrible thing when someone lingers on and suffers that way," she said in conclusion. "When your time comes I always say the quicker you go the better for all, including yourself."

Emma made no reply. Wally could sense her thoughts. They were on his father, of course, and the quick, tragic manner of his death. Why should she still care? Why had she ever loved him so much? He'd heard his brothers say things about his father and other women when they didn't think he would understand. He had understood, though. Since he was eight years old he had known about the ugly thing that went on between men and women. He didn't want to dwell on it. Above all, he couldn't bear to associate it with his mother and that big, overbearing man she had loved. He couldn't bear thinking of her that way. . . .

When he touched her arm, Emma seemed apart from him. He had a profile view of her face and did not need to see her eyes to know that they had the faraway look he had seen in them before.

His hand returned to the table as his mother said, "Belle, if you've finished your coffee you'd better go down cellar and bring up a quarter ham. We'll slice it and fry it for dinner."

"I'd better be running along myself," Mrs. McArdle observed without moving.

23

"Oh, have another cup of coffee before you go," Emma suggested hospitably.

"I don't mind if I do. It gives me a lift in the middle of the morning."

Wally retreated from the table to the silver service. He attacked the tarnished surfaces with vigor, bending over them to hide the tears of jealousy that would come to his eyes. He loved his mother more than his father ever had. Millions and millions of times more, he assured himself. But his mother didn't care about that. His love for her was just thrown in with what she had from all the others. She loved them in return, of course; Henry the most because he was, everyone said, his father all over again. "She loves me the least," Wally thought, looking at her straight back.

She had never restored him to the status of baby after Louise's death. "You're a big boy now, too big for my lap." That was what she had said. Nowadays an occasional pat on the head, a rare word of praise, was all he received. "I don't have much use for soft talk," she would explain with a laugh.

But he had lost still more ground with her since his father's death. Everything connected with that dreadful event was repugnant to her.

He picked up the fat cream pitcher and began to clean it.

At dinnertime the bell drew the young men and Virginia from the fields to assemble around the table in the dining room. They ate heartily. There were thick slices of home-cured ham; grape relish, new potatoes drenched in melted butter, new peas, radishes and lettuce from the garden, cucumbers with sour-cream sauce, warmed-up soda biscuit, and, for desert, rhubarb pie. The milk pitcher that held a gallon was emptied and refilled and almost emptied a second time as the meal progressed.

Emma sat at the head of the table and served the ham. Belle, making frequent trips to the kitchen, sat near the door to it. She was a large, awkward girl with heavy-set features and a mouth that hung adenoidally open so that she looked even less bright than she was. Henry had declared that her head was vacant; she lived by her spinal cord.

Over second helpings of pie there was visible relaxation on the part of the young men, who had been applying themselves steadily to the food. When Emma said, "Well, Ginny, didn't you wear a hat this morning? Your nose looks burnt," Henry answered for his sister. "Yes, she had on a hat but she kept pushing it back on her head and sticking that nose out for fear she'd miss something. That's why it got burnt."

It was friendly teasing; Henry was fond of Virginia. As he spoke to Wally a jeering note came into his voice.

"That was a nice little swap you and Ginny worked out this morning. Did she throw in one of her aprons for good measure? One with ruffles that would suit you to a T?"

"Now, Henry," Emma protested, "that will do." The rebuke was perfunctory, however. She shared the young men's laughter. Anything Henry said or did was sure to gain her indulgence.

Virginia shared it too. For all her domineering ways, away from home Virginia was inclined to pro-

25

tect Wally. Under the family roof she joined forces with her older brothers against him.

Wally's eyes moved over them, rested longest on Henry's face with its strongly modeled, high-bridged nose and mocking smile on full lips. A devil danced deep in Henry's eyes; it could be friendly to others; it showed only malice to Wally. He looked down at his plate.

Henry pushed back his chair and reached behind him to the sideboard for a toothpick. His glance fell on the rhododendron. "You're so clever with flowers, kid," he remarked lazily. "Fix me up a boutonniere for tonight, will you?"

Nick and Sam and Douglas grinned appreciatively as Henry got to his feet, yawning and stretching. Rolled-up sleeves revealed powerful biceps when he flexed his arms.

Wally, attending to his pie, did not answer. If there was some way to hurt Henry . . . if he could pinch him black and blue, bite him, kick him, hurt him horribly . . . Nothing else would satisfy the rage that swelled in him. He hunched his thin shoulders over the table. He was helpless. Henry was so much bigger; Henry could knock him across the room with one blow.

"One of these days I'll pay you back," Wally vowed to himself passionately. "I'll pay you back for everything. I'll make you wish you let me alone."

That day was far off; in the goading present no method of revenge presented itself.

During the afternoon, with the young men back in the fields and Virginia gone to visit a friend, Emma and Wally were alone on the porch. Before them was the winding dirt road that led to the Center, a mile away. In back of them were fields of rye, timothy, buckwheat, and corn; the garden and orchard and barn. Across the road was a pasture for the cows. Only the chimney of the nearest house was visible from where they sat. A fringe of trees bordered the river, a quarter of a mile from them, but the Kinnelly itself could not be seen from the porch.

Emma had a basket piled high with mending beside her chair. She darned and patched, rocking back and forth, the needle flashing. She was as quick and decisive in doing this work as she was in everything else.

The sky was a pale blue arc. Heat waves dazzled the eye. Jerseys moved ponderously, cropping the grass, their hides gleaming in the sunlight.

Two boys passed the house, bound for the river. "Why don't you go for a swim?" Emma inquired.

"Sam said I could go later with him," Wally told her. He was on the couch with a book in his lap, enjoying the quiet of the afternoon and the interval of having his mother to himself.

She shook her head in half-humorous disapproval. "I declare, you are a lazybones. If I were your age I'd make a beeline for that river so fast you wouldn't see my dust. And here you are moping around with a book all by yourself."

"I'm not by myself. You're here with me."

Emma shrugged. "An old woman like me."

Wally stared at her. "You're not an old woman at all! You're young, Mother." He spoke sharply. When people grew old they died. That must not happen to his mother.

27

She laughed. "I'm forty-seven. Not a chicken, boy."

"Yes, you are," he insisted. "And you look as young as young can be."

She was pleased by the compliment but would not show it. "Such silly talk," she said.

After dinner Emma had changed from a house dress to a white shirtwaist and blue linen skirt. She always changed in the afternoon. It was a point of pride with her. She kept a hired girl, she wasn't just a farm woman. Her face flushed with the heat and not a trace of gray in her dark hair, she did look young for her age.

"Is Henry going swimming too?" Was it Wally's imagination or did a softer note come into Emma's voice when she spoke his brother's name?

"No," he answered sulkily. "Only Sam and I are going. The others have dates. Sam said I could swim with him because of that," Wally continued in accents of martyrdom. "He wouldn't want me otherwise."

"I don't wonder none of them want you." Emma snapped off a thread and rethreaded the needle. "You're such a coward about the water that they have to push you off the dock to get you in."

"No." He sat up straight on the couch. "Not this summer. I'm not afraid any more. Nick says I'm getting to be quite a good swimmer, and fast too. Even Henry says so."

"Well, that's fine," his mother conceded. She took small, even stitches in a torn sheet. "Did you happen to hear the boys say where they were going tonight? Is Henry going out with that Sawyer girl Nick threw

28

over?" She wasn't successful in keeping a note of fastidious disdain out of her voice.

"I don't know. They don't tell me where they're going."

"Well," Emma began out of a silence and speaking more to herself than to her son, "it doesn't matter. Henry will be going to Boston in the fall. It's wonderful to think that he'll be an engineer, isn't it? We'll all be proud of him."

"I won't be," Wally thought. "Not ever."

At milking time it was his chore to herd the cows to the barn. He pumped water into the trough outside by the well where the milk was cooled and went inside. He liked to be there for the evening milking. He liked the clean smell of the cows, the hiss of milk rattling into the pails, the unhurried atmosphere of the end of the day.

He sat on a stool near the open door and watched the scene, taking no part in the talk and laughter that went on.

After supper he and Sam would cross the pasture, walking on Howard land right to the bank of the river. He would dive off the dock and he wouldn't be afraid; a straight dive would take him deep into the cool water, and when he came to the surface he'd lie on his back looking at the sunset and he wouldn't be afraid. Sam, alone with him, wouldn't try to duck him or make him swim out farther than he wanted to go. Nick and Sam—his gaze went to the two oldest of the brothers—alone with either of them, they were all right. He could never feel safe with Doug or Henry . . .

"For God's sake, Henry," Douglas was saying, "Nick's leavings. Haven't you any pride?"

"Hell, no." Henry was matter-of-fact. "I'm no pioneer. I take what's nearest to hand."

There was general laughter. "Besides," he continued, "with Nick having such a head start, where would I look for fresh pastures?"

"Not around Kinnelly," Sam agreed. "Any day now I expect to find one of the grays shod backward so they can't keep track of him when he's out whoring."

Nick was unmoved. "The trouble with you fellows is that you're not in my class. God knows it's not for lack of trying."

In this vein the talk went back and forth. Wally looked at his feet. He felt uncomfortable and yet there was dark fascination in listening that kept him fastened in his place. Even when Nick, pouring milk from the pail into the can for the creamery, glanced at the small figure and said, "Hey, little pitchers," Wally, although he reddened, stayed where he was.

"Little mama's boy," Henry remarked, grinning over his shoulder, "still believes in the stork."

"I do not!" The protest broke from Wally hotly. He must maintain his potential manhood, potential equality, with Henry. He could tell himself, he did tell himself, over and over that he wouldn't be like Henry, big, unimaginative dolt that he was, so sure of his world, his place in it, for anything. He would never admit the innermost truth of his envy of his brother, nearest him in age. He couldn't have lived with his own small body, his uncertainties and fears, if he had made such an admission.

Douglas had the last word, ignoring comment on Wally. He stood up with a full pail of milk and said to Henry, "But the lady is becoming a little too chippified even for Nick's taste."

It was Nick who drove the milk cart to the creamery. Wally rode with him, silent, preoccupied with images of himself that the talk in the barn had evoked. He was a tall, gallant man of the world with a dangerous reputation. The lady in the dream was beautiful, of course, although he was vague as to the details of her appearance. And she was innocent, pleading for chivalry in his treatment of her . . .

The dream, like all its counterparts, never seemed to end in the lady's embrace.

CHAPTER THREE — 1903

"But I don't like him," Virginia said, speaking in her positive way that was meant to settle a matter without further discussion.

"You could do a lot worse than Frank Beazley," Douglas commented.

"I could indeed," his sister agreed. "I could marry someone like my brothers; someone without respect for women or knowledge of how to treat them."

Henry whistled softly, with a wink for Douglas. "Shall we tell her what we think of her?"

"I think we ought to tell her to grab Frank Beazley if she can land him," Douglas replied with a judicious air. "She's twenty-one and no nearer a husband than ever. Mary was married at seventeen. We don't want Ginny on our hands indefinitely, trying to boss us around, do we?"

"God forbid!"

It was again summer. They were at the dinner table: Emma, four of her sons, Virginia, and Belle who had been with them for five years now. Only Nicholas, married two years earlier, and precipitately thereafter the father of a son, was missing from the group. Nick was reading law in the office of his father-in-law, the town-court judge. Agnes, Nick's wife, too pliant before marriage, had since displayed much energy and an iron will in more or less confining her husband to the domestic fold. With sound judgment, she pronounced his brothers' society an undesirable influence and did her best to keep him away from them.

"Pass the potatoes, please," Emma addressed Henry. "And stop teasing your sister."

"We're not teasing her. We're giving her some excellent advice. Aren't we, Sam? . . . Wally?"

Sam grunted what might have been an assent. He was sober-faced and quiet today. He had his own troubles.

At seventeen Wally had reached his full growth of five feet six. His gentle brown eyes seemed too large for his narrow face and gave him a perpetually wondering look. He was still too thin, and slight in bone structure, so that he appeared younger than he was. He said with primness, "Ginny has to suit herself. Perhaps she doesn't want to get married."

"I don't." Virginia was curt. Her eyes moved from one brother to another pointedly. "I've seen enough of men and their ways."

Only Wally knew her secret. Three years ago she had fallen in love with the new organist at the church. It was a hidden, desperate love. The organist, married, approaching forty, a shy, sensitive man, could not have known of the emotion he inspired.

33

Virginia was too proud for that. She held her red head high and was more aloof with him at choir practice than she need have been. But even the proudest must find an outlet, and one·night when Wally came upon her sobbing in the barn she swore him to secrecy and told him why she cried. "He's everything I admire or could look for," she said. "There'll never be anyone like him."

Last year the organist had left Kinnelly. What Virginia felt about him then Wally had no idea, nor did he dare to ask. Virginia was changing—hardening was the word he used to himself. She was a reserved, correct young lady. There were no more freckles since she had taken to guarding her skin. Her pallor had a creamy undercast, her cornet of braids was handsome, the fugitive attractiveness more constant. But Virginia discouraged all suitors.

"That's not a nice way to talk, Ginny," Emma reproved crisply. "Pertness isn't becoming in a young woman."

Henry lounged in his chair. "Y'know, Mother, I don't think Ginny much cares what is or isn't becoming in her."

Emma changed the subject. "Belle's sister was here this morning and said their mother had another bad spell yesterday. I thought one of you could drive Belle and me over to see her after supper tonight."

A general murmur of sympathy was directed at Belle, then Douglas and Henry said in unison, "I've got a date," and Douglas added, "Get Wally to take you. He can manage the buggy with Flower all right."

This was Wally's moment. He kept his face blank

34

with conscious effort. "I'm sorry, Mother, but I have a date myself," he said.

"What!" Douglas and Henry lay back in their chairs with exaggerated limpness. Even the preoccupied Sam showed interest. Every eye was on the youngest.

"Did you say a date?" Douglas inquired. "With a girl, you mean? A real date?"

"Certainly that's what I mean. Why shouldn't I?" Wally straightened himself, expanding his chest. "You people forget that I'm growing up. I'll be a senior in the fall."

"So you will," Henry acknowledged. "But good Lord!" He threw back his head and laughed. "You with a date."

"Look, kid, we'd better give you a long talk and some fatherly—" Douglas caught his mother's eye and subsided.

"Who's the girl?" Sam inquired.

Wally smiled secretively. "That's my affair."

He was enjoying the stir he had created. All of them were looking at him with new respect. It was possible, at the moment, to regard the impending adventure with less panic than it had been causing him since yesterday.

He had met Ethel Hotchkiss at the store. Their way home lay in the same direction, and she had attached herself to him. Ethel was at least a year older than he, a large, dark girl with bold eyes. As far back as two years ago at school he had known that she noticed him. But the nicer girls shunned Ethel. The most charitable thing they said about her was that she was a little fly.

Somehow, yesterday, going along Main Street with Ethel, uneasily adapting his pace to her saunter, he had let himself be inveigled into saying he'd take her for a walk by the river tonight. Wally wasn't sure how it had come about, except that it was Ethel's doing. Until he made his declaration to the family he hadn't even been sure he would see the thing through. Here at the table, however, he had committed himself. To the knot of nervous dread that settled in his stomach Wally said, "Why shouldn't you have a date with a girl? It's time you did, isn't it? What are you so scared of, anyway?"

"Well, no matter who has a date, I want to see Mrs. Powers tonight," Emma observed. "I'm going to make some custards this afternoon to take to her, so one of you will have to arrange to get me there."

"I'll take you," Sam volunteered. "I'm not doing anything special."

Belle served apple dumpling. Wally looked at the portion on his plate and thought better of eating it. As usual, his nerves were playing tricks with his stomach.

Across the table Henry was watching him through half-closed eyes. Henry was looking into his mind and knew how frightened he was. Henry was laughing at him. He must eat the dumpling and dismiss Ethel Hotchkiss from his thoughts.

He glanced at Henry and dropped his eyes quickly. Henry was a brute, a big male animal, exuding that assured, sickening maleness of his from every pore. Even though Henry had been away at the engineering institute most of the time for the last few years, he detested him as much as ever. Henry could shatter any carefully erected pretense with a laugh, a single derogatory word. Henry was like his father. No, he wouldn't think of his father. . . .

He swallowed a morsel of dumpling. Perhaps, after all, Ethel was the least upsetting choice for thought.

She had an incipient mustache on her upper lip, tiny, all but invisible black hairs. The whites of her eyes were conspicuous when she rolled their dark irises at him. Wally clenched one hand in his lap. She had large, full breasts and she had seemed to thrust them at him when they stood talking outside her gate. Her laughter was too quick and too noisy.

He swallowed more of the dumpling with its thick filling of sugared apple. His stomach churned in protest. But Henry was still watching him with amusement in his eyes.

"Ethel's just another girl," Wally told himself. "Heavens, she won't bite you."

Ethel Hotchkiss did do just that, however. At his suggestion they took the long way around for their walk to the river and did not pass the Howard farm. Summer twilight was blending into night when they reached the Howard dock. The river had turned into a black belt shot with gleams of light. On the opposite bank occasional points of lamplight starred the dusk.

Wally looked out over the water. He drew a deep breath of satisfaction, forgetful of the constraint that Ethel's company put upon him. "This is beautiful, isn't it?"

"Yeh."

His eyes followed the flight of a swallow, skimming the surface of the river and curving up over the tree tops and out of sight in a long graceful arc. "We've got a book home with a poem in it about swallows," he offered in a sudden burst of friendliness. "It's about a fleet sweet swallow . . . that's"— he hesitated, about to say "lovely," was afraid the word would sound girlish, and substituted—"that's nice, isn't it?"

"Yeh." Ethel was looking at him when his glance went to her. There was mystery in the glimmer of white that her face had become; her eyes were dark in the whiteness. She studied him with baffled interest. He was a funny kind of a kid: little, barely her height, skinny, soft-voiced, a good deal of a sissy. That was what the others kids in school called him. He never paid attention to any girl, and that was why she had got him to take her for a walk. A lock of lank brown hair fell over his forehead; he wasn't bad-looking, but he was—she groped for a descriptive phrase—much too different.

She put her thoughts into words. "You're a funny kind of fella, Wally."

"Am I?" She saw him stiffen. "Why?"

"Oh, I don't know . . ." The girl slapped at a mosquito on her arm. "Well, for one thing, most fellas down here with me wouldn't be talking poetry about swallows. They'd find something better to do, you can bet your life." She was half laughing, half petulant.

"What—would they be doing?"

It was then that Ethel reached for his hand, brought it up against her cheek, and gently bit the thumb. Her laughter was mocking, yet it carried an

38

invitation. "You give a guess," she said, moving nearer to him.

The palms of her hands were moist and hot against his face. She put them behind his head and pressed her mouth to his. Wally's first wild impulse to fling her off vanished. Critical faculties were lost in the rising, soaring excitement that drained his strength and the will to resist. He clutched her to him hard so that she gasped against his ear, "Wally, gee! You're—why, we'll have some fun after all, won't we?"

This was the prelude. The interlude for finding a secluded spot beside the river chilled the boy's courage, but Ethel, forward and resourceful, was not to be denied. . . .

When he had brought her as far as her gate he would have hurried away. "It's late," he reminded her. "What will your mother say?"

"She won't say nothing," Ethel informed him confidently. "She don't care."

This was the truth. Easygoing, shiftless Mrs. Hotchkiss kept no track of her brood. Ethel drew him into the shadows for a last kiss. Her vitality and robustness were repellent now. Her wet mouth was too eager. Arms tight around his neck, she whispered. "We had a swell time, didn't we, Wally? Nobody'd ever think to look at you . . . We'll do it lots more times, won't we? Tomorrow night?"

Wally unclasped her hands and stepped back. He looked away from her. "Tomorrow night? I don't know. I'd better not say for sure. I—er—I think we're going somewhere tomorrow. I—If you want me to, I'll stop by first chance I get and—I—well, we'll see what—"

The halting words were broken off by the slap she gave him, followed by another and another across his face. "You!" she spat at him. "You damn mollycoddle, you! I'm not good enough for you, am I? I was good enough a while ago, but now you want to sneak off home to your mama! Well, go ahead, and don't think I care. All I got to do is lift my little finger and I can have lots better than you'll ever be." She slapped him again. "What's keeping you? Don't stand there staring holes through me. No wonder the whole school laughs at you. They'd laugh harder if they knew you were afraid to have a little fun with a girl!"

She had to call the last part after him, for Wally was running from her, wholly intent on putting space between them before the final degradation of being sick to his stomach right in front of her should overtake him.

Half an hour later he let himself into the dark house and crept up the stairs to his room. He pulled off his clothes, drew his nightshirt over his head, and slid into bed. At first the single summer-weight quilt was not enough covering for his shivering body. Little by little he grew warmer, and as physical misery lessened, mental suffering became acute. The first rooster to signal the dawn was crowing before sleep blotted out all revulsion, all anguish. . . .

In the morning he pleaded illness and stayed in bed, swallowing without protest the dose of physic Emma gave him. His pallor, the black circles around his eyes, bore out the plea. He would have to face his brother's jeers at this reaction to his first date sometime, Wally knew, but not immediately. In the immediate present he couldn't face anything.

The misery he had endured through the night flailed him. He prayed that he would never see Ethel Hotchkiss again. When his thoughts became past bearing he also prayed quite earnestly to die and leave all woe behind him. As the day wore on he lay flat beneath the sheet and looked out the window at the summer sky. He was in full retreat from last night's experience. He never wanted to touch or speak to or even look at a girl again. What had happened was animal, awful, without grace or beauty . . .

Teeth and hands clenched at the memory of Ethel's full-bodied, shameless enjoyment of the act. "Never again," he whispered to himself fervidly. "Never. Not as long as I live."

When he had had enough of solitude and self-torture, Wally took a bath, dressed, and went downstairs.

His mother was on the porch, busy with the mending basket that was always full. Wally said hello to her through the screen door and gave her a wan smile. Belle was in the kitchen standing over a mound of vegetables that must be prepared for supper, but she left them long enough to warm a glass of milk for him. "You look bad," she told him. "Drink every bit of it. It'll settle your stomach."

She nodded encouragement as he emptied the glass. Belle liked the youngest son of the house. He was kind to her and in one important respect he

41

differed from his brothers: he never subjected her to small familiarities as they did.

The milk drunk, Wally went out to his mother. "Feeling better?" she inquired without looking up from the mending.

"A little."

"There's nothing like a good dose of physic to fix a person up," Emma stated with satisfaction. "It must have been those potato pancakes we had last night. Too heavy for you."

Now she did look at him as he sat down in a chair beside her. It was a disapproving look. "You ought to be outgrowing that delicate stomach of yours," she said. "None of the others ever had it; I don't know why you should." She shook her head in reminiscence. "The scares you gave me when you were a little fellow. Your second summer I was up night after night with you. I never thought you'd live though it."

"Here I am, though," Wally reminded her. He felt a trifle happier. It was good to hear that he had kept his mother from her bed, her place beside his father, and caused her so much anxiety. It gave him a sense of being important to her.

The sound of hoofbeats reached them. A buggy came around the bend, the top raised so that it cast a shadow over the man who held the reins. Emma squinted at it. "Who's coming? It must be someone for here." Since the Howard farm was the last dwelling on Nod Road, that much was obvious.

"It looks like Ad Winters' piebald mare," she remarked a moment later, a worried note in her voice.

Sam had been calling on Violet Winters for months past, and lately he hadn't been himself . . .

On the instant Emma's aroused maternal instinct told her that the visit meant trouble.

Ad Winters turned the buggy into the driveway with a slap of the reins. He got out slowly, tied the mare to the hitching post, and advanced toward them. He was a man of medium height with hard eyes and a hard mouth. Years of outdoor work had browned his face and dried it into innumerable lines.

Emma advanced to meet him when he reached the bottom of the steps. "Well, Mr. Winters, how are you?" She threw cordiality into the greeting. "Come and sit down . . . Wally, give Mr. Winters your chair . . . Run and ask Belle to pour a pitcher of cider. I'm sure Mr. Winters would like a drop on a warm day like this."

He was wearing his black Sunday suit and a stiff collar. For a busy farmer like him to leave his work at the height of the haying season, don his best clothes, and drive two miles across town meant something serious; something catastrophic, Emma thought apprehensively, while Mr. Winters was seating himself with the deliberateness that attended everything he did.

They spoke of the haying and how well the weather was holding; of the way the creamery had cut milk prices. Wally returned with a pitcher of cider and glasses. He set the tray on a table and would have taken another chair, but Ad Winters turned his hard glance on him and said to Emma, "Mis' Howard, my business is with you alone."

"Certainly . . . Wally, you heard Mr. Winters."

43

Wally went back into the house unwillingly. Emma stood up and poured cider.

"Just enough to wet my throat." Mr. Winters's gesture stayed her pouring. The road had been dusty, his throat was parched; half a glass of cider was a compromise between principle and need. Until his daughter's wrongs had been righted he mustn't accept the full measure of hospitality that Emma would have offered.

He had a harsh, carrying voice. Crouched beside an open window, Wally heard his every word as he cleared his throat and came to the point. "Mis' Howard, I came to tell you that your Sam has been carrying on with my daughter. He's got her in the family way. Near's my wife and I can make out, she's almost three months gone."

They were out of Wally's range of vision. But the creak of Emma's rocking chair ended abruptly. She was so long in making a reply that her eavesdropping son thought she would make none and expected to hear Ad Winters speak again. The farmer was patient, though, and waited. When her answer did come, it was a question. "Did Violet name Sam right out as the one responsible?"

"Certainly she named him!" The voice was louder and harsher still. "Who else would it be? He's the only fellow she had. I'll have you understand, Mis' Howard, my daughter is no chippy, running out with this one and that one."

"Of course not," Emma said quickly. "But this . . . It's a dreadful thing for a mother to hear about her son."

"It's not what a father wants to hear about his daughter, either," Ad Winters reminded her grimly.

A picture of Violet Winters took shape for Wally. She was blond, and pretty in an undecided way. She giggled easily. She was utterly unlike Ethel Hotchkiss, yet Sam and she . . . He felt his face grow hot. Sam hadn't been revolted by what they had done together. He had been courting her for months. They had done it again and again, probably.

And there had been many girls before Vi, of course. He had listened to enough of his brothers' talk to know that.

"This is a terrible thing," Emma was saying. "Just terrible. I can't begin to tell you how sorry I am, Mr. Winters."

"Being sorry won't mend matters," the farmer stated. "Vi's sorry enough herself, I guess. I took the strap to her after she told us, but her mother carried on until I stopped. They were crying their eyes out when I left." His voice was rising. He paused to get it under control. Nevertheless the suppressed fury with which he went on made Wally shudder. "The little fool!" he exclaimed. "I told her long ago that no good would come of a Howard courtship. I told her what hellions your boys are."

Emma cut in acidly, "I don't care to have you speak of my boys that way, Mr. Winters. When you get right down to it, you couldn't ask for better. They work hard, they've kept this farm going since their father died." The acidity was replaced suddenly by sweetness. "Of course boys will take advantage of a girl if they're given encouragement. I always taught my daughters to keep their distance."

A chair was pushed back with a grating rasp. Mr. Winters was evidently on his feet. His voice was thick with rage. "Mis' Howard, it's time you knew that your fine sons have the worst reputation in Kinnelly. No decent girl is safe with them. Like my Violet. What do you know about the young devils? While you're sitting here bragging about them they're off raising hell here, there, and everywhere!"

He walked back and forth with heavy tread. He added, "But what else could I expect a fool woman to say?"

"Do you come here to insult me, Mr. Winters?"

"No, ma'am. I came to see my daughter get her rights. The faster they're married the less talk there'll be." The harsh voice was measured and firm.

Wally heard the creak of his mother's rocker again. It was a rapid sound. She said, "Sam is a grown man. He'll have to decide for himself. If he loves Violet and wants to—"

"I'll decide for him," Ad Winters interrupted. "We'll leave love out of it. He'll have to marry her."

Wally hugged himself with nervous excitement. Sam was in for it this time. Mr. Winters was second selectman, a member of the school board, an important figure in the community. He had a large farm, another giggling daughter younger than Violet, but no sons. He was not a man to be trifled with. He appended, "If Sam don't want to marry her, maybe the sheriff can make him think twice about it."

"Naturally you want to protect your daughter," Emma said icily. "It's equally my duty to consider my son's best interests." The chair scraped the floor

46

as she stood up. "They're haying over at Eight-Acre this afternoon. I'll send Wally after Sam."

Wally flew from the window on tiptoe. He was at the far end of the room with a book open in his lap when his mother came in search of him. "Wally, run over to Eight-Acre and tell Sam to come home at once. Tell him Mr. Winters is here."

"Yes, Mother." Wally dropped the book and ran.

Sam pushed the broad-brimmed straw hat far back on his head, leaned on the pitchfork, and looked at his brother incredulously. "Old man Winters is here? Oh, Jesus!" he said.

He said nothing else. He left Douglas and Henry looking after him in astonishment as he let the pitchfork fall to the ground and walked away toward home with long strides that covered the ground quickly.

Wally, trotting behind, hoped for comment. Sam ignored him. When they reached the house Ad Winters and Emma were pacing up and down the lawn in front of it, and Sam went to them, saying, "Beat it," to Wally over his shoulder.

From the porch Wally watched the trio. The long conference was a heated one, to judge by gestures and expressions. Not a word of it could be overheard.

When Mr. Winters finally untied his mare, stepped into the buggy, and drove away, Emma and Sam remained on the lawn, still walking up and down, deep in talk.

At supper that night the atmosphere was subdued. Wally's gaze was drawn to Sam's lowering face. Violet Winters and he . . .

Wally felt a sense of superiority. He knew now what this thing was that his brothers pursued. It would never again drive him into disgusting intimacy with any girl. No outraged father would appear at the door for him. . . .

A week after Ad Winters came to the house Samuel Howard, reluctant, sullen, married Violet and went to live with her at the Winters farm. Ad Winters, that autumn, built them a house on his land. Since the farmer had no sons, Sam, sharing the responsibilities of the place with him, had reaped a sound financial harvest from his seduction of his daughter.

At the time Sam's house was being built Emma made her first sale of Howard land. Henry, back in Boston for his last year at the engineering institute, would not be staying at home to help with the farming. Wally, a high-school senior, had never showed any interest. Only Douglas was left. Emma hired a man to work the reduced acres with him and shed a few tears the night the deed of sale was drawn up. It was land her dead husband had bought. It seemed a repudiation of him to sell it.

CHAPTER FOUR — 1904

Emma said, "Well, if you're satisfied, I am. Everyone should make his own choice of what kind of work he wants." She sighed. "Times change. When your father was alive we'd make plans for you boys. He used to feel that farming was the best life a man could have. If you worked your own land you called no man master, he'd say. Perhaps if he had lived . . . But it's no use thinking of that, is it?"

The question did not demand an answer, but Wally said. "No," and with that inner recoil from mention of his father went on quickly, "Mr. Vance and I had quite a talk, Mother. He explained everything that I'd have to do, and it's diversified enough, he said, so that I'll learn a lot. There's the pay, too. Five dollars a week to start is good money."

"Education's a good thing too," Emma pointed out. "You know I've been putting by a little nest egg. I could give you a start if you wanted to go to college."

"I don't want to," Wally told her decisively. "I'm

perfectly contented with the arrangements I've made."

"I can't imagine why you don't want to go. You've always been so fond of books that I'd have thought the more learning you had the happier you'd be."

"Well, that isn't how I feel about it." He wouldn't tell anyone how relieved he was to have finished high school last week and to be separated from daily contact with the mass weight of his contemporaries. College would have meant leaving his mother and the world he knew; it would have meant four more years of being ridiculed and harassed by those who, in every group, enjoy tormenting the non-conformer, the weakling. Wally had long ago made up his mind that he would not go to college.

"But look at Henry." Pride was in Emma's voice. "Just think of his future with that job in South America. His prospects are brilliant." She nodded emphasis. "Yes indeed. Brilliant. Of course ever since he was a little fellow he's been taking things apart to see what made them go, and so interested in all the things they're doing with electricity these days. He's bound to make a good engineer."

Wally was silent. Compared with the colorful vista of years in South America, a clerkship at the Kinnelly bank was tepid stuff.

"Henry," Emma concluded fondly, "is the smartest one of all of you, I guess."

Always Henry. Henry could do no wrong. Wally clasped his hands in his lap and maintained his silence. Still thin, weighing only one hundred and nineteen pounds, he didn't fill the roomy chair he occupied as Henry would have filled it. He had on the blue serge suit that had been bought for graduation and that he had worn for his interview with Mr. Vance. With the stiff white collar, the new pearl stickpin in the dark tie, his hair parted in the middle, his pale complexion and small, well-kept hands, he looked suited to the work of clerking in a bank.

He picked up a book.

Emma, who was never idle, was knitting a sweater for one of her grandchildren.

For an interval neither spoke. The day was stormy and rain beat heavily against the windows. Emma glanced at her youngest, already lost in reading, and said impatiently, "For heaven's sake, Wally, go upstairs and change your clothes and go out to the barn. The boys are giving the milk cart a coat of paint. You'll find there's plenty you can do to make yourself useful."

"Oh Lord," Wally said in protest.

"Look at Henry," Emma continued. "He has his degree but he's not above helping out around here until it's time for him to go away."

Wally slammed shut the book. "Goddamn Henry," he said under his breath. He directed a bitter look at his mother. Would she never take sides with him in anything, large or small?

He had an answer to that question a few days later. It came at eight o'clock in the evening when Emma was setting bread and Wally, seated at a kitchen window, was talking with her.

He glanced out the window and stopped short in midsentence. Sam was coming through the orchard with lurching stride. Sam was drunk. He had been in town and come home drunk to find out that Wally

51

had borrowed and lamed his horse that day. He wouldn't listen to any explanation. . . .

"Mother!" Wally sprang to his feet. "Sam's coming and he's drunk!"

Emma ran to the window. Sam was almost at the gap in the hedge. She reached over to the table, turned down the lamp and blew it out. "Lock the door," she commanded.

"No, no, I'll run out the front way and hide." He started toward the dining room, but his mother caught his arm. "You'll stay right here, boy."

He tried to pull away. "Let me go, Mother! He's too big for me, I can't fight him. You know I can't. Why should I stay here and have him hurt me?" He was whimpering. "It's better to hide."

Scorn flashed across Emma's face. "You'll not run away, boy. And"—She caught up the strap of a harness that Douglas had been mending at the kitchen table—"if there's any hitting to be done around here, I'll do it."

Sam fell against the well sweep. He picked himself up and resumed his weaving progress through the yard, heading for the kitchen. Wally closed and locked the door.

A moment later his brother was hammering on it. "Let me in! I saw the light. I know you're there."

Wally's breath caught in his throat. In the shadowy twilight he waited for his mother to take the lead. The churning process began in his stomach. He could fight it off for a time but presently he would be sick.

"What do you want?" Emma called.

"I want to see Wally. I know he's there, tied to

your apron strings." Sam paused to make his tone conciliatory. "I just want to have a talk with him about Fancy," he added.

"You go along home, Sam. You've been drinking again. You can talk to Wally tomorrow."

Sam abandoned the pretense of friendliness and pounded anew at the door. "I'll talk to him now. By God, I'll do more than talk to him after the way he lamed Fancy! Open that door or I'll break it down."

"Sam Howard, you get away from here!"

Wally turned to flee, but Emma, gripping the strap in one hand, held his wrist with the other. "If you run now you're no son of mine," she hissed at him. "I'll be ashamed of you all my days."

Aloud she cried as the hammering continued, "Sam, if you don't stop, I'll have you arrested for breaking and entering!"

Sam was royally drunk. His reply was to send a fist smashing through one of the panes in the door. While splinters of glass were still tinkling to the floor a cut and bloody hand reached in to turn the key in the lock. He threw the door wide and staggered into the room, swaying back and forth, nursing his bleeding hand in the other one.

Wally retreated as far as his mother's grip on his wrist would allow. Sam would kill him. He was so drunk he wouldn't care what he did. . . .

"I'm awfully sorry about Fancy," he quavered. "I told Vi to get Doc Jennings and I'd pay for it and—"

"By God, you'll be sorrier yet before I'm through with you." Sam moved forward.

Emma dropped Wally's hand and stepped in front

53

of him, shoulders back, chin lifted purposefully. "Sam Howard, I won't have you in the house like this!"

Back against the wall, Wally saw Sam try to remove her bodily from his path. Her feet left the floor, swung out, and kicked viciously at her son's shins. He let her go with a cry of pain, came on and found a lashing tornado before him. The strap bit into his flesh; his arms went up to protect head and face. He stumbled over a footstool.

Wally flung his hands over his eyes as the crash of Sam's fall resounded. He heard him get back to his feet, his heavy breathing, his surly tone. "All right, Mother, I'm going."

When Wally's hands came down from his face Sam was on his way out the door. Emma stood with the strap hanging at her side. "I'll expect you back with an apology tomorrow—and a new pane of glass for the door."

Sam offered no reply. He was again nursing the injured hand as he went down the steps.

Emma watched him until he was across the orchard. She walked over to the shelf for matches and lighted the lamp. Her shoulders sagged a little while she paused at the table. With a deep sigh she tidied her hair, moved on to the sink where she washed and dried her hands, and turned back to the pan of bread dough.

"You can come out of that corner now, boy," she said over her shoulder. "We'll see no more of Sam tonight." Speaking to herself rather than to Wally, she added, "Poor Sam."

Wally held his hands against his stomach. Perhaps if he took a drink of water . . .

He drank and remarked with sudden venom, "Sam got what he asked for."

His mother's glance moved over him. There was no reproach in it. "I wasn't thinking of the way I hit him," she said curtly. "You'll find out one of these days that getting hit isn't the worst thing that can happen to you. I meant his marriage."

"He made his bed," Wally declared with piety.

"Oh, nonsense! Wait until you've faced a few temptations of your own before you take that tone." She waved him off with a floury hand. "Go away. I want a few minutes to myself."

In spite of his stomach and his mother's abrupt dismissal Wally was not unhappy as he wandered outdoors. How splendidly his mother had defended him! She had been a heroic figure standing up to Sam.

He lingered near the back porch, inhaling the fragrance of the honeysuckle vine that blanketed it. Watching darkness come and the stars gain brilliance, Wally remembered something his mother had said to a visitor when he was five. They had been talking about him, how small he was for his age, so different in that respect from his brothers.

With the adult assumption that children didn't listen to their elder's conversation, Emma had said, "He's always been a puny little thing, afraid of his own shadow." Her laughter held irritation. "I'm used to six-footers; men like his father and the other boys. Even though it's I he takes after in size, there are times when I feel he can't be my son. I must get over that, I know."

He remembered it well. But tonight it was far away. His mother had taken his part as she never had done before, and not against an outsider, either; against one of her own sons. He did matter more than he had dreamed of to her. . . .

Emma did not wait for Sam's arrival the next morning. Virginia and she took an early trolley to town for a day's shopping. It was raining and Douglas went fishing with the hired man, leaving Wally in the wagon shed with instructions to give the milk cart a second coat of paint.

Wally finished it quickly—he worked well with his hands—and returned to the house. It was only eleven o'clock, and if he could duck Henry with a suggestion of a new chore, he could get in an hour's reading on *Red Rock* before dinner.

The book was in his room. He went through the empty kitchen and up the back stairs. At the head of them he was brought up short. Belle was squealing, and the sound reminded him of nothing in the world but a pig getting its throat cut. Scuffling sounds accompanied the squeals. They came from the room that had been taken over by Henry after Nick and Sam were married. The door was closed. Belle's voice pierced it, rising in panic. "Let me go! You gotta let me go!"

Belle had been unfailing in her kindness to Wally. He had to do something. Not daring to think of what scene might meet his eyes or what might follow on it, he raced along the hall and flung the door open.

Half on the floor and half on the bed which she

56

had been making when Henry entered the room, Belle was fighting him, her skirts above her knees, her thick legs kicking out frantically.

His face dark and set, Henry was trying to pull her higher up on the bed when Wally burst in upon them. At his brother's entrance he sprang away from the girl and turned a formidable flare on him. "Why, you—you little—"

Belle was on her feet, darting past Henry and Wally into the hall. She clattered down the back stairs while Henry was smoothing his hair and straightening his clothes.

He advanced on his mesmerized brother, caught him by the shoulders, and shook him hard. "You goddamned little sneak," he gritted out and slapped his face, swung him off his feet, and sent him crashing against the dresser.

Wally crumpled to the floor. Henry stood over him, his handsome face showing naked fury. He said, "If you ever—ever—mention this to Mother, what I gave you just now will be nothing to what you'll get then. Is that clear?"

Wally, holding his head, did not speak until Henry prodded him with a foot. Then he muttered, "Yes."

"And," Henry continued, "if Belle says anything, you understand you're to keep your mouth shut. You're not to back her up."

"Yes," Wally muttered again.

For a space Henry stood looking down at him. "God," he thought, "what a miserable little creature he is."

He had hit him at will since Wally's earliest childhood, and Wally had never fought back. "If he had,"

Henry thought, "I'd have let him alone years ago and picked on someone my size."

He was beginning to be searingly ashamed of the whole episode. "Christ, if he'd just once make an effort to defend himself. If he weren't always such a rotten little coward."

There was nothing to stay for. Henry turned and left the scene of his humiliation. . . .

After supper that night Belle made her complaint to Emma in the kitchen. The girl had no gift for words; her schooling had ended at the fourth grade. She was embarrassed, too, and the story she told was obscure and confused.

The older woman, motionless by the range, said crisply, "Belle, you're imagining all this. Henry must have been fooling with you. He can be rough in his fooling, but he would never in the world . . ."

Her back to the sink, Belle faced the indignant mother, dull color suffusing her face. "He would so," she insisted. "He tried. He's tried other times, but not so hard as today. So has the rest of them, one time or another. All except Wally."

Emma's laugh was shrill. "My dear Belle, you're not that irresistible!"

Color deepened in the heavy face. "I know what I look like. And it isn't my looks your boys is after . . . You don't have to believe me about this morning. You ask Wally. It was him that saved me. Henry would've had the best of me if Wally didn't come in."

"Ask a mere boy a question like that? I should say not!"

Belle, slow to anger, was thoroughly aroused.

58

"Then I'll ask him myself. He's somewheres around the yard." She looked out the window. "Here he comes now."

"Belle, if you mention this story to him, I shall have to let you go."

The girl eyed her steadily. "I'm leaving anyways," she stated. "A respectable woman hadn't ought to work in this house. But I'm going to have my rights before I go. I'm not going to be called a liar to my face."

Wally came in through the back door and was instantly hit by the tension in the air. All day, with Henry's threat hanging over him, he had avoided Belle.

She took the lead. "Wally, you tell your mother what was going on this morning, will you?"

He turned his face away from her and looked down at the floor. He wanted to tell. He wanted his mother to know the whole sickening story of her precious Henry's conduct. Desperately vivid, however, was the knowledge of what Henry would do to him.

"Well, Wally, was Henry—roughhousing with Belle this morning?" Emma demanded.

This was his cue. He had to snatch at it while hatred of Henry lay on him weightily. "Yes, he was. Just—fooling."

"Wally!" The cry broke unbelievingly from Belle. "That ain't like it was. You know it ain't. Tell your mother."

He would not look at her, poor uncouth Belle who had been nice to him in many small ways. "There's

59

nothing to tell." He walked past the two women to the dining room.

Belle left the next morning directly after breakfast. Henry's manner was blandly innocent, with nothing to indicate that he was the cause of her departure. It was Wally whose sense of guilt was so great that he couldn't meet the girl's eyes. He loathed himself with a fierceness that was exceeded only by his loathing of Henry.

When Belle was gone Emma said to her favorite, "Henry, I don't want you ever again to be the least bit familiar with any girl who works here. A girl who's not too bright won't understand that you're only fooling. And you're a grown man now. It isn't dignified."

Henry lacked the grace to reveal embarrassment. He looked straight at Emma and said amiably, "You're right, Mother. I'll keep my distance with the next girl you hire."

Wally rushed out of the room. He couldn't stand it. Only one ray of light came through the blackness. In a few weeks Henry would be sailing for South America. He would be gone for years. The running sore of their relationship would surely heal when Henry was thousands of miles away.

CHAPTER FIVE — 1914

Because Martha Vanderbrouk was a widow and the mother of an infant son, born posthumously, she had a small, informal wedding. She married Douglas Howard in her own house that was surrounded by many acres of fine land. Martha was twenty-six, fair-haired, with a serene expression. She wore a light summer suit and smiled confidently at her bridegroom all through the ceremony.

Nick was his brother's best man. Nick's face was lined, his waistline bulged, but his height balanced the flesh he had gained and he was still a handsome man. His wild days were behind him. Tamed and ruled by his wife, Nick, the family man, had grown stodgy.

Virginia, also wearing a light suit, was bridesmaid. Her red braids were as beautiful as ever. There was sternness in her face, however, and she kept her lips pressed too tightly together. She had a rigid, holier-than-thou manner with people.

Wally was beside his mother. Mary and her husband and their two daughters and Nick's wife and children were present. The Howard family was represented to the fullest possible extent. Henry was not with them; he was in South America, and it was four years since he had been home. It was seven years since Sam had had a part in any family event. Seven years ago Sam, unhappy in his marriage, seeking solace increasingly in alcohol and association with many women, had been knifed in a saloon brawl. His widow had promptly remarried and left Kinnelly, so that the Howards had no contact with his son.

The June day was sunny and not too hot. A breeze stirred the curtains. They framed green fields and, in the distance, silver flashes of the Kinnelly River.

Emma's eyes were on her son. She was pleased with the marriage. Douglas was thirty-six, it was time he married; and Martha would make him a good wife. She would never, Emma's thoughts ran, have approved of some flighty girl of twenty or so for her third-born son.

She prayed a little. "God, please bless this marriage and cause it to prosper. Make Douglas be as good and faithful a husband to Martha as she will be wife to him. Don't let him go near Yvonne Beaumetz again. Nothing but evil can come of such a fast woman, so please, God, keep him away from her and satisfied with Martha . . ."

Across the room from Emma, the bride's aunt viewed the ceremony with disapproval scarcely concealed. She, too, had her attention fixed on the bridegroom. He was good-looking enough in a no-longer-young and somewhat dissipated fashion. He was tall, as all the Howards were except for the dandified little fellow over there by his mother. But there should be more to a man than his looks; more even than the ability to run a farm as well as Douglas Howard undoubtedly could. A woman needed a man she could trust. And how, Martha's aunt asked herself, could you trust a Howard? Father and son, they had never been content with one woman. Again she had to qualify her conclusion. The youngest son was different. His name had never been linked with that of any girl. But still . . .

"Forasmuch as Douglas Howard and Martha Vanderbrouk have consented together in holy wedlock . . ."

They were married. The group surged forward to shake hands with Douglas and kiss the bride.

A buffet supper was spread out in the dining room. The beverages were fruit punch and coffee, and, after the minister had departed, small glasses of wine.

Emma, in a new gray silk, noticed details. Martha had solid silver. The china was Haviland. The table linen was shimmering damask. The house was furnished with good pieces. Douglas was simply walking into all this. Not many men were so fortunate, she told herself.

She had inspected the second floor before the wedding began. There were four bedrooms. She withdrew quickly from the one where Robert Vanderbrouk, aged five months, lay asleep in his crib. The bathroom was tiled, whereas the Howard bathroom was merely painted. Such evidence of prosperity sent Emma downstairs filled with gratification.

The buffet supper could have been more abundant, she thought, when she was in the dining room inventorying the table. Cold baked ham, turkey, only three kinds of salad, two kinds of hot bread. Martha's thrift was a commendable trait, of course. . . .

"Go and sit down, Mother," Wally said to her. "I'll bring you a plate. What will you have?"

"A little of everything—of what there is."

In the parlor—Martha called it the living room, which Emma thought affected of her—she sat down beside Martha's aunt. Compared to this duenna, Emma, in her sixties, was still youthful.

"Nobody giving you anything to eat, Mrs. Howard?" The old lady peered at her out of eyes whose shriveled, overhanging lids gave her a hooded look.

"Oh yes, my son is taking care of me."

"Which one is that?"

"Wally, my youngest boy."

"That's the half-pint one, ain't it?"

"Well . . ."

The older woman reached for her coffee cup. "I never like my meals served up this way," she complained. "How can you do justice to the good food the Lord provides when it's on a plate in your lap? I want to eat in comfort." She was cleaning her plate as she spoke and looked expectantly at Wally when he arrived with his mother's serving.

"I'm sure Mrs. Opdyke will have something else," Emma said.

He took the plate the old lady thrust at him. "What can I get you?"

"Anything you see, young man, and plenty of it." When he was gone she wiped dribbles of food from her chin and said to Emma, "I've got lots to be thankful for. I'm seventy-eight but my digestion is good and I've got my own teeth. I can still enjoy my meals."

They shared a sofa. Emma set her coffee cup on the table before them and picked up her fork, moving out of reach of a beam of evening sunlight. "I'm glad they had such a beautiful day for the wedding," she observed. "It's supposed to be a good omen."

"I was married in York State in a downpour," Mrs. Opdyke announced. "The heaviest rainfall, 'twas said, within the memory of any living person." From her tone it seemed that she took personal credit for this demonstration of nature. "And I don't take any stock in the saying about happy the bride the sun shines on, because Will and I made out all right. He was a good provider; and he never looked at another woman right up to the day he died. Of course there's nothing," the old lady concluded, "that makes a woman happier than to know her man ain't out chippy chasing."

Emma's eyebrows went up. Mrs. Opdyke's comment was directed at Douglas. Everyone in Kinnelly knew about Yvonne Beaumetz. . . .

The old lady bludgeoned home her point. "So when I woke up this morning and saw what a nice day it was I said to myself, 'Well, I hope Martha's going to be happy; but the kind of wedding day she's got don't mean a thing, one way or the other.' "

Emma swallowed a mouthful of salad and did not answer.

"Then I said to myself," Mrs. Opdyke continued, "that who she married was Martha's outlook. Goodness knows, she had choice enough. A pretty woman like her with one of the finest pieces of property in town naturally had her pick of men."

This was the limit, Emma thought. "Douglas was in the same situation," she said, trying to keep her voice from betraying her maternal anger. "Since he was twenty there's always been one girl or another wanting to marry him. They never could resist him . . ." That wasn't the sort of thing she meant to say. She added hurriedly, "I couldn't count all the girls who thought he was such a catch."

Wally's return with Mrs. Opdyke's plate was the most welcome of diversions. Martha came to ask if they had everything they wanted. Emma looked at her new daughter-in-law and hoped that the quiet competence of Martha's manner would mean a great deal. It was not the mother's place to worry about Yvonne Beaumetz now. Martha should be capable of dealing with that complication. . . .

For once Wally didn't seek a chair near his mother. He brought her more coffee an_ left her. Emma, in a new dress with white ruching at the throat, her lovely gray hair, her figure still slender and erect, aroused no particular pride in the son today. She had wounded him too deeply last night for that.

Last night Virginia and Douglas were at Martha's, leaving Emma and him to enjoy the twilight together on the porch. Talk of the wedding tomorrow led Emma back to her own wedding day, forty-six years ago.

"I wore white satin," she said. "Hoop skirts were going out of style then, so I didn't wear one. Your father"—the dreamy note Wally resented came into her voice—"wore a black frock coat and white waist-coat. He looked—well, I never saw any man look handsomer than he did, smiling at me as I came up the aisle. He was so tall he towered over the minister—that was old Mr. Digby. You wouldn't remember him, he died when you were a baby. I was only sixteen, and I did look nice if I say so myself. What girl of sixteen wouldn't look nice on her wedding day? As for me"—her voice was a soft echo of old memory—"your father called me the lily maid of Astolot.

"Listen to me!" Embarrassment made her laughter sharp. "An old woman talking this way."

Wally's face was an oval blank in the dusk. He didn't want to hear about his father. Different echoes of different memories were aroused in him.

He was quiet in the chair. Nearly twenty years had passed. It was time to forget, to bury forever . . .

But the twilight seemed to bring back the past to his mother. She went on talking about her marriage and how happy she had been with his father. She said at last, "I'm glad Douglas is marrying tomorrow. It's time for you to think of it yourself. You've had another raise and been promoted to assistant teller. You could support a wife."

"I'm satisfied the way I am," Wally told her. "I'd rather stay with you."

The rocker creaked emphasis to Emma's gesture of protest. "That's foolish, boy. It's not natural for a young man to be tied to his mother. And it isn't as if I'd be alone. I have Virginia and, by the look of things, I'll always have her. It's disappointment enough to see her turning into an old maid. I don't

67

want you on my hands too, a cantankerous old bachelor."

His devotion to her never brought forth a response in kind. She had never even understood fully how he felt about her, how close he wanted to be to her. . . .

She rocked for a while and said, "I don't want you to miss the best in life. I had it with your father."

His father again. If she knew . . . If he told her . . .

"Your father meant everything to me," Emma added.

"But what about your children? Don't we—didn't we—count?"

"Yes, of course." The rocking stopped for a moment. "I'd still have been happy, though, if I'd never borne a single one of you as long as I had your father. That's the way it should be. Children grow up and lead their own lives. And sometimes when they're small and take up a lot of time they even come between a woman and her husband."

She was as good as saying she wished they'd never been born. No doubt she'd see them all dead in front of her if it would bring back their father . . . And this was the mother to whom he had given the most single-minded, unwavering devotion a man could give.

So, at the wedding, he didn't stay beside Emma. He felt repudiated and robbed of anchorage.

He stood in the dining room bay window, his plate in his hand, cup and saucer on the window sill. He was wearing a dark blue coat and white flannels. The customary attention to detail marked his appearance. His hair was parted in the center, so that the shape of his face and compact regularity of feature were more noticeable. The melancholy in his dark eyes lent him an air of wistfulness. This was Wally Howard at twenty-eight, attractive in a gentle, finely drawn fashion, keeping to himself in the midst of the wedding festivity.

He had met Janice Buell previously when Martha had entertained the Howards. With a high-school diploma and a summer course at the normal school for training, the girl had come to Kinnelly from northern Connecticut to teach at the second district school. Martha had boarded her, welcoming the companionship of the pleasant-mannered girl. In February, Douglas Howard began to court Martha in earnest, and the young widow found Janice's presence in the house a valuable check on the Howard impetuosity. Real affection had grown between them and, with the school term ended a week ago, Janice had stayed on in Kinnelly to help Martha with preparations for her wedding.

The girl came to stand beside Wally in the bay window. "Well, Mr. Howard, the whole thing has gone off beautifully, hasn't it?"

"I suppose it has." He was looking at Nicholas, who must have been drinking from some private source of supply. His face was red, his tone boisterous enough to bring his wife down upon him. He was slapping the bridegroom on the back and laughing at some jest between them.

"I think we're entitled to a little more enthusiasm,

Mr. Howard." Janice smiled reproof. "We've worked hard over this wedding."

She was two or three inches shorter than he and tilted her head back as she spoke. Wally found this agreeable. "I'm afraid I'm not a very good mixer," he told her. "I'm no judge of social affairs."

The attribute seemed to matter; the girl studied him with serious attention and said, "I'm afraid you don't really try to be sociable, do you?"

"Perhaps not." He expanded under the attention. "I'm a bookish, retiring sort of fellow by nature, Miss Buell. I like my own fireside too much, I guess, to stir away from it as often as I should."

He had found little to say to the girl when she had been seated opposite him last month at Martha's dinner table. Now he looked at her with real interest. She wasn't many inches over five feet tall. She was small-boned. Her blond hair, drawn back into a coil at the nape of her neck, was not worn in the current fashion, but the style was becoming to her. It showed off her fresh complexion and large blue eyes. Her voice was low and clear. She was ladylike, Wally reflected with pleasure, not one of these modern hoydens.

"Well," Janice remarked lightly, "if your own fireside suits you, I shouldn't take you to task, should I?"

"You think, then, that what suits people is always best for them?"

He was attracted by her habit of considering a question before she answered it. "Most of the time," she said, "I should think that would be true."

The trace of uncertainty and the way she looked

at him as though deferring to his judgment charged
Wally with recklessness. "Perhaps what I need is to
be shaken out of my moribund condition," he suggested.

He was smiling, and she smiled back at him, her
face lighting. "Perhaps that is what you need." She
gestured toward the table, where the guests were
crowding around Martha who was about to cut the
wedding cake. "Perhaps you should take part in
something like this."

Nick was calling, "Come and get it, folks. Come
and get your wedding cake. Take a piece home,
dream on it, and may your dreams come true."

There was much laughter. Douglas was beside
Martha, his hand over hers, as she cut the first slice.
He was a gallant figure bending to his bride.

Janice said, "Come and join in the fun, Mr. Howard."

If she had caught his hand to pull him forward,
Wally would have hung back. But her hands hung
at the sides of her ruffled dress. She only smiled at
him.

"Certainly," he told her.

Emma was in the press of people at the opposite
side of the table. Wally waved to her as he secured
pieces of cake for Janice and himself. He didn't go
to Emma. Last night she had rejected the too-close
tie; she had told him he must form other attach-
ments. Well, he would take her advice. He turned
his back on his mother resolutely.

Toasts were drunk. Under the stimulus of Janice's
smile Wally actually stepped forward to offer one of

71

his own to the bride and groom. His head was light, for Nick had laced the punch with brandy.

"It's nippy," he, the teetotaler, confided to the girl.

At seven-thirty Martha, after last instructions on her son's care to the cousin who was taking charge of him, came downstairs, ready to leave on her honeymoon. Douglas and she laughingly ducked through the shower of rice that awaited them outside and drove away in his car.

The guests began to leave. Nicholas sought out Janice. "We'd better be getting started, Miss Buell, if you want to catch your train."

Wally's new-found sociality was abruptly extinguished. "You're leaving Kinnelly tonight?" he asked.

"For the summer," Janice answered. "I'm going home. Your brother and his wife are driving me into town to get my train."

"But you're coming back in the fall to teach, aren't you?"

The girl was pleased that he was reluctant to have her go. "Perhaps you'd like to drive in with us," she suggested. "I'm sure your brother wouldn't mind."

Wally hesitated. "My mother . . ." Then he said, "But someone will see that she and Ginny get home all right. I'd like to go in to the train with you."

"That's lovely." Janice vanished upstairs.

She came down wearing a suit and hatted and veiled. In the meantime Wally told his mother he wouldn't be accompanying her home. "One of the

Blackstones will drive our carriage," he said airily. "Or Sister can drive."

The combination of Janice's interest and two glasses of punch were still at work in him. When they went out to Nick's open touring car Wally helped the girl into a duster and handed her into the rear seat with such assurance that the onlooker would have supposed it was a daily routine instead of his first experience of it.

Nick got in behind the steering wheel with Agnes beside him. The conversation was general on the topic of the wedding until the town was left behind. Then the car gathered speed and Nick gave his attention to his driving on the indifferently surfaced road.

"Do you drive?" Janice asked.

"Not yet," Wally replied. "But Doug says he'll teach me because Mother wants us to have a motorcar."

"I'd be terrified," Janice confided. "I'd never dare to touch a wheel."

Wally's smile came with masculine tolerance. "There's really not much to it. I've watched Doug."

She sat in the right-hand corner of the seat. He was a little distance away from her, and when a bump in the road threw them together Janice was quick to draw back. Wally found himself anticipating these occasional contacts as the ride progressed.

His hat was in his lap and he put his head back to look up at the darkening sky and enjoy the wind against his face. His thoughts left the girl next to him. Sometime soon now Doug and Martha would be arriving at the lake resort where they were to spend

73

their honeymoon. They would go to bed together. . . .

For Wally it was immediately Ethel Hotchkiss with whom Douglas would go to bed. The thing he would do would be done with Ethel. . . .

He made an effort to dislodge the association with Ethel from his mind. It was ten years ago that she had given him his only sexual experience. All women weren't like her, he reminded himself. Martha wasn't; the ladylike girl beside him was worlds removed from Ethel's coarseness . . .

But the act was basically the same; Ethel or Martha or Janice, none of them could escape the uses of their bodies. . . .

He smoothed back his hair and shifted uneasily. He had smothered the impulses of his own body until they had seemingly become atrophied. Tonight, however, they were coming to life because of this girl . . .

They left the open country behind. Houses appeared on either side of the road.

Janice broke the lengthy silence. "We're almost there."

"Yes. What time did you say your train left?"

"Quarter past nine."

"Isn't that late for you to be traveling alone?"

"It's only an hour's ride," Janice pointed out. "My father and mother are meeting me."

Time was flying by. He wanted to tell her how much the few hours they had spent together meant to him. Instead, what came out was a formal little speech. "I shall look forward to renewing our acquaintance in the autumn, Miss Buell."

Another man would have asked to see her during the summer, Janice reflected with some amusement. After all, she didn't live halfway around the globe from him. But Wallace Howard was incapable of such rapid strides. His gentleness and awkward advances appealed to her strong maternal instinct. She smiled at him assentingly.

They were in the city; Nick was stopping the car at the railroad station. They all accompanied the girl inside and walked out to the platform with her. There were no more pleasant moments of intimacy left for Wally. She held out her hand while the train was puffing to a halt. "Good-by, Mr. Howard."

He clasped it tightly. "Good-by, Miss Buell. I hope you'll have the nicest kind of summer." With Nick towering over him he couldn't bring himself to add that he would like to write to her. Apparently Janice read his mind, for she said, "If you find time, you might let me hear about yours. Martha has my address."

He moved in a happy daze going back to the car with Nick and Agnes. Janice liked him; she was encouraging his attentions. She hadn't laughed at him once or seemed to find him inadequate in any way, compared with other men.

Alone in the rear seat, Wally was in a blissful mood, putting his head back to look at the sky. This June night would always be good to remember.

The house was in darkness when Nick let him out in front of it, teasing him a little about what a fast worker he was and what a pretty girl he'd charmed. Wally enjoyed the teasing. He was on terms of equality with Nick, a man among men tonight.

In the corner room that had once been his oldest brother's, he went over every minute of the time he had spent with Janice, everything she had said, everything he had said.

Before he slept he tried to summon her exact image. Disturbingly, it wouldn't come clear. The face he saw rolled Ethel's black eyes at him; the delicate, trim body in the ruffled dress merged into Ethel's robust form pressed against him. . . .

CHAPTER SIX — 1916

One Tuesday evening in November Emma decided that she had pursued the course of non-interference between Wally and Janice long enough. "It's time someone prodded him along," she thought, looking at her son.

"You're not seeing Janice tonight?" she asked.

He glanced up from the newspaper in surprise. "Why, no. I saw her Sunday, Mother, and I'll see her tomorrow."

Sundays, Wednesdays, Saturdays; the schedule never varied. Emma suppressed an impatient sigh. She said, "A woman likes a little eagerness, boy. Janice could set her clock by you three times a week, and it looks as if it'll go on forever. That's not right." She turned to Virginia for confirmation. "Is it, Ginny?"

Virginia lifted her eyes from her book. "I'm not interested in men, Mother. So my opinion would be valueless."

The older woman shook her head. "Ginny, I wish you wouldn't talk like that."

"Why should I be a hypocrite?" Virginia demanded. "I shall always say just what I think." She resumed her reading.

Wally sat across the table from his sister, sharing the lamp. Emma was nearer the fireplace, hands linked in her lap, looking into the fire. Often enough Wally saw his mother with idle hands these days. She did no sewing for any of them and the great piles of mending were no more.

Her hair was entirely gray and growing white. A ripple of fear went through him as he studied her. She was getting old. The years had a way of slipping by, and his mother had been bowing to them little by little. The day must come . . .

He would not think of that day. He said, "There's no hurry, Mother. Janice is only twenty-one."

"But you're thirty, boy. And started on your third year of courting the girl. Is is fair to keep her dangling?"

Virginia emerged from her book to comment, "Perhaps it's not he who's keeping Janice dangling. Perhaps she's only marking time with him until someone better comes along."

Wally threw her an outraged glance. "I have no reason to doubt Janice's regard for me."

Virginia said, "Piffle!" and Emma interposed, "Then why don't you do something about it, Wally? Y'know, I heard the other day that old Mrs. Bennington's cottage is going to be put up for sale. It has six rooms, nice big ones. No improvements, of course, so it will sell cheap, and you and Janice could fix it up. No doubt—"

"Mother!" Wally's horrified gaze was turned on her. "I've had it in mind that if we did marry, with a big house like this and only you and Ginny to live in it, I'd bring Janice here."

Virginia laughed gratingly. "Good heavens, listen to that! And why should Mother and I have our lives upset by such an arrangement? What kind of man are you, Wally, anyway? Don't you want to have your wife to yourself and a home of your own?"

He reddened with resentment. "I merely thought, Sister, that—"

"You can spare us the details of what you thought. We wouldn't consider the idea for a moment."

"It's not just us, boy," Emma said. "Janice wouldn't consent to it either. Every woman wants her own home when she marries. It wouldn't be right to ask her to live with in-laws."

Wally's hands opened and closed on the edge of the newspaper. An abyss had opened before him. He had been a fool, of course, to hope that if he married Janice nothing would change.

His eyes swept over the room. Lamplight, firelight, familiar furnishings, many of them woven into his life since earliest memory. Upstairs was his pleasant corner room, his books and personal belongings all arranged just as he wanted them. . . .

He loved the house. The threat of being separated from it drove home the fact anew. He had taken it for granted; and his daily rotation between bank and home had been taken for granted too. His brothers gone, they lived quietly and contentedly—if Sister would marry and remove herself and her hectoring ways from them, utter perfection would be realized—but, failing that, he wanted everything to continue as it had been for the past several years. . . .

His mind went farther than the immediate surroundings. It roamed the wide lawn, the orchard, the garden, the barn, the wagon shed, converted into a garage last year when Emma bought their first car. It looked at the two saddle horses, the otherwise empty stalls in the barn. It wandered across the home pasture to the riverbank. All the farm land had been sold before Douglas's marriage. Out of the herd of Jerseys there was no longer even one left to supply them with their own milk. But the essentials, the house and land around it, remained; they were what meant the most. . . .

Janice was an enemy. She threatened to remove him from his home and, above all, from the aging beloved figure at its fireside.

The telephone rang. Virginia went to answer it and stayed in the hall talking.

When they were alone Emma asked, "Have you proposed to Janice?"

"No, not yet."

Her eyebrows rose. "All this time nothing's been said? There's no kind of understanding between you?"

"Not yet, Mother."

She looked at her youngest son, anxiety crinkling her forehead. Fears never faced had lifted when Wally began to call regularly on Janice. But the unacknowledged relief had long since faded. It could not last as she witnessed his slow, wavering, unenthusiastic approach to marriage.

She ended the discussion on a light note. "Well, Janice is just as slow as you are. I don't know what's come over girls nowadays. If I couldn't get a young man to pop the question before this, I'd think I was a pretty poor stick."

Wally laughed as he was expected to do. "If I could find a girl who was exactly like you, Mother, maybe I'd be quicker myself."

He took refuge in the newspaper and didn't read a word of it. Fright wove itself through his unhappy thoughts. What was he going to do about Janice? A lightning review of their association uncovered no instance when he had definitely committed himself. He had kissed her, yes; but she had permitted no other intimacies nor had he pressed for any.

At the moment he couldn't remember why her kisses warmed his blood so agreeably. Beyond the kisses . . . but he had never gone beyond them. Did he want to? Did he really want to?

There had been torturing doubt about that the whole two years . . .

He folded the newspaper neatly down the center and turned a page of it. Virginia completed her telephone call and returned to the book she was reading.

Janice had given him a standing such as he had never enjoyed before. He was not blind, not stupid. He had sensed the change at the bank, in the members of the family, in the community generally. Wally Howard was doing the natural thing at last. Like any other young man, he was courting a girl. He took her for walks. He took her into town now and then to a movie or play. He tried to teach her to ride, but she was afraid of horses. He hadn't told her of his own early terrors, of the fear of horses and the water that had been overcome. She admired his riding and swimming and ability to drive a car. He hadn't told her that he still undertook this latest accomplishment with inner misgivings.

Janice liked music and played well. He had sung to her accompaniment on the piano at her boarding house. He had taken her to concerts a few times. They had, in fact, done all the accepted things. But he hadn't committed himself; not definitely and finally.

What was the use of telling himself that? Everyone took it for granted that they would be married. How could he get out of it?

He pictured the Bennington cottage, low, rambling, and painted red. Separated from his mother and home, he was expected to live in it with Janice. It was to be his destination when he left the bank at night. In one of its bedrooms Janice would change from her cool, trim self . . .

His hands and face were damp with sweat. How could he go through with it? What was he to do?

Emma looked at the fire and made her plans. It was up to her to end his dillydallying. She would invite Janice to supper Sunday night and force the issue.

She could hear herself saying matter-of-factly at the table, "Janice, girl, Wally and I were talking about the Bennington cottage the other night. It's for sale. It would make a nice home for you and Wally when you're married. What do you think about it?"

That was what she would say. Let Wally try to blow hot and cold thereafter!

She glanced at her son with a little smile of triumph. The newspaper hid his face from her.

That Sunday afternoon they walked across the bridge that spanned Wolf Creek and followed a cart track through the wood. The day was somber, the sky overcast. The wind and the crackle of leaves underfoot were the only sounds in the quiet wood.

Janice tucked her hands in her muff. "November is a horrid month," she said.

"The month I was born in," Wally reminded her.

She smiled. "You showed poor judgment."

"On the contrary, I like it. You may have your fragrant springs, your full-blown summers, the garish part of autumn. I feel a special affinity for November days like this."

"Oh, Wally, you're just saying that." Her protest came laughingly. "These are the melancholy days, you know; they're associated with death, decay, moods of despair."

"Then," he declared, "that must be what I'm like; a true child of November."

"A perverse child, indeed," she told him.

"Perhaps."

Her quick glance found his expression serious. "What a silly conversation this is."

"I don't see why," he contradicted.

The cart track and the wood ended at a crumbling stone wall. It bordered on a pasture whose gate was formed by two rough bars laid vertically across an open space and fitted into uprights at either side.

Wally folded his arms across the upper bar. Dead matted grass, gray hills meeting a gray sky was the prospect spread before them.

The girl's gloved hand swept out to embrace the scene. "I suppose you like this too?"

"Yes."

She stood beside him. The wind had deepened her fresh color. She was wearing a brown suit, brown furs, and a close-fitting hat of brown velvet. Wally had complimented her on how attractive she looked when they set out for their walk. He took an interest in her clothes and had an eye for color harmonies and contrasts. Sometimes Janice considered it one of his nicest traits; at other times she took the customary view that it was a mark of virility for a man not to notice women's clothes, to say that he didn't know one color or material from another, he only knew whether or not he liked the general effect.

She said combatively, "I find it unspeakably dreary." She realized that her tone was sharper than it should be. She could tell herself that it was ridiculous to grow annoyed over a difference of opinion on the day; but annoyance grew, nevertheless. It was accompanied by a sense of helplessness as she looked at Wally's fine straight profile under the visor of his cap. She shivered exaggeratedly and said, "I'm cold. Let's go back."

Another man would have laughed and replied, "I'll keep you warm," and taken her in his arms. Not Wally, though. She saw his hands clench suddenly around the bar. He turned to her. "Oh, Janice! I don't know what—"

Rawest misery was in the cry. She reached for his hand. "What is it, Wally?"

"I—" Again he broke off. Could he tell her that he loved her and hated her, both at once? How could he explain his ambivalent attitude when he didn't understand it himself? What would she make of such inner confusion?

He had often been lonely. But never to the desperate degree of the present moment. He had read of true congeniality of spirit between two people; there had been times when he had thought it was, through Janice, within his grasp. Then it had slipped away before the barrier of her sex, the fear he felt of its potential. If he could say to her, "I should ask you to marry me. Everyone expects me to, you must expect it yourself. In a way, I want to ask you. But I never quite manage it because I'm afraid of what it will mean. And I look at you and actually hate you . . . and myself . . . Janice, can you understand? Can you help me?"

None of it was said. He stepped back from the gate, letting his arms drop to his sides. Janice drew her hand back and put it in her muff. His face was peaked with wretchedness as he swung around. When he saw the bewilderment in her eyes he forced a smile.

"Shall we go? It'll be dark by the time we get home."

She didn't move from her place by the gate. "Wally, what were you going to say?"

He was on the edge of decision, his future hanging

in the balance. If her tone had been gentler he would have asked her to marry him. But she was once more combative because he was often like this, retreating into himself, escaping her. There was too much between them that was obscure; he was too laggard a suitor—if he were a suitor at all.

So, in her voice, there was a trace of the commanding accent Virginia employed. It stiffened his basic resistance. "I wasn't going to say anything that mattered."

The girl could only fall into step beside him, half aware of the moment missed, caught again in the mesh of an unfulfilled relationship.

She had her intervals, too, of hating him, the shy, gentle young man who was one day her beau and another day no closer than any acquaintance. With little experience of men, Janice had no standard for comparison. But she sometimes knew with certainty that they didn't have a solid, satisfying association. At such times she fought his every symptom of withdrawal and quarreled with him; but even the quarrels were shadow quarrels in which they seemed to be only playing the part of lovers with emotions deeply aroused. There was no depth to them; they were as thin and sterile as Wally's courtship.

Both were silent on the homeward walk. The street lights came on when they were turning into Nod Road. The Howard house showed lights all over the first floor as they approached it through the dusk.

On the front porch Wally halted, his hand seeking hers. "Janice dear," he said softly, "have I ever told you how much you've brought into my life? Not just the hours that I've been happy with you—but a kind of balance . . ."

It was disarming. He opened the door and she smiled at him forgivingly. He smiled back, boyish and charming.

He followed her into the hall. The sound of animated voices reached them from the parlor. There was firelight, reflected on the woodwork, and laughter. It was masculine laughter, easy and gay, that brought Wally up short at the threshold of the room. He couldn't mistake that laughter although it was years since he had heard it.

Emma hurried to meet them, her face alight. "Come in, come in," she cried. "We've had such a surprise. Henry is home!"

CHAPTER SEVEN —

At the supper table Emma's plan for forwarding Wally's marriage was not put into effect. It was forgotten, blotted out, by the miracle of Henry's sudden arrival. She could talk of nothing else.

"I was through with the paper and there I sat by myself—Ginny was upstairs working on the household accounts—and I even cat-napped a little, I guess. It was such a gloomy afternoon I'd just made up my mind I might as well go up to my room and lie down sensibly . . ." Her hand reached out to cover Henry's. She confessed gaily, "My dear boy, I've turned into an old woman since you were last home. I sit nodding by the fire."

"I don't believe a word of it," Henry asserted. "You're as young and beautiful as ever."

She shook her head. "You save that kind of talk for your girls! Where was I?"

"You were saying you thought you'd take a nap," Janice prompted.

"Oh yes." Undemonstrative though Emma usually

was, she couldn't help touching Henry, rubbing his coat sleeve, placing a hand on his shoulder. When had he seen his mother as animated as this? Wally asked himself.

"Well, just as I stood up I heard a car stopping outside. I said to myself, 'Now who can that be?' and went to the window. And there was Ted Cornwall's jitney in the driveway and a man getting out. I kept looking and looking while he and Ted were pulling out the suitcases, and I thought I'd faint. I called Ginny—"

"You screamed at me," Virginia corrected her. "At the top of your lungs. You screamed that it looked like Henry outside. I almost fell down the stairs I came so fast."

Virginia, too, was animated, carried out of herself. The whole room seemed to vibrate with awareness of Henry's return. It was years since there had been so much gaiety at table.

"How long had you known you were coming?" Janice inquired.

It was the way his brother looked at the girl that had Wally on edge. All Henry said was, "Oh, I'd known for two or three months, Miss Buell. I didn't mention it in my letters because I wanted to surprise the family."

"Your letters," Virginia pointed out, "are so few and far between that you'd have been here ahead of your news anyway."

His answer came with a laugh and a shrug. "Ginny, old girl, you know I never was much of a letter writer."

"Then it should have been Wally who went away,"

Janice observed. "He's punctilious about things like that."

On the surface she was giving him credit; but to Wally, with jealousy eating at nerves and stomach, the virtue became a fault, a subject for mockery as Henry and she exchanged smiles. Henry's glance flickered over his brother with the old mixture of indifference and contempt. "Wally always was a proper little fellow," he said.

Commanding in presence, Henry lounged in the chair and, without apparent malice, pronounced the judgment that reduced Wally to a poor, ineffectual figure. Henry's white teeth shone when he laughed; the overhead lamp, suspended on a chain, picked out burnished lights in the thick cap of dark red hair that covered his handsome head. The younger brother thought that he looked like some unusually hearty exuberant breed of animal; that he had about as little sensitiveness as such an animal would have.

Hunched over the plate, Wally pushed food around with a fork. He couldn't eat. A hundred memories, all unpleasant, of the man across the table assailed him. If he could gouge out the hazel eyes that even now were resting on Janice in that caressing way of Henry's, perhaps the hatred that sickened him and cast a haze over his vision would vanish.

He hadn't the physical strength to do anything. There could be no ease, no surcease, for his hatred of Henry. There never had been; there never would be.

Henry was telling them about his trip through the Panama Canal. The three women hung on his every word. Wally was a nonentity. He picked up his water glass and drained it, his hand shaking so that some of the liquid spilled on the tablecloth.

Major, the collie who had taken Ned's place when the setter died of old age, came into the dining room and sat down beside Wally. His nose nuzzled Wally's palm. The dog was a steadying influence. He was devoted to Wally above all others in the family. Henry wouldn't be able to supplant his brother in Major's affections.

Wally looked at Janice, his pale, narrow face composed over inner turmoil. He loved her. All at once, he loved her without doubt or question. He always had loved her that way. . . .

She was leaning forward in her attentiveness to Henry, and her face had a sparkle Wally had not seen on it before. Again and again Henry's glance returned to her. She was lovely, his eyes told her, exquisite in her fairness and glowing color.

Emma's hand went up to Henry's head. "You need a haircut," she commented, running her fingers over the nape of his neck. It was only an excuse for touching him, Wally knew; she idolized the other. She had never idolized Wally like that nor been lavish with caresses. When had she last kissed her youngest son? She prided herself on not making a fuss over her children. Well, she was making fuss enough over one of them. And, of course, it would be Henry who was the recipient of the display; Henry was the one to whom people were drawn, whose life was brimming over with the admiration and affection that Wally had never inspired.

Henry flung a careless question at him. "How goes the bank? You're still a fixture there, I suppose."

The occupation of assistant bank teller was instantly reduced to milk-and-toast monotony.

Lena brought in dessert. It was peach cobbler with hard sauce. Wally stared at his serving and couldn't touch it. Whatever Emma had planned to have that night had been put aside for one of Henry's favorites. She must have ordered it the minute he was in the house.

"Nobody," Henry declared after the first mouthful, "preserves peaches the way you do, Mother. Thousands of miles away I could close my eyes and taste them."

"Listen to him!" Emma cried.

How long was he planning to stay? When would the household return to normal?

While Henry ate a second helping of dessert his brother had his answer. He had been transferred to the New York office, Henry announced. He would report to work there after a month's vacation at home. He had had enough of South America. "I'm not a kid any longer," he added. "It's time I settled down."

Emma was transported with happiness. Over and over she exclaimed that she couldn't believe it. "You'll be home weekends," she marveled. "We won't have to wait years to see you. You don't know what it means to me. The older I get the more I want my children near me."

It wasn't all of her children she wanted. It was Henry. "I could leave her," Wally thought, "and go around the world and she wouldn't care; not while she had Henry."

Janice said, "I'm so glad for you, Mrs. Howard. This means so much to you."

Wally gave the girl a sidewise glance. Her smile matched Emma's in radiance. She was glad for herself that Henry was back. She looked at him, great complacent slab of beef that he was, with delight.

"The house will be livelier now," Virginia remarked. "You and I are quiet, Mother, and you'd never know Wally was around. He's like a mouse. I certainly wouldn't want the old days back, when all the boys were home, but we can do with some stirring up."

That made the women's welcome unanimous. Only Wally was silent, and his voice was not missed in the flow of comment and question.

After supper Nick and Douglas arrived with their wives. Emma brought out her homemade wine and, in her benevolent mood, didn't keep track of how often her sons filled their glasses.

Wally refused the wine. He sat apart from the semicircle before the fire. They were in the front parlor with the handsome paneling around the fireplace and the big square piano at which Nick presently seated himself, trying to pick out, "Hail, Hail, the Gang's All Here" with one hand.

Henry had maneuvered himself into a place on the sofa beside Janice. He brought out snapshots he had taken on the voyage home. Their heads bent together to examine them.

No one else seemed to notice what was happening, except, perhaps, Martha. As the snapshots were passed around she left her chair to join the pair on the sofa and so broke up the tableau.

Wally's misery had become so acute that he felt feverish.

Douglas, Nick, and Henry were reminiscing at the moment, shouting with laughter. The anecdote had to do with Cal Burnham's heifer and the dawn when they wound up in Cal's barn and used the hoist rope to raise the heifer into the hay mow. Hidden there themselves, they smothered their mirth when Cal, old, slow-thinking, stood in the middle of the barn scratching his head and wondering how in thunder the heifer had got up there.

". . . and his brother-in-law said, 'Why, you so-and-so old fool, someone lifted her up,' " Nick reminded them, red with laughter.

"And then he asked Cal," Henry cut in, "if he thought the so-and-so heifer had grown wings during the night and flown up."

The women shook their heads over such antics. "Where the devil had we been that night that we weren't home until daylight?" Henry asked, shifting his position and stretching his legs out to the fire. "I don't remember."

"Why, to Skeet—" Douglas broke off abruptly. "Just out somewhere," he said, his glance divided between his mother and his wife. But Virginia was talking with Martha, and none of the women appeared to have caught the significance of what he had started to say.

Wally's eyes went in disgust from one brother to another. They had been to Skeet Corcoran's whorehouse, of course. Sam would have been with them. These were the pursuits in which his brothers had spent their youth.

Lowering his voice, Henry inquired, "What became of Skeet?"

"His old man died and he went back to Jersey to take care of his mother. He was about ready to retire anyway, I guess," Douglas answered. "He must have had a nice boodle."

Henry nodded thoughtfully. "I always liked him. He was a swell fellow."

The others agreed. Wally looked at them from under his brows. None of them saw anything incongruous in praise of a bordello master. Such were their standards.

When he walked home with Janice she talked of Henry. She was so far out of reach that the monosyllabic character of his replies went unnoticed.

She turned a cheek to his good-night kiss. When she had gone into the house he stood on the porch looking at the closed door. He had lost her, he knew; she was essential to happiness and he had lost her.

He walked home huddled in his overcoat, a slight, impotent figure, raging with jealousy. At the deserted corner of Nod Road he stopped and looked up at the low-hanging starless sky. All the oaths he had ever heard gushed from him. His hands clenched and unclenched futilely. What good were words?

He was sick to his stomach and numbed by the cold. He walked faster, his mind veering away from recollection of that other night when he had left a girl and afterward succumbed to nausea. He had to pass the run-down Hotchkiss farm and turned his head so as not to see it. Ethel no longer lived there. Years ago she had married a ne'er-do-well who repeated the pattern of her father. But not looking at the house had become a habit.

He went to bed. He heard Henry moving about in

the room he once shared with Douglas. Henry was back to torment his brother again; to rob him of Janice. To rob him effortlessly, which was bitterest of all. "I've given her two years of constant attention," Wally told himself. "Henry has only to smile at her and I no longer matter."

He should have asked Janice to marry him long ago—or even this afternoon when he had come close to asking her. Then they would have come home to take the spotlight from Henry with the announcement of their engagement. . . .

Wally pictured the scene; the exclamations from Emma, Virginia's more restrained good wishes, kisses all around. Kisses . . .

He turned over in the bed restlessly. Henry would have kissed Janice, claiming the privilege of relationship. Of course he would have, being Henry. And then it would have been no good anyway; once Henry turned that charm of his on her, that animal magnetism . . .

His head ached. The pillow felt hot and lumpy. He turned it over and smoothed it out, but the coolness was only momentary.

The house wasn't big enough to hold Henry and him. He would have to leave. "I will, I certainly will," he vowed in an undertone.

Even as he said it Wally knew he didn't mean it. It wasn't in him to go.

His month's vacation ended, Henry went to New York after Christmas. Every weekend, though, he was back in Kinnelly, and it became Wally's galling chore on Saturday afternoons to meet his brother's train with the car, weather and the condition of the road to town permitting.

It was Janice who brought Henry home so often. Once, at the table, Emma said, "Look here, are you trying to cut Wally out?" and Henry answered good-humoredly, "Is he in the running? I've had the impression that he wasn't serious."

His glance brushed over Wally in dismissal, and Emma said no more on that occasion.

She did, however, make other protests on behalf of her youngest son. But her position was weak because Wally had never mentioned marriage to Janice; nor could Emma believe, in view of his dilatory wooing, that his affections were deeply engaged. The protests went unheeded. Henry continued to usurp his brother's place on Saturday and Sunday. Only Wednesday evening was left for Wally.

He didn't know why he hung on at all. It wasn't in the hope of offering Henry competition; he didn't want to, he told himself. Janice had shown the true shallowness of her nature when she immediately preferred Henry's flashier attributes to the lasting quality of his own love for her. Henry was welcome to her. . . .

Still he went on seeing her whenever he could.

Emma tried to talk with him about his ambiguous position. He waved her aside airily. "Janice and I have been friends for a long time, Mother. What lies between Henry and her is their business."

His mother wouldn't let herself see that his eyes were forlorn. She wanted to accept Wally's interpretation. It left her free to hope that Henry would marry Janice. He was in his middle thirties. A wife and home ties would keep him from wandering off to some outlandish spot another time. She wanted nothing so much as to have him near her for the years she had left.

On Washington's Birthday Wally took Janice to a party. On the way home she told him she was going to marry Henry. "He asked me last weekend," she said. "There was never any question about what my answer would be." She was trying to keep her voice subdued, not to flaunt her bliss; but the bliss crept through, it wouldn't be denied. "Since the night I met him I've realized how I felt," she added.

It shouldn't have come as a surprise. It didn't, really. From the start Wally had known Henry was not launched on any philandering path. Janice would never have been one of his easy conquests.

He walked beside her in silence until she touched his arm. "Wally, aren't you going to wish me happiness?"

He kept his voice steady to meet the moment that had lain in wait for him since the night Henry came home. "Oh yes, I wish you happiness. Naturally. But what I wish . . ."

The girl was not angered by the implication that she would have little prospect of happiness with his brother. She said quietly, "Do you truly mind, Wally? I don't believe you do—except that it's Henry. I've sometimes thought that you resented everything about him."

"Of course not!"

She ignored the denial and went on, "We've been friends . . . and that's all you've wanted, isn't it?"

"My Lord, Janice!"

She was fond of Wally. Before Henry appeared on the scene she had thought she was fond enough of Wally to marry him. At least she had wanted to take care of him. She had read uncertainty and self-deprecation in his eyes and persuaded herself that she could banish such shadows and find her own happiness in doing so. Then she had met Henry. . . .

Speaking with the lilt that wouldn't stay out of her voice, she said, "It isn't as if we'd been engaged, Wally. You had left me perfectly free to do as I liked when I met Henry."

How she lingered over his name! Wally merely nodded assent and took what satisfaction he could from the fact that she apparently felt obliged to go on talking about how free she had been when she met his brother. She was applying salve to his wounded pride. Quite rightly, her conscience was none too easy.

Fury shook him with such force that he moved away from Janice so that she wouldn't know how his body was being racked. The degree of his emotion alarmed him. He could have turned on the blind, foolish creature at his side; he could have taken her throat between his hands . . . so that Henry wouldn't have her. . . .

Henry and Janice were married in April 1917, two weeks after the declaration of war on Germany. A month later Henry received his commission in the engineers.

CHAPTER EIGHT —1925

Janice died in childbirth eight years after her marriage. In death she looked younger. The shadow of sorrow—the memory of a dead child, of her husband's lapses from the standard of perfection she had believed him to represent—was gone from her face. Artificial color applied to cheeks and lips helped to create the illusion of a young girl.

That was how Wally saw her. Henry had sent her body to Kinnelly, and Wally waited until late at night when the household was in bed to slip downstairs and look at her.

She lay near the front windows, surrounded by flowers. A single wall light had been left burning. It furnished little illumination in the spaciousness of the room, remodeled several years ago by removal of the partition between front and back parlors.

It seemed to Wally that he was looking at the girl who had come to talk to him at Douglas's wedding. There was sadness in recalling the way she smiled that day, the ruffled dress she wore, the ride to town together in Nick's car.

His hands were clasped behind his back as he studied her. They had dressed her in blue; that was her favorite color, the color the ruffled dress had been. He was glad she hadn't cut her hair short as all the women were doing nowadays.

Wally had not yet undressed for the night. He was in a gray suit, a slight, boyish figure in the dim light. If there had been anyone to see him, he would have seemed no more than twenty himself.

"Well," he thought, "here she lies." He moved to the door and pressed the switch that turned on the overhead lights.

They swept away illusion. His hair was graying at the temples, his skin was sallow, with lines around the eyes and more of them puckering his mouth, giving it a petulant cast. And Janice was not a young girl; she was a dead woman with rouged cheeks and lips. Her fair hair, drawn back loosely from a center part, was the only thing about her that was really unchanged. She was thirty years old.

"Well, here she lies," Wally thought again. Sadness had fled before the bright light in the room. He pursed his lips, almost in satisfaction. Janice had preferred Henry to him; she had gone South with his brother after the war and the climate hadn't agreed with her. She had borne Henry two children and lost her life giving birth to the second one. Henry, like all the Howards, couldn't have been a faithful husband. She must have shed her share of tears. . . .

He, Wally reflected, was not like his brothers. He

lacked their strain of infidelity. They were their father's sons; he was apart from them. If Janice had married him and remained in Kinnelly, content with household tasks in the Bennington cottage, no demands beyond her strength would have been made on her. She would have spent no sleepless nights waiting for him to come home. It was Henry who had been too much for her; her routine with Wally would have suited her in its tranquillity. But she hadn't understood that. Dazzled by Henry's superficial appeal, she had flung away her life on him. . . .

She had brought about her own untimely death, then; and it was atonement for the way she had treated Wally. She had earned forgiveness. But he would never forgive Henry for robbing him of her and of the home and family associations he should have had.

He went on looking at her. He believed with all his heart that she had been the great love of his life— there had been no other. He believed that his lagging courtship of her had been the height of romantic ardor.

When Henry had robbed him of her, he had taken everything.

A board creaked on the porch. One of the french doors was opened and his brother stepped into the room. His eyes flicked over Wally tiredly. "Oh, it's you."

"I wasn't in the mood for bed," Wally told him. "I felt like coming downstairs to see Janice . . . alone."

Sacs of flesh sagged under Henry's eyes. The ruddy color he had always had was deeper; his jowls were more pronounced, his face heavier. But his auburn hair was still thick and wavy; he was still a striking figure of a man as he stood beside Wally, reducing the latter to insignificance.

Wally glanced at him. Weariness glazed his brother's face, his shoulders were slouched under the weight of it. Still, neither time nor fatigue had yet stripped Henry of that something—you could call it a kind of hard, brutal charm, Wally supposed—that made the older man's way easy for him. The subdued air he had would serve only to arouse more sympathy; no one would be able to do enough for him in his grief, while he, Wally, wouldn't count. No one would remember or care that he had loved Janice first.

Even as he was thinking this, Henry paid his sense of being a lonely, tragic figure some tribute. He said, "That's right, you were rather sweet on Janice once yourself, weren't you?"

Wally's clasped hands tightened their grip on each other. "Damn the clod!" was his inner cry. "It's just like him to belittle my feelings this way!"

Aloud he said coldly, "I think I'll go to bed. Good night." Henry glanced at him from under strongly marked brows and said, "Good night. Turn off the overhead lights as you go out, will you?"

Wally pressed the switch by the door and left the room. From the gloom of the hall he looked back at his brother. Henry stood, hands in pockets, gazing down at his dead wife. While Wally watched him, he raised one hand and rubbed his forehead slowly. There was infinite sorrow in his attitude.

There should be, Wally thought spitefully. He

should suffer, he should endure every conceivable torture of remorse. That ugly sexual drive of his had caused Janice's death. He should never have got her pregnant a second time after the first child had been born dead and she had had such a bad time herself. But had Henry thought of that? Of course not. He had always been a great hulk of selfishness from whom you could expect no kindness or consideration.

He went upstairs to bed. He was no longer sustained by a sense of righteousness as he lay remembering his courtship of Janice and the pleasant hours they had spent together. He shed tears for that lost time and for the emptiness of his life that had never, somehow, been right. Henry, he acknowledged to himself, had at least lived fully. Henry must have memories of Janice that would always be good to call to mind. Far back—how far back?—things had begun to be mixed up for him, Wally . . .

If he had been as big as his brothers . . . if he hadn't been afraid. . . . The devious ways had been stamped on him, though. . . .

There had been the time when he was eight and Henry had hit him for something and he had got his revenge by putting Paris green in the food Henry gave his pet squirrel. The squirrel had died. . . .

If it hadn't been for—— But he had never been at ease with girls anyway. He hadn't been at ease with anyone, actually, except his mother. Seven years ago it seemed that he had found the perfect companion when he met Art Treadwell, a new teacher at the high school, gentle and intelligent. They had had fine talks . . . Then had come the camping trip and that

104

little incident born of Art's stupid lack of understanding . . .

But that was another of the things he never dwelt
upon. . . .

Deep into the night Wally lay weeping.

Anne Howard, aged two weeks, was coming North
in the care of a nurse to make her home with her
grandmother. The day after Janice's funeral the plan
was talked over by Emma, Henry, and Virginia. Apparently it didn't occur to them to consult Wally; he
was at the bank when the decision was made and
was informed of it at the supper table. He looked at
his mother blankly. Janice's and Henry's child was
to be thrust upon him. Henry would be making more
frequent trips to see the brat. There would be little
respite from Henry now.

Virginia said, "I've been wondering if we
shouldn't make some changes in the rooms, Wally.
Yours get lots of sun and air and——"

"No!" he interrupted shrilly. "Give up your room
if you like; let Mother give up hers."

"Mine's at the back and doesn't get enough sun;
and of course we wouldn't think of disturbing
Mother. She's had the same room since she and Father were married."

"No!" Wally said again, pushing back his chair
and getting to his feet. "It's your plan, Sister. You
figure out where you want to put the child. But it
won't be in my room."

"Now, Wally, it was just an idea," Emma said.
"Sit down."

"Yes, sit down." Henry was watching him, an eyebrow raised. "Keep your shirt on. My old room will do very well for a nursery. I see no reason why the baby should upset the household any more than she has to."

Coming from Henry to Wally, it was placatory. Wally, still wanting to leave yet not wanting to let the older brother outdo him in the urbane attitude, sat down slowly.

As though there had been no argument, Henry began to talk of train schedules and the most satisfactory arrangements that could be made for bringing the baby to Kinnelly. Only Emma looked often and thoughtfully at her youngest son. Her gaze went from him to Virginia. She found Virginia, in her forties, an object for pity.

Years ago, when it became clear that Virginia wouldn't marry, she should have had some training. Nursing, Emma reflected vaguely, or perhaps Ginny could have gone on with her music. Anything would have been better than to see her arrived at middle age with her life lacking any vital interest. Wally at least had his work at the bank. Wally . . .

She looked at him and sighed to herself. "You bear children," she thought, "and you have such hopes for them. You think they're going to be outstanding in some way. That's nothing but maternal pride. They don't turn out at all as you want them to."

Virginia's usual austerity was transformed into eagerness as she talked about the baby. The care of the child could be mostly left to her, Emma reflected. "I'm seventy-three," she reminded herself.

"I'm ready to avoid responsibility. I can see that Wally doesn't want the baby here, but I don't want to go into his reasons for feeling that way."

What she did want was to live on the surface of the lives around her. Let them keep their troubles to themselves, she thought. She'd kept hers from them as much as she could. At her time of life it was her privilege to sit in a rocking chair and cherish memories of her young days and of Nicholas Howard, dead for so many years.

The nurse stayed for a week after her arrival with the baby, instructing Virginia on the intricacies of infant care. Henry's old room was repainted, its heavy furniture moved to the attic, linoleum laid on the floor, and nursery pieces installed. Virginia took charge of the activity. Not since her girlhood had she shown such zest for any project.

No demands were made on Wally, his routine was in no way changed, when the baby came. Nonetheless, during the first weeks that she was in the house he made a point of mentioning it at breakfast whenever he had heard her crying in the night.

He had expected to experience some profound emotion the first time he looked at Anne Howard. Either he must feel violent hatred for her or great tenderness. He fancied the latter; it would indicate nobility of nature on his part. He played with the idea of a strong bond developing between the child and him. As she grew older he would hold first place in her affections, ahead of her own father. Would there ever be a more delicate balancing of the scales of justice than if this took place?

However, his first glimpse of the child had no particular effect on him. She lay in her crib when he came home from the bank and went upstairs to look at her. She was a month old and had a fuzz of red hair. She was asleep, just a small baby like any other.

With the passage of time he discovered that he had no interest in children after all. He had no knack for playing with them or amusing them.

At Christmas, Henry was home for a week, pronouncing approval of the way Anne Howard had grown and letting his sister take full credit for it. He was more interested in his daughter than he had expected to be; she showed off for him and laughed at everything he did to entertain her.

She was seventeen months old when he came again. She was walking and putting words together and delighted him with her engaging curiosity about her enlarging world. Before his three weeks' stay was over Henry had become devoted to her and the devotion was a mutual affair. At no time had she ever bestowed caresses on her uncle Wally as lavishly as she gave them to her father. It was the familiar pattern repeated, Wally told himself. It didn't occur to him that a child as young as Anne could sense his indifference to her.

Henry returned to the South. There was an exchange of letters with Emma. He wanted to be near his daughter, he wrote. His company would transfer him to its Connecticut office; he could live in Kinnelly and commute to work.

Emma read the letter aloud to Wally. He walked

up and down in front of her agitatedly. "Why, of all the—— Why, the thing's—it's just not to be thought of!" he sputtered. "I don't want him back. You know Henry and I never got along. I'm the one who stayed here with you all these years, Mother. I'm the one who should be considered first."

"Henry is my son too," Emma pointed out. "With his wife dead and his child with us, this is still his home. He has his rights. I'd be a poor kind of mother if I didn't write him to come, that the spare room would be ready for him."

Wally argued, but Emma wouldn't change her decision. The last threat of all—to leave himself if Henry came home—hung on his lips without being spoken. He didn't dare to give it voice. His mother would let him go. She would say that she couldn't sacrifice Henry's need to his unreasonableness, but it wouldn't be that. If she were forced to choose, there could never be any doubt of what her choice would be.

CHAPTER NINE — 1929

On an autumn afternoon Wally's face was set in anger as he hurried out to the barn. Henry and he had just had hot words over Anne. The child had got into his room and scribbled in his books and torn several pages. He hadn't thought himself unduly severe with her, but the little girl had cried and that had brought Henry to her defense.

It was years since he had struck his younger brother. At the height of their quarrel, however, it had seemed that he might.

Wally flung a saddle over the aging mare that was the only horse left in the barn, buckling straps with fingers that shook and fumbled their task. He talked to her as he led her outside. "I'd have killed him if he laid a hand on me," he declared through his teeth. "So help me God, I would have."

He was a trim figure on a horse; erect and relaxed, he gained size and dignity from the animal. He rode down the driveway past the house. Anne, with a child's quick forgetfulness of a scolding, waved to him from the porch, but he pretended not to see her. On Nod Road a touch on the reins headed Lady toward the river.

It was a sunny September afternoon with only feathery white clouds to break the limitless blue of the sky.

Lady moved at an easy trot on the dirt road that paralleled the river while Wally's high pitch of anger gradually abated. It became possible to review the exchange with Henry without beginning to tremble again. His hatred of his brother was like a fever chart, shooting up to sharp peaks, zigzagging down to lesser levels, but always fixed in him.

A little later he was saying aloud, "How can we go on like this? There's no room in the house—there's no room in the world—for both of us any more. I'll end up killing him one of these days."

He hadn't expected to hear himself say that; he hadn't thought it out; it had come of itself.

He rode on for a space, looking at the satiny sheen of Lady's neck in the sunlight. He didn't quite believe what he had just said. After all, he was Wallace Howard, teller at the bank, member and regular worshiper at the church on the green. He believed in God and the Christian virtues He represented. It seemed to Wally that there was nothing in his background to lend credibility to his words.

Big, overwhelming, quick-tempered, the figure of Nicholas Howard sprang unbidden to his mind. It moved before him on the road. There was blood on the face. Wally shut his eyes tight. He had seen that blood; and he had been standing beside his baby sister when she turned her head to the side, a bubble

111

of froth on her lips as she died. Death had been familiar since childhood; it had served him in good stead. . . .

His heels urged the mare into a gallop that outran old memories. The road wound away from the river through a patch of wood and across a meadow.

Lady slowed to a walk, and he began to think about Anne. Between them Ginny and Henry were ruining the child. At four she was stubborn and strong-willed. When she started to do something and was told to stop she wouldn't obey. She was persistent and tiresome about everything she undertook. There was nothing of Janice about her except, perhaps, her smile. She had her father's temper. She had his hair and hazel eyes and deliberate charm which she used consciously to get her own way. She was quite spoiled. Emma Howard had reared her family on the maxim that sparing the rod spoiled the child, but over her granddaughter she exercised no control. Indeed, she attempted none. She watched Ginny and Henry give in to Anne and smiled approval and said, "She's only a baby."

Wally concentrated on Anne's faults, trying to keep his mind from darker thoughts. But even while his niece was in the foreground a picture of Henry intruded itself.

Henry was dead and, like Janice, lay surrounded by flowers in the living room. Wally stood looking at him as he had looked at Janice and was filled with relief. The weight of Henry had rested heavily on him all his life and it was removed. Henry would never trouble him again. . . .

The road dipped gently into a hollow and climbed

112

up to join a hard-surfaced road that went past Douglas's. Reining in the mare at the top of the slope, Wally could see Douglas's house across the hollow. It was square-built with a square porch jutting out at the front. The upper half was finished with brown-stained shingles; the lower part was clapboarding painted yellow. It was solid and comfortable, and that was the most that could be said for it.

The mare stood patiently while her master made up his mind to call on Martha. He liked his sister-in-law. She would ask him to supper and he would stay. It would be pleasant to ride home at twilight, and by the time he got there Henry would have gone out for the evening. No one asked Henry, a man in his late forties, where he was going, but Wally knew that his brother was taking out women again. Janice was forgotten.

The mare ambled down into the hollow and went up the opposite rise. He would ask Bob Vanderbrouk, Martha's son by her first marriage, to ride with him tomorrow, Wally decided. Bob was growing up to be as nice a boy as you could ask for. There was no physical resemblance between tall, stocky, blond Bob and Wally, but the latter found traces of his own youth in the boy. Bob had a deep affection for his mother and treated her with more consideration than was usual at his age. He wasn't rough or brutal with anyone. He borrowed books from Wally and listened to the older man's opinion of them with respect.

Bob seemed to get on well with his stepfather. Douglas had turned exclusively to dairy farming, and the boy helped him outside of school hours. Wally had never known them to be at odds and yet he hadn't finally concluded that Bob was fond of his stepfather.

How could he be? Wally reflected that Bob, at fifteen, must have heard some of the gossip about his stepfather and Yvonne Beaumetz. Their affair, predating Douglas's marriage, had been a town scandal for so long that it had almost taken on the stature of respectability. After all these years Martha surely knew about it. Douglas was not the man to bother with much effort at sneaking around corners.

He felt indignant on Martha's behalf. Yvonne Beaumetz was trash. Martha had it all over her for looks, for ladylike behavior, for character. Yvonne didn't even have youth in her favor. She was every day as old as Martha, if not older. What Douglas could see in the slut . . .

It was sex, of course. The creature was without Martha's refinement and must keep Douglas in her clutches with behavior too disgustingly abandoned to think about. . . .

Bob was in the barn when the older man dismounted at the open door. He came forward to meet him. "Hello, Uncle Wally. Here, I'll take Lady for you."

Wally was looping the reins over a post. "If you'll just give her a drink of water, little man. I don't know yet how long I'll be staying."

He lingered to chat for an interval and then crossed the yard to the front, thinking with approval of Bob. The boy was as sound as his mother.

Behind him, arms akimbo, Bob grinned as he watched him. Wally was a funny old guy but likable

114

in a way. And rather pathetic, somehow, when you got right down to it. . . .

The screen door slammed while Wally was rounding the corner of the house. A thick mat of vine on the porch trellis hid Douglas and Martha from him, so that he heard their voices before he saw them. Martha was saying, "I tell you I won't have it, Doug. I've kept quiet long enough. I didn't sleep last night thinking of that remark Bob made yesterday. He's got to be con—"

It was a bitter dispute, apparently. Martha sounded all but hysterical. Wally paused, uncertain of what to do. Then Douglas crossed the porch and saw his brother. Relief was in his greeting. "Hello, there," he called heartily. "How are you? I'm just leaving—a couple of errands—but Martha's here to keep you company."

"Hello." Wally mounted the steps with hesitant tread, looking from one to the other. Douglas had an expression compounded of obstinacy and sullenness. Martha was flushed and her lips were tight-pressed.

"How are you?" Wally asked her, trying to act as if nothing were out of the ordinary, pulling off his gloves and dropping them on a table.

"Good." Martha barely parted her lips.

"Well, I'll be running along," Douglas began. "I've got a lot—"

"Don't you dare!"

One foot hung suspended in the motion of going down the steps. Douglas drew it back and turned to look at his wife. "Y'know, Martha, I don't like that tone used to me."

"And I don't like your behavior. I said I wouldn't stand for it and I meant it! Just because I've been putting up with it for years doesn't mean that I'll continue to now that Bob is growing up and said yesterday that——"

"What I do is none of Bob's business. It never was and it never will be."

Wally was forgotten as they faced each other. He moved back to the house wall, wanting to leave and not knowing how to effect his departure.

Martha's hand rested on the table. She picked up Wally's gloves and began to smooth them out, not even knowing she had them. Her voice was lifted. "I meant what I said. If you go near that Beaumetz woman today or any other day, don't come back here! The doors will be locked, and they'll stay locked as far as you're concerned."

Douglas's scowl was formidable. He thrust his head forward. "By God, I'm past fifty years old. I never let anyone tell me what I could or couldn't do since I was a boy. I don't intend to start now. When I want to see Yvonne I'll see her, and if you lock any door in this house I'll break it down!"

Afterward it seemed to Wally that much time went by while Martha looked at her husband, her hands working at the gloves. There was time to think she would rip them apart, time to hear Bob's footsteps coming through the hall toward them, time to draw in breath to say, "Here's Bob," and end the scene.

The warning went unuttered. Douglas was standing at the edge of the steps, his back to them, when Martha lifted the gloves to strike him across the face, crying, "Why, you—you——"

He threw up an arm to hold off the blow and lost his balance.

There were only four steps to the ground. But at the bottom Douglas's head struck heavily against the stone baluster. Before Wally could grasp what had happened Bob rushed out of the house.

Martha's arm fell to her side. Her head came around and she stared at her son as if she couldn't identify him. She said, "Go back in the house, Bob. Go now! You didn't see a thing."

"But, Mother——"

She screamed at him, a termagant he didn't know. "Go back in the house this minute! Go to your room and stay there until I tell you to come down!"

The boy's gaze went from her to Wally. Without another word he turned to the door. They heard him ascending the stairs.

Wally swallowed hard and moved forward until he stood beside Martha looking at his brother.

Douglas lay sprawled out at the bottom of the steps, his head twisted in such a fashion as Wally had never seen before. No living man had ever held his head like that against his shoulder.

The sun glinted on red hair touched with gray. Douglas faced the other way. Wally could have gone down one step and touched his brother's foot with his own. It was inconceivable that anyone should die from a fall as short as that.

He couldn't, himself, make sure that the inconceivable had happened. He said to Martha in a thread of speech, "He's hurt. You'd better see—how much . . ."

"He's dead," Martha stated, and her voice came out clearly. "You know he's dead."

Wally moved back. "I'll call a doctor. We've got to have one right away."

"He's dead," Martha repeated. "What good will a doctor do?" She was still pulling at the gloves and then, suddenly conscious of what was in her hands, dropped them on the table.

"We have to call a doctor—as soon as I get my breath." Wally sank into the nearest chair.

The road was empty in the warm light of late afternoon. But any moment a car might appear for its occupants to see the peculiar tableau: a man limp in a chair, another man spread out dead at the foot of the steps, a woman fixed at the top of them.

The plaintive moo of a cow came from the pasture. Wally glanced across the road and saw the brown herd moving about. It was close to milking time. The two men Doug employed would be coming from the dairy barn. They had to do something . . . He had to do something, he corrected himself, his eyes going to his sister-in-law. Martha was like a woman in a dream. She couldn't do a thing.

He said in a firm, strong voice, "Martha, I'll call Dr. Harshbarger."

"Yes." All at once she was shaking from head to foot and leaned against a pillar for support. "It's my fault. I killed him."

"No, you didn't. You never touched him. I saw the whole thing. He lost his balance and fell. It was an accident."

She shook her head and flung an arm over her

face. "It was because I was going to hit him . . . with your gloves . . ."

Wally's eyes narrowed. His gloves. Was she trying to involve him? Of course she wasn't. She didn't know what she was saying in that smothered voice.

She straightened herself and walked down the steps to kneel beside Douglas. She touched his twisted head and picked up his hand. A flood of tears came. "Doug . . . oh, Douglas . . ."

Wally fled to the hall and telephoned the family doctor. He knew what he was going to say. It came from him effortlessly. "This is Wally Howard speaking, Doctor. I'm over at my brother Douglas's. There's been a dreadful accident. He lost his balance and fell down the porch steps. I'm afraid his neck is broken. Will you come right away, please?"

The doctor said he would come immediately. Wally cradled the receiver, went back to the porch and down the steps to his sister-in-law, picking his way so as not to brush against the dead man's legs.

He caught Martha's shoulder and shook the sobbing woman. "Martha, I've called the doctor. Martha . . ."

A car came toward them, the porch in full view of the man at the wheel. He slowed to a stop across the road and stuck his head out the window. He was no one Wally knew.

"What's the matter?" he called.

"There's been an accident," Wally answered. "But the doctor's on his way and there's nothing you can do."

"Well . . ." The man put the car in gear and drove on slowly for about a hundred feet. He stopped again

119

and sat with his head out the window, looking back at them.

"Martha!" Wally shook her with increased vigor. "You've got to pull yourself together. The doctor will be here."

"I can't," Martha sobbed, her face against her husband's shoulder. "I——Oh, don't talk—don't bother me!"

"I must." Wally drew her away from his brother and helped her to her feet. "You've got to listen to me. Dr. Harshbarger is coming. I told him Doug fell and that his neck was broken. That's all he has to know . . . Are you listening?" His hands dug into her shoulders urgently. "Are you?"

"Yes." She raised her head so that he saw her tear-stained face.

"We don't want a scandal." Wally enunciated his words carefully, to aid her in understanding them. "All we have to say is that the three of us were talking here on the porch. Doug was getting ready to leave to do some errands. He didn't seem to realize how near he was to the edge of the porch, because he stepped back and fell."

He brought his face close to hers, looking anxiously into her lackluster eyes. "Martha, is that clear?"

She pulled away from him. "I couldn't say that. It isn't true. I was going to hit him. That's why he fell. I killed him."

"Oh, my God." Wally began to pace the walk. "What good will it do to bring disgrace on yourself? It won't bring Douglas back to life. And my mother . . . think of my mother. This will be shock enough to her as it is. She could never stand knowing what had really happened. And Bob . . . my God, Martha . . ." He caught her shoulders again. "Your own son! He's a fine boy, and you'll ruin him if you don't keep quiet about it. Your highest duty is to him now."

"He saw it all anyway," Martha reminded him dully. "I can't keep it from him."

"You can keep him from being ruined by it," Wally insisted. "As he would be if every detail of what went on here came out . . . As all of us would be. Martha, I've got to make you see it this way. If you tell the whole story, what good will it do? Douglas's death will still be an accident. I'm prepared to swear in any court in the land that you never touched him. You didn't, you know . . ."

He said the same things over and over with mounting desperation. Dr. Harshbarger was due any moment. If Martha persisted in the folly of martyring herself, the town would ring with the story by nightfall. His mother, all of them, would share the disgrace as every detail of the Yvonne Beaumctz affair was told and retold . . . And what would the conservative bank officials say to having one of their tellers involved in such a lurid business? But it was no use telling this stubborn woman that he would, no doubt, have to resign the position he had held for so long. . . .

He finally concentrated on the harm she could do her son. That was the note to strike; intelligence came back into her eyes when he kept telling her she must protect Bob.

The doctor's car stopped in the driveway. Dr. Harshbarger jumped out and hurried across the lawn, a tall, lanky figure who held their future in his hands.

He knelt beside Douglas's body and made a brief examination. As he got to his feet Wally placed a reassuring arm around Martha. The doctor addressed her. "I suppose you know your husband is dead, Mrs. Howard?"

Martha nodded. Her eyes went to Wally.

It was he who gave an account of what had happened. "I'd just arrived, Doctor. Doug was about to start downtown and we stood talking on the porch. Doug was at the edge of the steps facing us. He lifted his hand to brush away some bug—a bee, I think—that lighted on him and lost his balance. Before either of us could move to help him he went down the steps backward and struck his head . . ."

Wally let his voice trail off and reached for a handkerchief. He blew his nose hard. There was time now to feel a little sorry for the dead brother. After all, Douglas had been eight years his senior and had never treated him with the harshness Henry showed. Tears that were partly for his brother's death and partly for himself, caught up in the violence and suddenness of it, sprang to his eyes.

"You'd never in the world," he added brokenly, "expect a little fall like that . . ."

"Falls are tricky things," the doctor remarked.

His expression was sympathetic as he looked at Martha. Wally could feel her body taut against his arm. But she didn't speak. She didn't challenge his story. Once she became involved in her present silence she must keep to it.

Wally let his tears flow unchecked. He could do the talking. He could take care of everything.

CHAPTER TEN — 1931

No one ever shortened Alfred Lodge's first name to Al. Alfred suited him. It suited his dreamy-looking, myopic blue eyes, his pink-and-white complexion, the lock of fair hair that fell forward over his high forehead. It suited his shy manner, his soft voice, his old-fashioned air of diffidence toward his elders.

Alfred came to Kinnelly late in 1930 to take up his duties as pharmacist at the Kinnelly drugstore. That was where Wally met him for the first time; afterward he fell into the habit of stopping by frequently to talk with the tall, wispy young man. It was spring, however, before he invited Alfred to visit him at home, where Henry subjected him to a brief scrutiny and ignored him. When the visits increased Henry began to refer to Alfred as Wally's soul mate. By early summer he was thoroughly disagreeable about the friendship.

It still had its tentative aspects. Wally was only beginning to open his heart to the young man as he had once done with Art Treadwell, the high-school teacher. This time there was to be no camping trip nor repetition of its disaster.

Zoology was Alfred's hobby. In the Howard car Wally and he toured museums within driving radius. They read works on it together. Like Janice long ago, Wally's new companion couldn't be persuaded to take an interest in riding. But when Wally rode on Saturday afternoons Alfred, during his hours off from the drugstore, would meet the older man at some appointed place and walk back to the Howard house beside him and the mare.

Alfred was still young enough to embark on long earnest conversations about God and immortality. He enjoyed discussions of the compulsions that motivated human behavior. And he shared Wally's liking for poetry.

A hot Sunday afternoon in July invited them outdoors to the Howard orchard. Stretched out on the grass, they took turns reading aloud. The heat induced languor. They read slowly.

Henry came upon them in the orchard. Dressed in swimming trunks and tennis shoes, he was strolling about with Anne tagging after him in bathing suit and sandals. They were waiting for Bob Vanderbrouk, who was bicycling over to go swimming with them.

Henry had a tall glass, misty with coldness, in his hand. Tom Collinses were his personal prescription for withstanding the heat.

Wally and Alfred had their heads close together over the volume of poetry. Wally read Whitman's words:

Here is the efflux of the soul,

The efflux of the soul comes from within through embower'd gates, ever provoking questions,

These yearnings why are they? these thoughts in the darkness why are they?

"Well, why?" Henry demanded from behind them.

They hadn't heard him coming across the grass. Wally, lying face down, supporting himself on his elbows, swung around to look at his brother.

Henry stood over them with his legs wide apart, the swimming trunks revealing the depth and breadth of his chest under its mat of red hair, the flatness of his stomach, the heavy biceps in his arms. He was smiling; at least his teeth gleamed white in the ruddiness of his face. It wasn't a pleasant smile; it let them see his mockery of them.

"Tell me some more," he urged, dropping down on his haunches. "These yearnings of yours, Wally—I don't know that I understand them very well."

Wally rolled over and sat up, and Alfred did the same. Alfred was scarlet, his glance going uneasily from one brother to the other. He waited for Wally to deal with the situation.

"Well?" Henry prodded and drank deeply from his glass.

"We're—reading," Wally brought out unsteadily. "We'd rather—you didn't interrupt."

"Oh yes. I can appreciate your reticence." The older brother settled back on the grass, resting on one elbow. "But go ahead and read to me. I promise not to interrupt at all."

Alfred stood up. "I think I'd better be running along," he muttered, not meeting their eyes.

For Wally the young man's embarrassment was painful to witness. His tall body that still had the awkward, bony look of adolescence, his scarlet face and lowered gaze made him seem unbearably vulnerable. The instinct to protect his youthful companion swept Wally to his feet, forgetful of fear of his brother.

He covered the short distance between them and glared down at Henry. "Get out," he said furiously. "Alfred is visiting me. I didn't ask him here to be driven away by you. It's not his place to leave. It's yours."

Henry set aside his empty glass and let his eyes travel over Wally indolently and come to rest on the latter's set face. "I've got as much right in the orchard as you have," he pointed out. "I should think you'd want me to stay and acquire a little culture. God knows you've made it plain enough that you think I'm a terrible boor. Maybe"—he pulled up a blade of grass and inserted it between his teeth—"if I stick around you'll see an improvement."

"I insist that you go!"

"This passion for privacy . . ." Henry deplored it with a shrug. He was openly laughing at the younger man.

"Damn you, get out of here!" Beside himself, Wally grabbed his brother's arm and tried to drag him to his feet.

Henry's answer was to sit up and slap Wally's face. It was not a hard slap, indeed it was given almost lazily, but it caught Wally by surprise and sent him sprawling to the earth. Henry stood up, looked at Alfred whose jaw sagged and at Wally, coming back to his knees. He couldn't miss the hatred in his younger brother's face. It blazed from the dark eyes, it showed itself nakedly in the distortion of the prim mouth, the paper-white pallor of the skin.

It startled Henry. He could neither share nor comprehend it. He had only been alleviating boredom on a hot afternoon; when Wally rose to the bait, he had kept the thing going. He hadn't meant to hit him or to bring such feeling to the surface.

"You asked for that, you know," he said, and he was apologizing. He pulled at the strap of his trunks and bent to pick up the glass. Still he hesitated. Some graceful means of withdrawal should offer itself, some casual phrase or gesture that would restore the crouching figure on the grass to normality.

Six-year-old Anne Howard witnessed the scene. Lagging behind her father on his stroll, she had been kneeling over an anthill, absorbed in watching the insects, until Wally's raised voice caught her attention. She stuck her head around the hedge that separated garden and orchard in time to see her father hit her uncle. Henry's back was toward her, but she had a good view of Wally, facing him. His expression frightened her. She drew closer to the hedge, watching him apprehensively.

"Don't look at my daddy that way," she whispered. "You stop it, Uncle Wally. Stop it now." This made her feel a trifle better, but only a trifle.

There was another witness. Bob Vanderbrouk,

skirting the far edge of the hedge, unaware of Anne's presence, arrived in time to see what was happening. It was he, racing across the orchard, who solved Henry's dilemma of what to do next.

Two years ago Wally had saved Bob's mother from disgrace; this was an opportunity to discharge a fraction of the everlasting debt of gratitude he owed him.

He stooped and helped him to his feet and turned on Henry. "You damned well ought to be ashamed of yourself, Uncle Henry! Why don't you pick on someone your own size?"

Next to her father, Bob Vanderbrouk was Anne's idol. The episode was more inexplicable than ever to her. Bob, too, it seemed, was mad at her father, lashing out at him with bitter words. Her father wasn't mad, though. He talked quietly. She saw him lift his shoulders in defeat and shake his head. Bob lowered his voice after a while, and at last the whole group moved toward her. She heard her father say, "Look, I've told you I'm sorry. Now let's forget it. Wally, for God's sake, shake hands and drop it, will you?"

Anne was certain that Uncle Wally didn't want to shake hands, but Bob was urging him and finally he did. He no longer looked as he had a few minutes ago; there was no expression of any kind to be seen on his face. Alfred, Uncle Wally's friend, trailed along with the others, hanging back and looking sad. Not sad exactly, Anne corrected herself; she didn't know any word to cover the way he looked. Bob wasn't mad now; he was smiling at her father. It was Henry who looked troubled, with deep lines creasing his forehead. Anne studied him anxiously; she was a faithful reflection of his moods.

They were drawing close to her. The child stood up, the hedge higher than her head, and ran noiselessly away. . . .

Weeks were to pass before the scene in the orchard lost its vividness. It never was quite forgotten. Years later Anne would recall it, not in detail but as an impression of Wally against her father with Bob taking her uncle's part, eventually to become, in her recollection, an integral part of the quarrel.

That night Wally walked alone by the river. He stood on the dock, hands in his pockets, brooding over what had happened. He was steeped in humiliation.

"Today was the end," he announced in the night silence. "I'm going to kill him. He's brought it on himself. He's closed the door on everything else."

He paced the dock. Up and down it he went, shoulders drawn in, letting hate engulf him, hugging it to him with a finality that meant it must find an outlet.

Wally couldn't bear to think of Alfred. "I love the boy," he admitted to himself. And Alfred had looked up to him, admired him, until today. . . .

They would still be friends, yes. Alfred had been sympathetic about the whole wretched affair. But how could any admiration be left in the other's regard for him? He had seen Wally insulted, struck in the face, unable to retaliate. He had heard Henry's nasty gibes at their friendship that stripped it of the glamour it had held . . .

"Christ above," Wally cried to the dark water, "how I hate Henry!"

The one aspect of the afternoon that bore contemplation was Bob Vanderbrouk's championing of his cause. It eased humiliation to review the boy's attitude there in the orchard. He liked Henry, and Henry's daughter adored him; yet he had taken Wally's side today and elicited a formal apology from Henry to his brother. Gratitude was not altogether dead in the human heart.

Wally was sometimes uneasy about the gratitude Bob displayed to him. A few days after Douglas's death Bob had tried to thank him for what he had done. The older man, feeling sorry for him, had cut the conversation short. Afterward, sorting out Bob's halting words, he realized that the boy thought his mother had actually hit Douglas, causing his fall. He had been at the screen door. From that different angle it looked that way to him.

Twelve paces to the edge of the dock and twelve paces back. Wally counted them. One of these days he must correct that idea; it would mean a lot to Bob if he knew his mother hadn't played such a direct role in his stepfather's death. On the other hand, it might lessen the sense of gratitude toward himself.

Perhaps he would wait a while longer to tell him the truth.

The brief time that Bob could deflect his thoughts from Henry came to an end. Nothing could keep Henry out of them for long tonight. His fate was settled. It was merely a question of ways and means. . . .

Wally went on pacing the dock, his eyes on the water, seeking the answer.

CHAPTER ELEVEN —

Wally put Paisley's *Household Poisons and Their Remedies* back on the shelf. He returned to the chair where he had done his reading to consider what he had learned about aconite.

There wasn't the least possibility of securing any monkshood, grinding up its roots, and serving it to Henry as horseradish. . . .

Aconitine, though . . . He had been in the back room of the drugstore where prescriptions were compounded; he knew which drawer Alfred went to when he wanted the key to the cabinet where poisons were kept. . . .

It was eleven o'clock at night. Emma and Virginia had gone to bed an hour ago. Anne had been in bed since seven-thirty, and Lena had climbed the stairs to her attic room at nine. Henry was out and not likely to return before midnight. In the quiet of the living room, with only the lamp beside the chair turned on, Wally had uninterrupted leisure for contemplating a feasible means of ending his brother's life.

Days had passed since Henry had struck him in front of Alfred, but his resolution had not faltered. Not even the anguish he must cause his mother nor the necessity of including a six-year-old child in his plan could weaken Wally's resolve. The thing could be broken down into mathematical calculations. Henry had crowded every possible experience into half a century of living. What could he look forward to that he hadn't already had?

But Wally himself—what about him? Henry had robbed him of Janice, the children he might have had; he had cast his hulking shadow over the whole of his younger brother's life.

If Wally should live the allotted seventy years, he had twenty-five of them left. It was his right to make the most of them; Henry had had too much; he had had too little. Henry must make way for him at last.

Since childhood God had worn two faces for Wally, the churchgoer. In forbearance His face was benevolent and kind. But when forbearance had been shattered He turned the other face of wrath and punishment. It was the latter face that Wally pictured, bearded and stern, bidding him act as its instrument.

He moved restlessly in the chair. The quiet and dimness of the room, the late hour, gave imagination full play. He could look past the bookshelves into the shadows and conjure up the face of a baby sister, her life wished away by a boy of five. That boy, locking in his terror and remorse, had thought of himself as the instrument. . . .

He could turn his head the other way and see a big redheaded man lolling against the cushions of the window seat. He lacked half a face; where it should have been there was an open wound and blood. Wally's hands went up involuntarily to cover his eyes. He had never been the instrument of such an awful sight as that. . . .

To break the spell he had himself evoked, he got to his feet, crossed the room to the french doors, and went out on the porch. He stood at the railing looking across the pasture. A faint mist rose from it in peaks and spirals that could be said to take on shapes almost human if one looked at them long enough. Somewhere in the mist a whippoorwill raised a constant plaint. "Whippoor-*will*, whippoor-*will* . . ."

His hands closed on the porch railing. He would keep Alfred and the drugstore out of it by using tincture of aconite. He would get it from Dr. Sheehan, the family dentist. Every so often when Emma's plate irritated her gum, Dr. Sheehan used the tincture to relieve its soreness. He must have it, then, available at his office.

"Whippoor-*will* . . ." The plaintive, disembodied cry kept coming from the mists.

"Aco-*nite* . . ." Wally heard himself employing the same accent. He turned back to the house.

On his lunch hour, which coincided with the dentist's, Wally crossed the green from the bank and climbed the stairs to Dr. Sheehan's office. The dentist and his nurse were absent, but since no particular care about locking doors was taken in Kinnelly, a turn of the knob let him into the waiting room. Nor was the inner door locked. Wally skirted the dental chair and stood before the supply cabinet. That, too, was unlocked. It contained a two-ounce bottle of tincture of aconite that was nearly full. The label carried a warning that it was poisonous, but nevertheless there it was, waiting for the first comer.

He shook his head over such carelessness, slipped the bottle into his pocket, and went out. . . .

Emma helped him to launch his plan that Saturday afternoon. She fanned herself with a folded newspaper and said first of all, "Goodness, this heat!"

The awning shaded the side porch. Anne was stretched out on the grass rug at her grandmother's feet with water colors and a paint book. Wally, inert in the glider, looked as if he had nothing on his mind. Henry had a radio on the table beside him. Wearing old flannels, he was deep in a chair, dividing his attention between the morning *Courant* and the baseball game being broadcast. Only Virginia was missing from the family group. She had driven to town for treatment by a chiropractor in whom she had great faith. Virginia, within the last few years, had decided there was something wrong with her back.

Emma continued, "I should think you'd all go for a swim. If I were your age I certainly would."

She was nowhere near any of their ages, of course. She was nearly eighty, enjoying the amazement of new acquaintances that she should be as old as that when she didn't look within ten years of it. She had on a flowered dress. Her snowy hair was waved and worn in rolls back from her face. Her dark eyes were clear and bright and she used glasses only for reading.

Wally glanced at her and looked away quickly. If his plan succeeded . . .

Anne raised her head. She had been experimenting with holding the handle of the brush between her teeth as she painted. It was still there, interfering with speech, as she asked eagerly, "Are we going swimming, Gram?"

Emma smiled at her. "Ask your father or uncle Wally."

"Daddy!" Anne whirled around to him, her thick red braids swinging out from her head. "Will you take me swimming?"

"Oh Lord," Henry groaned.

This was the moment. Wally said, "It might be a good idea to take our supper along and cook it by the river. What do you think, Anne?"

"Yes, yes, let's have a picnic," the child cried delightedly, jumping to her feet.

There wasn't any question of what must follow after that. Henry was free to be as bored as he pleased, but he couldn't say no to his daughter. He stipulated that they must wait until the game was over. Anne raced to the kitchen and importuned Lena to pack the picnic basket. She flew back to the porch. "Daddy, may I ask Bob to come?"

Henry grinned. "Bob? I'm going to sue that kid for alienation of your affections before I'm through. Sure, go ahead and call him."

Wally hadn't counted on Bob. Hand in his pocket, he fingered the bottle that hadn't left his person since the day he had obtained it. He was in the grip of frustration. If Bob should come he'd have to give the whole thing up until another time.

As he thought it over, however, he changed his mind. At the crucial time he would get rid of the boy somehow. He'd work it out. . . .

He couldn't face a postponement. He might never be able to go on with it if he did. His gaze wandered back and forth between Henry and Emma while the ball game drew to a close. He had insulated himself against breaking under the strain; in his view he was no more than an instrument of justice. But his heart pounded heavily while he waited; his breath came in shallow gasps.

Anne ran back and forth, reporting that she had telephoned Bob and he was coming, that Lena said they could have broilers and some of the tarts she'd baked that morning. She leaped about, her small face aglow.

The game ended as Bob arrived on his bicycle. Bob had finished high school that June and was going to the agricultural college in the autumn. "Another year," Henry told him, "and you won't be bothered with fuddyduddies like Wally and me and kids like Anne. I don't know why anyone goes on a picnic of his own free will anyway."

Wally got to his feet. He hadn't been sure his legs would hold him up, but they did. They even carried him upstairs, where he put on a bathing suit and a pair of flannels over it that were as old and stained as the ones Henry wore.

His brother was in the hall when Wally came down. He followed the older man to the dining room and watched him fill a small pocket flask at the sideboard. He had been counting on that; his plan was built around the flask. And Henry hadn't disappointed him. Henry was cooperating in every possible way.

He trailed his brother out to the porch. There was morbid fascination in following each move Henry made as he selected a cigarette from his case, lit it, and exhaled smoke. The man was about to die, and his smallest gesture took on significance because so few of them were left to him.

Bob picked up the picnic basket. Anne was allowed to carry the old tin coffeepot and swung it back and forth so that the chain on the lid made a light tinkling sound. The evening newspaper had arrived, and Henry took that and tucked it under his arm with the blanket he meant to spread on the grass. All that Wally carried was the grid for broiling the chickens and the bottle in his pocket.

Emma stood at the screen door to see them go. Henry gave her arm a squeeze. "Bye, Mother. Enjoy a nice quiet dinner by yourself . . . unless you want to come too?"

He was grinning at her, and the moment before her answer came was long. Wally knew he couldn't kill his brother before her eyes.

Emma shook her head and laughed. "I'll take my meals at table, boy."

"Sensible woman." Henry patted her shoulder and opened the door. This was their parting, Wally thought, and didn't look at his mother when he said good-by to her.

Later he would look at her and kneel beside her to offer comfort in her grief. She would at last turn

137

to him as she never had before. He would do everything he could to make it up to her for the sorrow
she must feel. She would get over it in time. She had
stood up so well to the loss of Sam and, only two
years ago, to the shock of Douglas's death. . . .

Emma was the center of the world. She could
stand up to anything.

The bars were still there at the pasture gate although no cows had grazed on the lush grass for
many years. Henry let the bars down and they went
through, with Wally, last in line, putting them back
in place.

Anne held her father's hand, with Bob on the
other side of her. She hopped along, first on one foot
and then on the other, the chain on the coffeepot
keeping up a cheerful accompaniment to her chat-
ter.

Wally's eyes were on his brother's broad back. It
was Henry's last walk, the last time he would look
at a summer sky, the last time his feet would follow
the path they had helped to wear smooth to the river. He was telling Bob about the pheasant he had
seen the other day in the wooded land next to the
pasture. He had seen railbirds there too, he added,
and began to talk of the hunting season. He wouldn't
be raising a gun to his shoulder again on an autumn
morning while that beautiful setter of his flushed
game.

Henry had only himself to blame. In his arro-
gance, he had been building for this day. Wally was
but the trembling, nerve-racked instrument . . .

He drew closer to the trio ahead and heard Anne
saying, "Wait till you see how good I can do it."

138

"All right," Bob answered. "We'll see. Just remember, though, young lady, that one more belly flop off that dock and I quit giving diving lessons." Over her head, his eyes met Henry's. "The trouble with your daughter is she doesn't listen when you explain how something is done."

"How can she listen when she's talking herself every minute?" Henry inquired. "Her tongue isn't still from the time she leaves her bed in the morning until she's back in it at night."

"Oh no," Anne protested. "Aunt Ginny says I'm learning not to interrupt when other people are talking. She says I'm getting to be a little lady and wait my turn."

Henry looked down into her upturned face with affectionate amusement. "I hadn't noticed the improvement, Daughter," he said.

They were at the river. It glittered under the sun. Far down at the bend a sailboat's canvas was a dazzling spot of white. Here at the town itself the river was deep and wide and clean above the mills that polluted its waters where it joined the Connecticut.

Henry spread the blanket out on the grass. On either side the fence that bordered the Howard pasture ran to the river's edge. Years ago they had built a fireplace on the bank and they kept a cache of wood in the hollow stump of a tree. It had been the scene of many family picnics. Henry had lately added an outboard motor to the rowboat that was tied to the dock.

It was he who unbuttoned Anne's pinafore and helped her into her one-piece bathing suit. His large hands were unexpectedly skillful in anything he did

139

for his daughter. When she was ready and tucking her braids under a rubber cap he kissed the tip of her nose and said, "In with you now. You can tell me how the water is."

Bob had already dived off the dock. He swam out with a smooth crawl stroke that the older men had never learned and turned to laugh at Anne's call to wait for her.

Henry stepped out of his flannels and left them in a heap on the grass. Before Wally had removed his shirt his brother was in the water giving encouragement to Anne, who stood at the edge of the dock. The little girl executed a dive in which she just missed hitting the water flat on her stomach and came to the surface crying, "See, Bob! I did a good dive, didn't I?"

There was a drop of several feet to the river. Wally, sitting on the grass, kept his eyes on the bobbing heads below while he reached for Henry's flannels and the four-ounce flask in the hip pocket. He had difficulty with the cap in unscrewing it. He had difficulty with the cork in the bottle he carried. He couldn't keep his hands from shaking as he poured whiskey out on the ground and added tincture of aconite to what was left. He screwed on the cap and shook the flask, his body shielding his actions from the three in the water. They weren't watching him in any case. Bob was treading water and Anne was clinging to his shoulder. Henry and he were laughing and teasing her.

The only post-mortem signs were those of asphyxia, according to Paisley. Numbness and tingling of the mouth were the first symptoms. . . .

The flask was back in the pocket. Wally took off his shirt and trousers, walked down to the dock, and dived into the river.

When the swim was over Anne, meaning to help, hindered him in building a fire. He sent Bob to the spring near by for water when he saw Henry, rubbing himself with a towel, get out the flask. He had trouble with his voice, speaking to Bob. It was little more than a croak when he suggested to Anne that she unpack the paper plates.

Henry removed the top from the flask, tilted his head back, and drank. Wally watched his Adam's apple slide up and down. His hand went to his throat. His own mouth was too dry for swallowing.

His brother blew out his breath, said, "God, that's strong," and put the flask back in the flannels. He lit a cigarette, took a few puffs, and did what Wally had seen him do innumerable times before and had counted on him doing today. He wandered down to the dock, walked out to the edge, and sat down with his feet hanging out over the water, his shoulders propped against a post.

The fire was crackling briskly. Wally left it and followed his brother. A backward glance showed Bob coming into sight with the coffeepot. The boy was perhaps a hundred yards away, moving along the bank toward them.

He had to hurry. He ran the last few feet out to the dock. The whole scene was clear cut before him as he ran. There was Henry, smoking and looking out over the water; across the river a rowboat had put out from shore with a man at the oars and two women facing him; the trees on the opposite bank raised an uneven green pattern against the sky.

Wally reached his brother, cried, "Come on in, the water's fine," and shoved Henry off the dock. He went in after him, hitting the water cleanly in a shallow dive, and began to swim out with a fast overhand stroke as Henry broke surface, sputtering and swearing.

The older man shook water from his eyes, shouted, "By God, you'll get what's coming to you for that one!" and started in pursuit of his brother.

"You'll have to catch me first," Wally called back over his shoulder.

"I'll catch you all right."

Anne was watching from the bank and urging her father on. "Catch him, Daddy, and duck him good." She spied Bob approaching and beckoned to him. "Hurry up, Bob! Daddy's going to duck Uncle Wally."

Her laughter floated out over the water. Wally was a fast swimmer, Henry was a stronger one. The head start he had and his speed carried Wally far ahead. The ugly travesty of water sport continued as he shouted, "You'll have to do better than that, old boy!"

He looked back. Henry's face was twisted in agony, his arms shot up into the air.

The rowboat was coming toward them. One of the women facing the scene screamed. She pointed at the spot where Henry was going down, but Wally pretended not to understand. "What's the matter?" He swam faster toward the boat, putting more distance between his brother and himself and postponing the moment when he must go to Henry's assistance.

The boat and Wally were approximately at midstream. He heard Bob shouting behind him and Anne's frantic sobbing. He could delay no longer. He turned back in time to see Henry thrashing about in the water and to catch a last glimpse of his contorted face as he went under.

Wally added his voice to the commotion. Bob had dived in and Anne followed him. Wally could hear the boy telling her to go back. In the sudden lull every sound they made was loud in the stillness of the afternoon. The little girl sobbed a refusal to return to shore, and Bob had to slow down to swim beside her.

Some distance away from where he had seen Henry disappear Wally began to dive for him. With a sweep of the oars the man in the rowboat came up beside him. "Downstream more," he cried. "More to your left. For God's sake, don't let the current take him!"

Wally had counted on the swift current. It eddied about him, and the water was ten feet deep. He dived repeatedly, keeping his eyes shut under water, afraid of what he might see. On one dive his foot brushed something and he surfaced with his teeth chattering. It had been a submerged branch, surely; or an old barrel; not his brother's body.

Minutes were speeding by. Hampered by Anne, Bob hadn't yet reached them. He yelled to the man in the boat, "My God, come and get this kid, will you?"

The boat was quickly beside them. The man lifted

143

Anne into it. She crouched on the bottom, looking over the edge. One of the women tried to draw her close, saying, "Oh, you poor child," but Anne pulled away from her. The tragedy had left her without words. She could only look prayerfully at Bob as he swam away.

Wally and he kept on diving over an ever-widening area and couldn't find Henry. The older man's lips were blue, his face bloodless. Looking at him, Bob said at last, "You'd better get rowed to shore and go for help. You're all in. I'll keep on diving."

"I can't go," Wally answered. "We'll send this man here with his boat and I'll stay. I can't leave while there's the least hope of saving Henry."

That hope was gone, Bob felt. The ineffectual little man had himself muffed what chance there might have been. He had been fatally slow in understanding that his brother was in trouble. "If only I'd been the one who was with him," Bob thought. "I'd have got to him."

Wally was persuaded to climb over the side of the boat, and sat in the prow huddled together in exhaustion. He didn't look at Anne. He wished he need never look at her again.

CHAPTER TWELVE —

It was growing dark that night when Henry's body was found. By flashlight on the riverbank the characteristic foam of the drowned man was visible on lip and nostril. The medical examiner was satisfied. No question of an autopsy arose.

Wally moved away from his dead brother. It was over. He must go now and tell Emma Howard that Henry was found.

He was quiet during the drive home, sitting alone in the back seat of the car while Bob sat with the driver. All feeling was wrung from him.

"Are you okay?" Bob asked during the ride.

"Yes," Wally said. "But the strain . . ."

It had been the greatest of his life. It was over. Henry had lost the power to hurt him. Henry lay on a blanket, statuelike, dead. He had drowned. What had brought about his drowning was beside the point.

The uncorked bottle of aconite was at the bottom of the river. Henry's flask was in Wally's pocket. All that was left to do was to rinse it out and put it back with Henry's things. There was that one small task remaining . . . And there was his mother.

Virginia opened the front door the moment the headlights swept the yard. He went up the steps to the porch, looked at his sister, and nodded slowly. Her spare figure was rigid against the screen door.

"They—did they try a pulmotor?"

"He'd been in the water for hours," Wally reminded her. "He was completely, unmistakably dead." He walked past her into the house.

Emma sat in her low rocker at the far end of the living room. Nick and his family were away on a vacation trip, but Mary had been summoned and had come with her husband. Martha was there. Each pair of eyes fastened on Wally crossing the threshold. He went the length of room to his mother and dropped down beside her, taking her hands.

"Mother . . ."

She threw off his clasp, got to her feet, and moved away from him. At the french doors she stood plucking at the curtains. No one spoke. She turned and said harshly, "He drowned before your eyes. It seems you could have saved him!"

"Mother!" Wally sprang to his feet and met the bitter, accusing gaze. "I tried. I did everything I could."

"Did you?" From now on no one would tell Emma that she looked younger than she was. Time had caught up with her in the hours since she had heard about Henry.

Mary went to her. "Come and sit down, Mother," she said soothingly. "I'm sure Wally did his best. It will make a wreck of you if you keep thinking of what might have been done."

"I'll never be able to stop thinking of it."

"You don't realize what you're saying!" Wally cried.

"Oh yes, I do." Her glance appraised her youngest son. "If it had been the other way around . . ."

Mary took her mother's arm on one side, Martha on the other. "Mother, you mustn't stand here like this," Mary said. "You've got to rest."

Emma's face was, indeed, twitching. Her eyes looked blind, but apparently they still saw Wally and couldn't bear what they saw. She turned her head away from him.

He stood behind the chair and repeated tiredly, "I did everything I could."

"Of course you did." It was Martha who spoke. "You're all in, Wally. I'll get you some coffee."

"No." He leaned sidewise against the back of the chair and felt the pressure of Henry's flask. "Yes, I will have some. But I'll get it myself."

Between them Mary and her sister-in-law were settling Emma on a sofa. Wally stared at her and felt dazed. Only two or three minutes had gone by since he had entered the room, and in that short period of time his mother had become estranged from him.

"I'm going to call the doctor," Mary said to him in an undertone. He scarcely heard her.

It was Virginia, coming in with Bob, who called the doctor, disregarding Emma's protests that he could do nothing for her. They covered her with an afghan and Mary sat beside her, stroking her hand. Wally was unnoticed as he slipped out to the kitchen.

The percolator stood ready on the range. He turned on the gas under it and sank into a chair. He held his head in his hands. Even after death Henry stood in his way; his mother blamed Wally because her favorite son was dead.

It didn't matter much just then. The day had drained him of the capacity to react positively to anything.

The percolator bubbled and he lacked the energy to shut off the gas.

He was like this when Martha came out to him. She made him a sandwich, poured coffee, and insisted that he draw the chair up to the table and eat.

It was a chicken sandwich. Lena had packed broilers that had never been eaten in the picnic basket. His stomach contracted. He pushed the plate aside, fighting nausea.

Virginia came to get a glass of water for her mother. Her eyes were red with crying. Wally remembered that Henry had been her favorite too. He took a sip of the black coffee and said to Martha without interest, "Is Anne all right? Who brought her home?"

"She's in bed. The women who were in the rowboat brought her home."

It was they, then, who had talked so loosely about Wally's slowness in going to the aid of his brother. It was they who were the cause of Emma Howard's outburst in the living room. But what difference did it make?

He took another sip of the coffee. Martha went away and he sat on at the table. Leaning back in the

148

chair, he felt again the pressure of Henry's flask against his thigh.

Anne, waking up from the light disturbed sleep in which Virginia had left her an hour before, came down the back stairs. The door at the bottom was ajar, but her bare feet made no sound. She stood on the landing and shaded her eyes against the bright light.

Her uncle was at the sink. He had her father's flask and emptied it down the drain. It wasn't, she knew, what people usually did with liquor.

She saw him run water into it not once but four times, rinsing it carefully and drying it with a towel. He went into the dining room, carrying the flask with him. Anne, following noiselessly, watched him pour a small quantity of liquor into it. She retreated to the landing when he turned away from the sideboard.

Her father's flannels, the picnic basket, the blanket, had all been left by someone on a chair beside the refrigerator. Her uncle picked up the trousers and put the flask in one of the pockets. He put them back with the other things and sat down again at the table.

Anne asked, "Why did you take Daddy's flask?"

His chair shot back and was knocked over in the haste of his rising. He spun around to look at his niece, standing like a small white wraith in her nightgown on the landing.

How long had she been there?

"Good Lord, child, you startled me. What are you doing downstairs at this time of night?"

He hadn't answered her question. Instead he was

asking one of his own. Contrary to the persistence of childhood, she didn't repeat hers. There was something threatening about the way his eyes were fixed on her that kept her silent.

"Go back to bed," he said. "Your aunt Ginny wouldn't like to have you wandering about this way. And it's not nice to creep up on people. It makes you seem . . . sly."

Her eyes were large in her small face and clouded with misery. "Did you—find Daddy?"

Wally hadn't wanted to use her in his plan. But no other method of getting Henry to accompany him to the river had presented itself. He had been forced to use Henry's daughter because his brother wouldn't have gone alone with him. Making her a witness to the tragedy had been, in the last analysis, Henry's own fault, the result of his slighting treatment of Wally.

He could remind himself of that; but here was Anne looking at him with unhappy eyes and quivering lips, and what could they be but a reproach to him?

"I'll find your aunt Ginny," he told her. "She'll put you back to bed."

Virginia came and took the little girl upstairs. Compassion for his niece soon dwindled with her removal from his sight. He moved uneasily around the kitchen. How much of that business with the flask had Anne seen? He had taken the wisest course in ignoring her question about it. The less that was said the less likely it was to make an impression on her. . . .

He went to the foot of the stairs and listened.

Anne's room was opposite the upper landing, and the door must be open, for he could hear the murmur of Ginny's voice.

Would the child tell Ginny about the flask? She was crying now. His sister had probably told her that Henry's body had been found. Yes, Anne was crying steadily.

It was a pity, a great pity, that she had had to see Henry drown. She was six years old; that was old enough never to forget it.

But look what had happened to him when he was only nine—his father dead before his eyes. It had been much worse than Henry's drowning, and he had had to get over it. . . .

Had she seen him empty and rinse the flask at the sink? He hoped not. It could lead to awkward questions. "Little minx," he muttered in exasperation. "Sneaking up on me like that."

Abovestairs the anguished crying went on. The slam of a car door broke in on it. That would be the doctor for his mother.

"If it were I who lay dead tonight, there'd be no such goings on," he thought. "I never counted the way Henry did."

He closed the door at the stair landing to cut off the sound of Anne's crying.

The doctor took a grave view of Emma's condition. When she had been put to bed and was asleep under a sedative he talked about her age and the shock she had experienced. She must have complete rest and quiet, the doctor said.

It was midnight. Martha and Bob went home. The others, including Wally, went upstairs to bed.

Wally said good night and was at last by himself in his room. He walked the floor in the dark.

How could he have anticipated the rending accusation in eye and tone with which his mother had attacked him? How could he have known that Henry's death would affect her like this? Sam had died; Douglas had died. She had grieved, yes; but not as she grieved tonight. Tonight she was limp, empty-faced, like a broken thing, under the doctor's ministrations.

Her sons had had that affinity for non-conformity in them, and they couldn't be expected to die peaceably in their beds. She must have recognized that long ago. She had accepted what had happened to the others and should display the same fortitude toward the loss of Henry. It wasn't right for her to play favorites so flagrantly. The exact amount of sorrow she had felt for Sam and Doug should be Henry's meed; not one tear, not one regret more for him than for them.

But she had never been impartial where Henry was concerned. She had looked at him with hatred because Henry was dead.

Wally struck his palms together. "I had to do it, God," he whispered. "You meant me to, didn't you? You showed me the way."

His head went up in a listening attitude, as if an answer must come. The silence became a physical weight.

His mother had looked at him with hatred . . . He wept, stifling any sound.

"God, please listen! Help Mother to get over this quickly. Make her realize how much I love her and always will. Teach her to love me as she loved Henry."

He was calmer after prayer. When the first shock of Henry's death had passed, his mother would turn to him. The brother who had come between them would no longer be there. They would be close to each other as they never had been before.

It must be that way. Otherwise, because of what he has done . . . "No! I won't even think of that. Everything will be all right." His voice was loud in the quiet of the room. He clapped a hand to his mouth.

In the morning Emma got out of bed, fell, and couldn't get up. When Ginny went in to her, the right side of Emma's face was awry, her right arm and leg were paralyzed.

A nurse, Miss Drake, arrived at the house the day before Henry's funeral. The sight of her in her white uniform struck terror in Wally's heart. He tried to reassure himself; Emma would soon be well again; this was a temporary state of affairs. . . .

Miss Drake remained twenty-one months. For that length of time Emma survived her favorite child. The nurse was efficient and constant in the care of her patient. Wally grew to loathe her after a while.

He blamed her for standing between his mother and him. She was too often in the room when he visited Emma. Private talk was impossible with that starched watchdog underfoot, he complained to Ginny. But Miss Drake was a good nurse, and Emma quickly came to rely on her.

She improved that winter. She was able to sit up for hours at a time in a chair near the windows. She

153

watched the snow melt in the pasture and the first signs of spring appear. Summer came and autumn. By imperceptible degrees Emma lost the ground she had gained. Only the vitality that remained in her wiry body kept her alive so long.

It was a period of drawn-out misery for Wally. He had other worries in addition to his mother's health. At the bank rumors of change were bandied about after Roosevelt's election. The bank president, who had been a friend of Wally's father, died. There was talk of reorganization, of younger men, new blood.

The habit of talking aloud to himself became fixed in Wally during this period. In his conversations with himself he was able to justify everything he had done. But his mother didn't get better.

His friendship with Alfred Lodge was all that offered solace. In the first weeks after Emma's illness began he had avoided Alfred. The younger man was involved in it. Wally had been driven to kill Henry at last because his brother had humiliated him so frightfully in front of Alfred. Action against Henry had brought on Emma's shock.

So Wally reasoned and kept away from Alfred until the latter reproached him for his neglect and asked for an explanation of it. Wally made excuses, and afterward they were back on the old footing. Alfred's sympathy, the long talks they had, became Wally's chief support. . . .

One March afternoon he went in to see his mother and found her alone, sitting at the windows. Sunlight fell across her, and her appearance was like the stab of a knife to him. She was failing every day; her hands, folded in her lap, seemed transparent in their thinness.

He stood in the doorway studying her with helpless anger. This was Henry's work. Henry had left her for years at a time, had married and lived his own life as he pleased. And yet, with that easy manner of his, he had so insinuated himself into Emma's affections that his death was destroying her.

"There must be some way to bring her out of this," Wally thought frantically.

He went to her, drew a chair close, and sat down. He didn't attempt to take her hand, having been hurt often enough by having his mother evade his touch. "How are you today, dear?" he asked.

"Pretty well, thank you." Her voice was flat. She barely glanced at him before she returned her gaze to the windows. That was better, at least, than having her stare at him. Sometimes she did it in a way that made him uncomfortable.

"How was your lunch?"

"Good."

"And did you eat every bit of it?"

"No . . . I wasn't very hungry."

Wally shook his head and rested a hand on her arm for a moment. "Mother dear, how are you to get well if you don't eat?"

"I'm eighty-one years old. Why should you expect me to get well?" She looked at him. The padding of flesh was gone from her face so that the bones stood out under the skin.

"Oh, but you must," Wally pleaded. "You must make more effort. We all need you. I do especially,

155

Mother. I don't want to even imagine what my life would be like without you!"

Her expression softened at the despairing note in his voice. She said, "I've been through a lot, boy. I've got five graves ahead of mine over there in the cemetery. The last one"—still, he noticed, she didn't use Henry's name—"was too much for me."

She turned her head to the windows again, but she had spoken with more feeling than he could remember hearing in her voice since she had had the shock. The oblique reference to the dead man, whom she hadn't mentioned in his presence all this while, his own impotency before the obstinacy of her grief, brought out a comment he didn't mean to make.

He spat it at her. "Henry was never worth your sorrow for him! What did he do to earn it? I'm the one who stayed home with you and put you ahead of—"

He stopped short when he saw her face, deathly white, with fire leaping into the sunken eyes. "You were always jealous of him! Your own nature was too small to grasp the bigness of his." Her hands clutched the chair arms as if to rise. "I forbid you to speak to me of him again. Ever!"

She panted for breath that failed her. "You didn't try—to save—"

Wally ran to the thermos beside the bed and poured water into a glass, slopping it over on the table in his haste. "Here, Mother, drink this."

The brief flare was over. She drank from the glass and lay back in the chair. Her son watched her anxiously. "I'm sorry I upset you like that. I didn't mean to."

Her gesture waved aside the incident. She closed her eyes and murmured, "I'm sorry too. I ought to know by now that people are the way they are. If you—got lost—a long time ago . . . well, it must be my fault as much as yours."

Wally ventured to take her hand. It lay inert in his. "Maybe we've never understood each other as we should, Mother."

"Maybe we haven't." Emma half raised her eyelids and let them fall again. "What's the use of talking about that now, though?" She was faintly querulous. "It's all past and done, boy."

Wally ignored the dissent and went on, "I've been a disappointment to you all my life. I never could please you as Hen—as the others could." His hand tightened on hers. "But has it been all my fault, Mother? There've been things against me . . ."

His voice trailed off into silence. Her face with the closed lids was a mask. If only, he thought, she would understand. If only this once they could open their hearts to each other fully.

Emma shifted her head to look at him, her hand responding to the pressure of his. "Poor Wally," she said pityingly. "Poor boy."

"Mother—"

It was Virginia who interrupted them. She came into the room with Anne, bringing the child for her regular afternoon visit to her grandmother. She said, "Goodness, Mother, what have you been doing?" Her eyes went to Wally and she frowned. "Wally, have you been talking too much? Mother looks tired."

"We've just been having a little chat." Wally tried

not to sound on the defensive and didn't succeed. He returned her gaze with dislike in his. Ginny was more domineering with every year that passed.

"Well, you'd better leave now. You've certainly tired Mother out." Her nose and chin had sharpened. She pointed them at him suspiciously, looking from him to Emma while she drew Anne forward.

"Give Gram a kiss, child," she commanded. "And then you'd better run along too. I'll call Miss Drake and we'll get your grandmother back to bed."

The little girl went to Emma and kissed the fleshless cheek affectionately. "I picked you some pussy willows after lunch, lots and lots of them," she said. "Aunt Ginny told me I could bring them up, but I forgot. Shall I get them now?"

"Yes, do, pet." Emma drew close for a moment and let her go. "Bring them right up. I always did like pussy willows."

"All right." Anne ran from the room, and Virginia said, "I'll call Miss Drake, Mother. But I'm not going to let the child stay. She'll only tire you more, the way she chatters."

"No, she won't," Emma declared. "I enjoy listening to her."

Miss Drake bustled in with rustling uniform and toothy smile and gray frizzed curls.

Wally gave it up. The talk that might have been wouldn't take place.

The chance to have it didn't come again. As April gave way to May, Emma grew weaker and kept to her bed.

Miss Drake lost her cheerful manner with Wally. She said to him, "Mr. Howard, I felt it my duty to tell Dr. Harshbarger that for some reason you seem to upset your mother. He thinks you'd better make your visits very short. . . . Just for now, of course," she added hastily, seeing the pain the interdict gave him. "Just until she's a little stronger."

He went to his room without answering. He was told to stay away from his mother. His presence disturbed her. She looked at him and looked at him and read—his mind?—his heart?

She knew about Henry. In some fashion, born of her love for the other, she had known from the first. Not about the aconite. She believed Wally could have saved his brother and had deliberately let him drown.

This was what had resulted from accepting himself as the instrument of Henry's destruction. A man less sure of the rightness of his act would call it punishment. . . .

"I'd do it again," Wally avowed passionately. "I've never regretted it as far as Henry was concerned. I never will. He got what he deserved."

But there was his mother in the room across the hall. . . .

CHAPTER THIRTEEN — 1933

Emma died one night at the end of May. The minister had spent an hour with her during the afternoon. The doctor had paid a final visit. She was left with her children.

The New Testament was in her hands. Her mind was clear and she retained consciousness.

Wally stood back from the bed. Here was the moment before which all previous sorrow lost meaning. His mother was dying. Still within sight and touch, she was slipping away from him and he couldn't hold her back. She would die tonight; he would never again be able to turn to her, talk to her, draw comfort and strength from the fact of her existence.

Because speech was a struggle, she beckoned to Virginia. "Read," she whispered, lifting the Bible.

Her daughter took it. "St. John, Mother?"

Emma nodded, and Virginia opened the book at the chapter that was a favorite of her mother's. She read:

" 'Let not your heart be troubled: ye believe in God, believe also in me . . .' "

They stood around the bed, their heads bowed as they listened to Virginia's clear, unfaltering voice.

" '. . . Jesus saith unto him, I am the way, the truth, and the life: no man cometh unto the Father, but by me . . .' "

A sob escaped from Wally and he moved back a step. But his mother's eyes followed the sound and rested on him. They weren't searching and weighing him as they had for all the months past. There was such pity in them that it almost broke his self-control entirely.

Virginia read the whole chapter. Her mother listened and seemed a little removed from her body's effort to breathe.

The rug deadened the fall of Nick's footsteps walking back and forth. It was the women who hovered over the bed, shifting the pillows and supporting Emma in attempts to ease her. A man could grieve, but there was nothing for him to do.

Only suggestions, the merest traces, remained in Nicholas Howard of the handsome, lighthearted young man who had come back from the war thirty-five years ago. His marriage to Agnes and the passage of time had changed him into a bulky, slow-moving man of sixty, all recklessness squeezed out of him, his hair nearly white, his heavy face set in sober lines.

Emma kissed them good-by, signaling them to come to her. By unspoken agreement they went in the order of their seniority, Mary, Nick, Virginia, Wally. She gasped to Virginia, "Take—care—Wally."

Wally, the last, bent over her, raising her slightly while he brought his face down to hers. Her lips were cold and damp against it. She lay back and looked at him. He was blinded by tears, but he heard, as they all did, what she said. "Poor—wretched—one. God—our refuge—"

She didn't speak again. Mary was propping her up when her head dropped on her daughter's arm. Miss Drake sprang forward, but Emma had no further need of her. . . .

It was Alfred to whom Wally turned for comfort the next day. His grief drove him out of the house. He had to see Alfred.

The younger man took him into the prescription department at the rear of the store and provided him with a chair. Wally wept while Alfred hung over him sympathetically and tried to offer consolation.

"Think how fortunate you've been to have her so long, Wally. It's been more than half the average lifetime. Not many of us are that lucky. Look at me. My mother died when I was eleven."

"I know." Wally groped for and pressed Alfred's hand. He clung to it in a passion of tears. "Dear boy . . ."

Alfred patted his shoulder. "Think of the love she gave you, the memories you'll always have. You're a man who believes in God, Wally. You expect to be with her again."

"I know . . ." But the comfort Alfred gave wasn't in what he said; it was in his presence and the clasp of his hand.

Wally rested his tear-wet face against it. It would have been a relief to tell Alfred that his mother hadn't given him the full measure of her love because she had given it to Henry; and, before Henry, to Wally's father. He couldn't tell Alfred, though. He couldn't tell him about the hatred and jealousy of his brother that had eaten into the center of his being and laid its corroding touch on his lifelong relationship with his mother. Nor could he tell Alfred how frightened he had been by what his mother had said before she died. "Poor, wretched one," she had called him. The rest of them might think she meant only his general apartness from other people, but he knew better. She had meant everything, all the way back to his baby sister. At the very end nothing in his life had eluded her. . . .

Alfred said more soothing words, more of the obvious things. His exquisite face was warm with affection as he bent over the older man. Alfred had his own place. He couldn't fill the vacuum Emma's death had left; he couldn't straighten out the inner processes that were awry in Wally; but he had his own large place.

Wally leaned on him, smoldering his sobs against the other's arm.

"I'm perfectly satisfied, Sister," he said. "it was a very fair will."

They were at dinner. Lena had served coffee and retired to the kitchen. June sunlight slanted through the blinds from the west, falling short of the table.

Wally repeated himself. "It was a very fair will," he said again.

Emma had died a week ago. By the terms of her

163

will, read that day, each of her children received a cash bequest of two thousand dollars. Life use of the house and its furnishings was given to Wally and Virginia. When they died, the others or their heirs were to inherit an equal interest in it. The balance of Emma's estate was left to Virginia, with the explanation that she was unmarried and was beyond the age to start earning her own living.

Opposite Wally at the table, Anne watched him out of large hazel eyes. They were Henry's eyes, Wally reflected, as he had many times before. The child was her father's daughter through and through. Wasn't it probable that she shared responsibility for the new will Emma Howard had made after Henry's death? During his mother's long illness her granddaughter and she must have talked often of Henry. Anne would have told her every circumstance relating to her father's death. . . .

A smile concealed the antipathy she aroused in Wally. "You've finished your dessert, I see," he said to her. "You may leave the table."

Anne slid out of the chair, bobbed her head at them as Virginia had taught her to do, and left the room.

"She's getting so tall," her aunt commented, looking after her.

"She's eight years old. They don't stay babies."

"I know. It crossed my mind just now that Henry would find such a change in her if he could come back. It's nearly two years."

Virginia's eyes were more brown than hazel. She adjusted her glasses with a sigh that blew out her long upper lip and returned her attention to her brother. "Mother talked over the will with me before it was drawn up," she said. For once she was on the defensive, lacking her customary self-assurance.

With Ginny, Wally thought; not with him, but with Ginny, his mother had talked over the final rejection of the son who had devoted his life to her.

He had made no complaint when he learned the terms of the will. Virginia was on the defensive with him because they both knew that in the earlier will he had shared the estate in equal portions with Henry and her.

Virginia herself didn't quite understand why her mother had made the change. The older woman had been evasive about it. All she would say was that Wally wasn't practical; the money would slip through his fingers; Virginia must look after him.

But if his mother felt that way about him, why had she made greater provision for him in the earlier will?

Virginia gave up speculation. Of course money did slip through Wally's fingers. Still, his maximum salary had been fifty dollars a week, and that had been cut to forty since the Depression. Out of it he had paid for the upkeep of a horse until the last one he owned had died two years ago; he shared the expenses of the family car; he paid board . . . How could he save very much? And he had a nice collection of books upstairs, many first editions, poetry, mostly, and not too valuable; but it represented some money. As for that Lodge boy who was too often about the place—there wasn't the least doubt but that he sponged on Wally everywhere they went together. It was . . .

She just wouldn't let herself think about Alfred Lodge. . . .

The most convenient view to adopt was her mother's: Wally wasn't capable of taking care of himself and needed looking after.

He said tonelessly, "I wouldn't presume to question Mother's judgment."

His sister gave him a sharp glance. Was there irony in the comment?

He was a neat little man. His dark hair, thickly sprinkled with gray, was combed back from his forehead. The navy-blue suit he wore, the white shirt and black bow tie were part of him. The light struck his horn-rimmed glasses so that she couldn't see his eyes; but his thin, colorless face, with deep grooves at the mouth, was blank.

She couldn't find any fault with him over his attitude toward the will.

Wally moved back from the table and lit a cigarette, dropping the used match on his saucer.

"Do get an ash tray," Virginia ordered. "If you will smoke at table."

There was a stack of crystal ash trays on the sideboard. He got up and took one. "You know I always smoke with coffee," he complained. "Why don't you have Lena put an ash tray at my place?"

"And I've always considered it a disgusting habit, even if everyone does do it nowadays," Virginia retorted. "I shan't encourage it."

She poured more coffee. Wally brooded over his cup. He felt lost and lonely. The feeling grew until

166

he was impelled to seek sympathy. "I just can't get used to her being gone." Tears filled his eyes. He took out a handkerchief and wiped them away. "If I could only have her back, Sister. My heart's broken. I don't think I'll ever get over it."

If she had stretched out a hand to him and answered, "I know how you feel. We're going through it together." If she had been gentle . . .

She drank her coffee and set the cup back on the saucer before she made any reply. Then she said with her usual crispness, "You'll have to make the best of it. We all have to stand on our own feet now. It's selfish to want her back. Her health was gone and she was eighty-one years old."

She patted her mouth with her napkin, laid it aside, and stood up. "Excuse me, Wally. While I think of it, I want to remind Lena to put beans to soak for tomorrow."

She went past his chair. No consoling hand rested on his shoulders. She left him there, looking after her tall erect figure as she went through the swinging door into the kitchen.

Wally was thrown back into himself. Any vague, unformed hope he might have had of transferring the affection he had given the mother to the sister vanished. Ginny was a cold, selfish woman, sufficient unto herself. Emma Howard's death hadn't softened her. Nothing would. She moved within the shell of her own righteousness.

For the first time in his life Wally came face to face with the truth about his feeling toward his sister. He hated her. Why, he had hated her for years! It was his mother who had stood between him and the truth. She had schooled him to be thoughtful of his sister, to defer to her . . .

A shiver went over him. Hatred should have died with Henry. But now there was Ginny.

What was the matter with him? Was he incomplete without a focus for hatred? Did it give him the illusion of a completeness that was never in him and never had been?

Virginia spent an afternoon with Nicholas at his office. When she was home she waited until Anne was in bed to tell Wally what she had done that day.

They sat on the porch. The sun had set and it was growing dark. Often Wally had sat here at this hour with his mother. It was painful to him to have Ginny occupy Emma's rocker and to hear its familiar creak. He closed his eyes. In the twilight couldn't he place his mother there?

He couldn't, of course. He could only remember other twilights with her and resent his sister's usurpation of Emma's chair. He moved restlessly, so that the glider swayed and creaked in unison with the rocker.

Virginia began, "I saw Nick today. He's going to draw up my will."

"Yes?" Wally became motionless.

"It concerns you, so I thought I'd tell you about it."

"Yes?"

"Anne is, naturally, my heir."

"Why naturally?" Wally wanted to ask. "I'm

closer to you by blood than she is." What he said was, "Yes, naturally."

"She will receive outright one half of my estate when she's twenty-five if I die before then. The other half will establish a trust fund and you'll draw the income from that for life, Wally. When you die the principal will revert to Anne.

"Of course," she continued, "Nick brought up the question of the child dying ahead of us, so I took care of that. If she should, you'd have life use of the income from the whole estate; on your death it would be divided among the rest of the family."

She rocked back and forth. Unmentioned between them hung the fact that under no circumstances was Wally to control the principal of the estate. He was deeply hurt at the lack of confidence in his ability to handle money, he who had worked for years in a bank.

But even Virginia, for all her forthrightness, couldn't bring herself to tell him that she had no intention of allowing the money Emma Howard had husbanded so long to be spent on people like Alfred Lodge—"Degenerates," she reflected.

Wally's comment was slow in coming. He had to be sure his voice wouldn't betray the soreness he felt. "This is generous of you, Sister," he said, without emphasis.

Virginia replied abruptly, "Someone has to look after you when you're too old to work. I promised Mother I would."

The dusk obscured Wally's expression. He allowed himself the luxury of sending her a venomous glance. "I can't help wondering," he ventured, setting the glider in motion, "just how I'll manage to keep up the house on half of your income, Ginny . . . assuming you should go ahead of me, which I hope won't happen."

She made an impatient gesture. "You needn't live here. Why should you want to stay on in a big place like this if you were alone? You could rent it and find something smaller."

His jaw dropped. "Leave the house where I was born? Where our forebears have lived for a hundred and fifty years? Oh no, Sister!"

"That's a lot of sentimental nonsense," Virginia retorted.

He looked at her. She meant what she said. She had no respect for the past. She would, he realized with fright and dismay, be ready to sell the house over his head. Thank God she couldn't!

But what if she refused to keep it up? He certainly couldn't live here alone on his salary and have Ginny, no doubt, demanding rent for her half interest in the place. She would make that demand, too. She was exacting. . . .

His eyes devoured the serene, familiar surroundings like one about to be wrenched away from them forever.

The rumored changes were made at the bank that autumn. Wally was past forty, nearing fifty, in fact, when all over the nation emphasis was laid on youth. There were other factors in his dismissal. With the choice lying between two old employees, the other married and the father of a family, it was Wally who had to go. The intangible, too, weighed against him; the remarks that had been made for years, the knowing glances.

In a daze, he went home to Virginia with the news. She said, "That's too bad." Her tone said, "It's what I expected."

"I'll get something else," he assured her. "They're going to pay my salary for two years."

"They should. You've been with them nearly thirty."

That was the sympathy he received when his safe world was torn from its foundation, his ego crushed, his belief in himself as a man of affairs destroyed.

"Yes," he said. "I've had nearly thirty years' experience. I shouldn't have much trouble getting another job. I'll try the banks in town."

He tried them all. None of them, in the autumn of 1933, the winter of 1934, the spring, the summer, had any place for a small, anxious man approaching fifty who couldn't altogether hide his fear of his own inadequacy to cope with the unfamiliar.

In the autumn he did get a job as cashier in a busy cafeteria near the railroad station. But the pay was meager, the hours long, and the pressure of work continuous. Wally held the job for five months, leaving Kinnelly early in the morning to return on a late bus at night. He retreated from it into an illness that was diagnosed as neuralgia.

"You'd better forget about that halfpenny job of yours," Virginia told him one day. "I'd rather feed you than have you sick on my hands."

His recovery was rapid after that pronouncement. Virginia dismissed the man who had come twice weekly to mow the lawn and do odd jobs about the property, and Wally took over these tasks. He repaired an Adams secretary for Mrs. McArdle, and what began as a neighborly matter ended with his being paid to completely refinish the old piece. He discovered that he had some talent for such work. He started to earn small sums of money for doing it.

Wally enjoyed the new-found leisure, the little puttering things he did. The following spring, when Alfred suggested that he might be taken on as a clerk at the drugstore, the older man turned down the proposal. It would be pleasant, of course, to be near Alfred so much of the time. On the other hand, they saw each other often as it was, and there could be drawbacks to daily proximity. The truth was, he didn't relish the prospect of being tied again to regular working hours. He was content with his mode of life even though, in one respect, the price of it was high. Virginia ordered him about; Virginia ruled him.

Unconsciously, moving toward adolescence, Anne aped her aunt's attitude toward him. He was discounted as of no importance. The unintentional snubs, the thoughtless behavior of a child, should have been overlooked. But Wally stored it in his mind in a kind of general mental file labeled "Henry's daughter."

At odd moments he thought of how convenient it would be if something happened to Anne, who was Virginia's heir. But nothing would happen to her; his sister watched over the child too closely.

172

He was pleasant to his niece. No hint of his ponderings ever found its way into his manner toward her.

CHAPTER FOURTEEN — 1946

"Oh no, Aunt Ginny, not the cottage," Anne protested. "We've had such wonderful summers there. Look . . ." She swung her head around with the vigor that, in childhood, had set her braids swinging. Now it was a loose swirl of auburn hair that followed the movement of her head. "Why don't you take some of my money if you're hard up?"

"My dear child, I'm not exactly what you call hard up," Ginny said stiffly. "I need to be careful, though. That automobile stock keeps dropping and dropping. It's off half a point again today. And it seemed such a good buy that I took a lot of it, listening to that fool of a broker."

"How much did you buy?" Wally asked.

Virginia never would give her brother details of financial transactions. She said, "Quite a lot; more than I should have."

Anne, home for the week end from the college at New London where she was nearing the end of her third year, sat cross-legged before the fire, wearing dark green slacks. She missed beauty because her face and nose were too long and too thin. Her skin was good, however, her hazel eyes large and brilliant, and she had Henry's infectious smile and easy manner. She had, too, the thick wavy mass of auburn hair that instantly caught the eye. There was no lack of young men who found Anne suited to their taste.

She said, "Aunt Ginny, there's that money, my father's insurance and so on, that you're going to turn over to me when I'm twenty-one, isn't there?"

"Several thousand," Virginia conceded.

"Well, I want you to use some of it." The girl flashed a smile at the older woman. "In payment for services rendered, darling. Free room and board and attention all these years."

"That's absurd!" When Virginia was moved she became more brusque. "I don't know how we got into this discussion. I merely remarked that since I picked up the cottage on the Cape for next to nothing twelve years ago, this seemed a good time to sell it. It's a seller's market. But we'll say no more about it."

"Couldn't I buy it from you, then?" Anne persisted.

"No." Virginia rose. "I don't know why I'm sitting here when I have so many things to do." She left the room.

Anne locked her hands around her knees and moved closer to the fire. "It's none too warm in here," she commented.

"Sister thinks that as soon as it's April the thermostat should be set back to sixty-five. The temperature outside has nothing to do with it." Wally's tone was light but the criticism was there.

The girl's defense of her aunt was automatic. She took sides without thinking about it and said with a shrug, "Oh well, usually it doesn't matter. It's just that it's raining today. We have to take Aunt Ginny's little ways as we find them, I guess."

"Yes. In everything." Although the tone was still light, Anne glanced up at her uncle. Uncle Wally under Aunt Ginny's thumb had been part of her life as far back as she could remember. It was not something one questioned; one simply accepted it.

And yet the glance became a scrutiny. Dark eyes, bulwarked by rimless glasses, returned it blandly. The narrow head with thinning gray hair rested against the back of the chair. Uncle Wally was the most inoffensive little man imaginable. . . .

Anne suddenly felt sorry for him because of something—self-deprecation, perhaps, or overanxiety to please—that marked his manner. It was a subtle thing rather than a pronounced one. It was, she concluded, the result of years of financial dependence on Aunt Ginny.

It couldn't be good for a man to live like that. Reversing the normal order couldn't be good for anyone. No wonder Uncle Wally found what escape he could in the petty gibe, the peevish thrust.

"I must be nicer to him," Anne told herself. "I've got a bad habit of not noticing him much."

To consult him would make as good a starting point as any, so she shifted her position in order to face him directly and asked, "Is Aunt Ginny in real financial trouble, do you think? Like needing to sell the cottage?"

He made a steeple of his fingers and pressed them to his nose. "Sister has been crying poor mouth since your grandmother died. After all, has she actually lost money on that automobile stock? No. The shares have dropped, but she owns them outright. It's a new company, under good management. They'll go up again. The talk about economizing is just her way of reminding us that she holds the purse strings, child."

The casual air fell away. Spite broke through as he lowered his voice. "To hear her, you'd think she was headed for the poorhouse. But it's all put on; most of the time for my benefit, but right now for yours. She knows you're almost twenty-one and will control your own money. She's deep, child. Once she's sure of your sympathy, she'll be into your pocket if you don't watch out."

Wally leaned forward, his eyes holding hers. "Never let her. Take it from me, Anne, there's nothing in the world like your own dollar."

He pursed his lips. The girl stared at him. Something showed in his eyes. It was only for a moment; then he was relaxed in the chair, his smile benevolent. "Did I surprise you, child? I was just talking. I'm getting old. I ramble deplorably."

Anne drew in a long breath. The gloom of the dark rainy afternoon lent spurs to the imagination. Hatred slipping the leash, some mental refraction, couldn't have looked out of the gentle brown eyes a few feet away.

She jumped to her feet. "The fire's dying. I'll stir it up good."

The incident was over and thrust into the back of her mind. She came home for other weekends; the days ran into each other and it was June. When she returned to Kinnelly for summer vacation she helped her aunt and Lena with preparations to go to the Cape. Their departure was postponed so that Anne could be one of the bridesmaids at a large wedding. She was inclined to be a little dreamy-eyed about the best man, who said charming things to her and began to put them in writing as soon as he reached his home in Ohio. She went on overlooking her uncle Wally in spite of good intentions.

In the end their departure for the Cape wasn't delayed quite long enough from the girl's point of view. The day before they were to leave Kinnelly, Martha telephoned. Bob had written her from a separation center in the West, she announced. He would have his discharge and be home next week.

"That's lovely," Anne said. "You must be terribly thrilled."

"Well, I should say! It's been almost three years."

It was almost five years since Anne had seen him. Four and a half years, she corrected herself. Right after Pearl Harbor. He had had leaves, yes, but she had missed them. She had been away on a visit to a cousin, the only maternal relative left, or at the Cape, and, during his last leave, in New London. It hadn't occurred to him to come there to see her before he was sent to the Pacific. He had known how she had idolized him as a child, but he hadn't troubled to say good-by to her. He could have been killed; he had known that when he left, of course, but still he hadn't said good-by to her. He had sent her two postcards in five years, the last one about nineteen months ago.

She sat by the telephone making a litany of Bob Vanderbrouk's neglect of her, but the knowledge of it couldn't dampen her excitement. He was coming home. He wasn't married or engaged and he was coming home. He was quite old now—she counted back and discovered that he was thirty-two—but it wasn't possible to believe that any change had taken place in him. He was immune to time and all the other human hazards. He had mended her toys and repaired her bicycle and given her quite a lot of latitude in following him around. He had gone out of his way to be kind to her when her father died.

Anne sat still, the glow dimmed by memory of sunlit water, a struggling figure, and herself screaming. The depressed interval was brief. It was an old, familiar tragedy, and apart from that last afternoon there were only isolated images of Henry Howard left to her.

She went out to the porch and leaned against the railing, bemused by the magic promise of Bob's return. They would be at the Cape when he came home, but she would write to Aunt Martha—or, better yet, have Aunt Ginny do it—and invite them up. She was bound to see him again soon.

Her aunt Ginny drove into the yard. Wally left his cellar workshop to join them and was told by his sister to change his clothes, it was nearly dinnertime. This he had intended to do in any case, but he didn't say so; he merely nodded and went upstairs.

At the table Anne told them about Bob. There was delight in talking about him, but the news couldn't be spun out indefinitely. Uncle and aunt said how nice it was for Martha, and that, apparently, was all the meaning the great event had for them.

The girl looked at them in discouragement. Virginia's braids were white, Wally's hair was gray. They were sixty-four and sixty; old, she thought. Their hearts were past quickening at the sound of a name—if they ever had.

Lena came in with the coffee. She moved heavily. Lena was old too. She had worked for the Howards for forty years.

"Oh dear, I wish someone young lived with us," Anne thought and felt a sense of guilt and disloyalty. These three couldn't check the passage of the years. She must one day grow old herself. . . .

She sighed.

Virginia produced her own news. "I met Abe Hollister downtown this afternoon," she announced. "We got to talking about the Barth place. It's going to be put up for sale shortly. The Barths are building, you know."

She was speaking to both of them. Wally's spoon slipped from his hand to the floor. He bent to retrieve it and used it to stir his coffee without even wiping it on his napkin. Virginia interrupted herself to exclaim, "Good heavens, Wally, what are you doing? You could have asked for a clean spoon."

He couldn't have asked for one. A blanket of fog cut her off from him. His head was whirling. Ginny was going to take the step that he had been afraid for years she would take. She was going to impose the necessity of stopping her upon him. . . .

He didn't need to hear what she said, although much of it penetrated his consciousness.

". . . The rent office would set a high figure on this house, he thinks . . . Only three bedrooms, but there's a room downstairs that Edith Barth used for a sewing room . . . A studio couch for you, Wally, and make you quite comfortable . . . So much work here and Lena's not getting any younger . . . Furnished, I told him . . . A three-year lease would be the minimum I'd consider . . . I gave him our address on the Cape. . . ."

Wally's glance roamed wildly about the room. Its wide-boarded floor gleamed with wax. Its mahogany furniture had belonged to their great-grandmother. Thirty-odd years ago he had helped Emma Howard select the rug under his feet. The sailing-ship models on the mantelshelf had been carved by his great-great-grandfather who had also set in the paneling around the fireplace.

Since his mother had died he had known this must come. He looked at Ginny, and her face wavered before his eyes. To think that a money-grabbing old bitch like her was the rock against which his life could be broken!

But he wouldn't let it be like that.

He stayed at the Cape only a few days, reminding Virginia that he had three repair jobs on furniture waiting for him in his workshop at home. Actually there was no hurry about them; they were an excuse for leaving.

He never spent the summer at his sister's cottage. He came and went for occasional weekends, enjoying, in the meantime, the freedom of the house in Kinnelly with Ginny out of it. He did his own cooking, entertaining Alfred, who returned the hospitality now and then in his own bachelor quarters over the drugstore, and entertaining other young men of his acquaintance. He liked reading late at night alone in the silent, empty house. Sometimes he carried on long conversations with the dead.

So Wally came back to Kinnelly. He invited Martha and Bob to dinner two days after the latter reached home. He was fond of both of them. Their arrival was a welcome respite from the thoughts that harried him.

He shook Bob's hand vigorously. "Well, little man, this is splendid!"

Bob, towering over him, grinned and returned the handshake. "I'm glad to see you."

He was wearing slacks and a sport shirt. "I hoped you'd still be in uniform," Wally told him. "You looked so well in yours."

"I'm damn glad to be out of it for good."

His hair was cut shorter, he was deeply tanned, there were crow's-feet at the corners of his eyes, his mouth had hardened somewhat. Otherwise Wally, taking stock of him, found little change.

Bob strolled into the living room and came back to the porch, where he stood looking out at the pasture. "Everything's the same," he said with satisfaction. "In a mad world this place doesn't alter a hairbreadth. At home it's another story." He grinned at his mother over his shoulder. "Ma's had the living room done over, new furniture and all. It was like hitting a strange house when I went into it."

"The living room was a sight," Martha declared. "I had to buy new things."

"Still," Wally said, "I'm glad there's someone like me around. I don't like change. I can't"—his voice went high—"stand change."

He caught Bob's glance and summoned a beaming smile. "Come in, little man, and let's investigate the sideboard. I know you and your mother would enjoy a cocktail. Personally, I don't care for the things, and I know so little about the mysteries of putting them together that I'll have to ask you to help me."

Affection was blended with the amusement Bob felt. He would never lose sight of what he owed to Wally Howard, who had done so much for his mother and him.

Wally couldn't resist the pleasure of slipping an arm through the younger man's as they went into the house. The solid bulge of muscle reminded him of Henry. But Bob wasn't like Henry. For all his size, he was quiet and slow-moving, so that you couldn't imagine him using his strength with Henry's hotheaded savagery.

While they mixed cocktails Wally's gaze kept returning to Bob. He was a wonderful fellow, blond, good-looking, mature. You could sense the same hard core of maleness in him that Henry and the other Howard brothers had had, but it wasn't obtrusive as theirs had been. Yes, he thought, Bob had turned out to be a grand person.

"How's the kid?" the younger man asked. "Haven't seen her in years."

"Kid? Oh, you mean Anne."

Martha, who had followed them to the kitchen, laughed. "Anne is a young lady now, Bob. Beaus, college, everything. You'll be surprised when you see her. She won't be tagging after you as she used to. She doesn't have to tag after any man these days."

Wally saw the flicker of interest in Bob's eyes. He had seen it many times in many men's eyes at the mention of an attractive woman. It was as old as time, and he had remained outside its influence. . . .

His own excitement over Bob died away.

Wally sat on the porch, Virginia's letter in his lap. He looked out across the road.

Virginia had written that Abe Hollister had a prospective tenant for the Howard house. The Barths would sell to her in the autumn, when they were sure of occupancy of the new house they were building.

"I don't suppose you'll be pleased with the plan," Virginia had written. "You never are pleased with any plans I make for economizing. I do realize, too, that you're attached to the old place; but after all, I'm the one who has to think of making ends meet. I'm worried about the way that stock of mine has dropped, and I want to look ahead. You know how I feel; my greatest dread is that through some misfortune I might come to a penniless old age . . ."

In additional apology she had added, "And it's

only for three years. We'll move back then if all goes well financially . . ."

Three years was a long time when you were sixty; a big slice, perhaps, of the remainder of your life. And what assurance had he that Ginny would keep her promise? She would have got used to the Barth place, and the rent money from this house would look good to her. . . .

"Mother," Wally said aloud, "you'd never have stood for this. You wouldn't want me to stand for it either, would you?"

He went inside and upstairs to his room. He walked around it, touching the possessions of a lifetime. He walked down the hall to his boyhood sliver of a room next to the bath. Here he had put up shelves and they were filled with his books.

At the Barth place he would sleep on a studio couch in Edith Barth's sewing room.

He went into his mother's room, opening the door gently and walking with reverence. It was just as she had left it. Many of her things were still in the dresser drawers. They would have to be cleared out, of course, if strangers came.

Wally had never before opened the top drawer of the highboy that held his father's gun. Today he opened it and took out the gun, wrapped in cloths. He examined it. Someone—Nick, probably—must have oiled it a number of times in the past half century, for it seemed to be in good condition.

He took it downstairs, oiled it again, and wiped it clean. It was a .45, and there were cartridges to fit it in a box in the drawer. Back in his mother's bedroom, Wally loaded it. His father had taught him how to do it. He hadn't touched this gun or any other since the day his father died, and he found it odd that he should still remember the way it was done.

He wrapped up the weapon and put it back in its place, closing the drawer and leaning against it. He was spent as if from hard labor, his legs trembling and his hands shaking. He didn't know why he had made the .45 ready for use; not, certainly, because he had any idea of turning it on Virginia.

With the blinds drawn the room was dark. His father had died here. Right near the windows he had sagged to the floor. He was there now! He was trying to lift himself up . . .

Wally fled, locking the door behind him. But still his father followed him, mouth open in a guffaw that made no sound, feet silent on the stairs. Wally ran until he had gained the porch, where sunlight routed the burly figure at his heels.

Tincture of aconite led to aconitine in a pattern that varied only slightly. Virginia herself had laid the groundwork three years ago with a coronary attack. It hadn't been repeated, but Nick had died of one. Dr. Harshbarger advised Virginia to be careful and not overdo in any physical exertion. He had given her a prescription for a sedative.

Virginia, in her letter, had asked Wally to have it refilled for her. Well, she should have it.

Aconitine wasn't in general use any longer; it was a dangerous, powerful poison. This Wally gleaned from Alfred's pharmacopoeia at the drugstore. But the older man had the freedom of the prescription department; he knew where the key to the poisons cabinet was kept. When Alfred was busy with a customer he opened the cabinet and discovered that it still contained a bottle of the powder. He shook some of it out into an envelope, sealed it, and put it in his pocket.

When Alfred came back to him Wally was reading a copy of *Time*. He glanced up from the magazine. "Ah, dear boy, before I forget—will you make up Sister's prescription? She wrote me that she's running low on it."

Alfred made up the prescription, and Wally took the package home with him. That evening he wrote to Virginia protesting her decision, begging her to change it. He was giving her a reprieve, he thought, putting a stamp on the letter and taking it across the road to the mailbox. Sister had a right to her life, but she mustn't trample on his rights, his most sacred feelings, either.

A gold and red and violet sunset held him on the porch. Once when he was three or four and just such a sunset as this had flamed in the sky his mother had sat here with him on her lap reading to him. . . .

Wally was pierced with longing for that far-off time, for his mother. It was so intense and painful that it drove him into the house away from the scene that had evoked it.

And yet the moment of nostalgia stiffened resolution. He had lost the youth that, in retrospect, seemed bright and full of promise. He had lost his mother. The house and all its associations he would hold.

Virginia's reply to his plea arrived a week later. The lease, she wrote, would be drawn up to be signed when she returned from the cape. The lessee, a man from Chicago, was moving his family to Connecticut the first of November and would like to take possession of the house on that date.

"I'm afraid I can't allow sentiment to stand in the way of practical considerations," Virginia wrote. "And I'm a better judge of them than you are. Through Mr. Hollister I'm taking an option on the Barth place this week. I feel sure you'll be quite contented there once you've settled down."

Wally laid the letter on a table. It closed with a reminder that she hadn't received her prescription yet.

The capsules came apart. He separated one of them, emptied out the seconal powder in it, and substituted aconitine.

He was calm, putting the capsule together again, dropping it back in the bottle with the others, and shaking them up so that he no longer knew which one carried death in it. He was calm because he had no choice. His sister had settled her own fate. She must suffer what would appear to be a fatal attack of coronary thrombosis.

He walked out to the porch. The night was clear, but mist rose from the pasture, white and faintly luminous in the starlight.

There had been mist that other time too, before Henry's death; and a whippoorwill calling. Mist often shrouded the pasture, though, after a hot day. There was no reason for finding a ghostly symbolism in it.

Still he listened for the cry of a whippoorwill that did not come.

CHAPTER FIFTEEN —

Wally called Bob the next day. "When are you driving to the Cape to bring your mother home from her visit?" he asked.

"I'm leaving Friday afternoon—as early as I can get away." Bob laughed. "The things I've forgotten! I'm learning dairy farming all over again these days."

"Well, will you stop by and pick up Sister's medicine? She wrote me to have her prescription filled for her?"

"Okay," Bob said. "I'll pick it up."

The small bottle of clear glass held fifteen capsules. Wally had counted them. He gave the bottle to Bob that Friday afternoon, told him repeatedly to give it to Ginny, and waved to the younger man as the car went out of the driveway.

The thing was out of his hands now. He must quiet the terror that seized him when the car was gone. The sane course was to ask himself if he even had a part in Ginny's death. After all, he wouldn't be forcing the capsule down her throat. She fussed too much about her health; about her heart and that imaginary back ailment of hers. It was just nonsense. If she'd stop it, she needn't touch the bottle . . .

Wally crossed the porch and dropped down on the glider.

He said, "There was nothing else for me to do, Mother. You know what I've put up with all these years. I haven't complained about the way she ran my life and ordered me around . . .

"You used to say when we were small that I had to give in to her because she was a girl. But not in this, Mother! You loved this house too. You meant us to live here the rest of our lives. It's Sister who's flouting your intention . . .

"Mother, you understand what I've had to do, don't you?"

Wally cocked his head to listen. The drowsy golden stillness of the late afternoon kept its own counsel.

He became petulant. "I don't like to say so, Mother, but it's really your fault. It's that will you made, giving Sister control of every cent . . . You did it because of Henry, didn't you?"

He buried his face in his hands and began to cry. "He wouldn't let me lead my own life either. He never gave me a moment's peace . . ."

Because she was eager to see Bob, Anne made it a point not to be at the cottage when he arrived. It didn't do, was the girl's theory, to pamper your emotions. There was another angle too. If Bob were the

190

least bit interested in seeing her again—which of course he wasn't—it would do him no harm to wait. She had waited long enough between postcards.

It was, then, nearly midnight when she returned from a movie date in Hyannis. She saw the car pulled up close to the cottage and the group on the porch. She sat and waited for Bill Kensington, who had taken her to the movie, to come around and open the car door for her. She could have winged her way up the walk, but she lingered to talk, saying that she had enjoyed the show and yes, he could come over to swim with her tomorrow.

Going toward the porch, Anne lifted a hand in greeting and paused to look back at the stretch of white sand and the glimmering expanse of ocean. The effect must be what she wanted: that of a young woman in no hurry to see anyone.

She was wearing white; it accentuated the light tan that was all her fair skin had yet been able to acquire. She had combed her hair and put on fresh lipstick when she left the movie theater. A last quick inspection in her handbag mirror had satisfied her that she looked as well as she possibly could.

Bob came forward to open the screen door and loomed over her, silhouetted against the light in the living room. "Hello, Anne," he said. "How are you?"

The girl tipped back her head to look at him. "Why, hello, Bob." Her voice somehow held back her deep excitement. "It's nice to see you again."

Ginny, Mary, and Martha were on the porch with him. Anne mounted the steps and shook hands. Bob studied her appreciatively and glanced past her to the three women.

"Lord, how she's changed!"

"You've been gone awhile," Anne reminded him and sat down, selecting a seat at the far end of the porch where the shadows hid her.

At first, after Bob had stretched himself out in a reclining chair again, the girl avoided looking at him. She answered Martha's questions about the picture she had seen and presently let her eyes stray in his direction.

He hadn't changed too much, she decided, except that he was even better looking than she remembered him being. She listened as he spoke to his mother about something at the farm. His voice had a ring of authority; it was deep-toned, all that a man's voice should be.

She was sitting a little apart from the others, not joining in their talk. Bob seemed not to notice, but finally he turned to look at her. "What's the matter, Anne? You haven't turned out to be the silent type, have you?"

"The sun will rise in the west when that happens," Virginia commented dryly.

The girl produced a yawn. "I'm tired."

"Why don't you go to bed, then?" Mary inquired.

"I shall," her niece replied without moving. "I've always been in love with him," she was thinking. "Even when I was too young to know what being in love was."

It was he who put an end to the evening, standing up and saying with a yawn, "Ladies, I've been on the move since six this morning. And that drive. I'm going to hit the sack."

"So should all of us," Virginia said, getting to her feet. "It's late and the wind's quite chilly . . . Anne, child, I believe you're nodding in the chair."

The girl shot an indignant glance at her. As if she would be nodding in the chair like an old grandmother! Why, she had never felt so keyed up in her life. She wouldn't sleep a wink tonight.

Before she went to bed—where, contrary to expectation, she fell asleep in a short time—there occurred a small incident that was meaningless then but that Anne was to dwell on afterward. The five of them were in the living room and Aunt Ginny locked the door. Martha asked Bob if he had taken the car key out of the ignition. He reached in a pocket to make sure he had, and his hand came out holding a bottle.

"Oh, here's the medicine Uncle Wally gave me." He grinned at Virginia. "It's lucky Mother asked about the key. Otherwise I'd probably have taken it right back to Kinnelly with me."

"Thank you." Virginia took the bottle. "I'd have skinned you alive, young man, if you'd forgotten it," she added. "I'm down to one capsule."

Anne reflected that age had its compensations. When you were as old as Aunt Ginny you could take a familiar scolding tone with a blond young man who stood with his hands in his pockets and gave you a careless grin. When you were young it was different. She was certain that she herself would never feel at ease with him as she once had before the war.

By daylight, however, Anne's attitude changed.

Bob was matter-of-fact, eliciting matter-of-factness in return. His pedestal was not so lofty as she had thought.

He came out to the beach at noon, having slept the morning away. Anne lay on the sand beside Bill Kensington.

"How's the water?" Bob inquired, dropping down on the other side of the girl.

"Arctic," she told him. "Bill . . . She nudged the youth beside her, who was lethargic from sunbathing. "Your manners . . . This is Bill Kensington . . . Bob Vanderbrouk."

Bill propped himself up on an elbow and reached a hand across her to Bob. "Glad to know you."

"He's a sort of a cousin," Anne appended.

Bob contradicted her. "We're not related at all."

"By marriage," she finished.

"Well, have it your way." He stretched out on the sand and lit a cigarette.

"Aren't you going swimming?" the girl asked.

"I'll let the tide come in and catch up with me."

The talk was desultory. It was enough to lie there warmed by the sun and lulled by the rhythm of the surf.

Bill, still gawky at twenty-two, lavishing mooning glances on Anne, stayed with them until far off on the beach his younger sister shrieked, "Bill, lunch is ready! Come on."

"Coming!" He rolled over and clambered reluctantly to his feet. "See you later," he said. "Anne, wanna play tennis this afternoon?"

Bob squinted at him in the sunlight. "She's got

responsibilities this afternoon, Bill. I'm a guest. She's got to show me the sights."

Nothing gay or bright, nothing that struck the right note, occurred to Anne. She said lamely, "Oh yes . . . yes, of course, Bob. I'd like to."

"Well . . . I'll stop by later." Bill was not pleased as he left them.

They went for a drive that afternoon, and Bob took her to dinner at one of the places renowned for sea food, where Anne ordered Southern-fried chicken. This, he said, reminded him that she had always been contrary as a child.

"But I don't much care for sea food. I never have," Anne told him.

They had talked all afternoon; a little about his army experiences, more about family matters and town gossip. By now most of the constraint the girl felt in his presence had vanished. She remarked over the first course, "Y'know, last night I thought you hadn't changed. Today, though, it seems that your face used to be rounder."

"Sure it was. Growing up, I used to look like a Dutch boy in a musical comedy. All I needed was the wooden shoes." He cocked an eyebrow at her. "Don't you find me more romantic this way? The lean, Lincoln look, I mean?"

"It doesn't much matter what a face is like," Anne replied sedately. "Not really. It's not supposed to, anyway."

"Ah, there speaks your aunt Ginny. 'Handsome is as handsome does, child.' "

His imitation of her aunt's severest manner was

exact. Anne laughed. "She can be pretty formidable, can't she?"

"Formidable is the word." He shook his head meditatively. "Then there's your uncle Wally, a character in his own right. May I say, Miss Howard, that your family runs to them?"

Consistent in her attitude toward her uncle, the girl dismissed him with a gesture. "The only trouble with him is that he's a born old maid."

They spent two hours at dinner on a porch overlooking the ocean. In her happiness Anne thought, "This is the nicest time I've ever had. I wish it would never end."

But it had to come to a close. It was she herself who said, "We really should go."

Bob agreed and then remarked unexpectedly, "Your hair is beautiful. Was it always as dark a shade as it is now?"

The tone was casual, but for a moment Anne thought his eyes weren't casual in the least. He added, "You forget about things like that when you're away awhile," and his eyes held nothing in particular.

The drive home passed all too quickly. They had the ocean on their left. The clouds that hid the moon, broken and edged with its glow, were lovelier than moonlight. With any of her contemporaries, the girl knew, she would be staving off suggestions to sit a little closer. But Bob kept both hands on the wheel and talked about the old whaling days at New Bedford.

The next day Bill Kensington and other young people from cottages near by were much in evidence. Lena served the usual heavy Sunday dinner that left them with a torpid feeling during the afternoon hours on the beach. In the evening Martha initiated a bridge game, so there were no more blissful interludes alone with Bob; nor did he, Anne noticed with despair, attempt to create any. Virginia complained of her back, and the girl said she would take her to the chiropractor in Hyannis for treatment.

That was the evening. Monday morning Bob and his mother made an early start for Connecticut, and Anne watched the car until it was out of sight. The promise of Saturday had trickled away into a family Sunday and a brisk handshake and, "See you in the fall, Anne," on Monday.

With a sense of discouragement, she went back into the cottage to wait for her aunt Ginny to be ready for the chiropractor's. Aunt Mary decided to accompany them, and Lena too, to do some marketing. There would be other expeditions like it; the month of August stretched ahead, a desert.

Each time the telephone rang that week Wally raced to answer it. But the suspense spun itself out, torturingly fine; the call he expected didn't come. When he could stand it no longer he telephoned Bob and took a joking tone. "You young scamp, I'll bet you forgot to give Sister her medicine."

"No, I didn't. I gave it to her the night I got there."

"Good. I had a letter from her yesterday and she didn't mention it, so I wondered if you'd forgotten."

That was all that it was necessary to say, but he

went on, "Well, I'm glad she has it. To tell you the truth, Bob, I can't help worrying about Sister and that heart attack she had. Dr. Harshbarger seems to think she's coming along nicely, though . . . Still, she needs her medicine and I did wonder if you'd forgotten or if the bottle might have been broken or something . . . I'm certainly glad to hear that she has it . . ."

Wally didn't know how to extricate himself from the conversation.

It was Bob, growing bored, who said, "Well, she got the stuff all right. I know Mother called and told you about her visit, so I won't keep you, Uncle Wally."

"No, no, not at all. Good-by and thank you."

"You're quite welcome."

The older man put the telephone back in its cradle. He couldn't think why he had become so nervous all at once. There was no need of it, of course. Bob wouldn't give a second thought to the call.

He must pull himself together and behave naturally. The day Martha had telephoned, for example, he could have asked her if Ginny had her medicine; but he hadn't dared to mention it. That showed you what uncertainty you could let yourself in for when there was no reason for it.

Ginny had had the capsules for a week. He sat by the telephone picturing the bottle and his sister shaking a capsule out into her hand. Suddenly the bottle looked different. Its inner surface was cloudy.

Wally hurried to the medicine cabinet to verify his new source of apprehension. Yes, here was a bottle like the other one. There were a few capsules for

198

a cold left in it and it had a film of white powder on the inside; a sifting, a slight leakage, he supposed.

What if that happened to Ginny's bottle?

The thing to do was to get hold of it right after she died. He would wash it out thoroughly and then replace whatever capsules there were in it.

His fears were not altogether quieted by this decision. They wouldn't be, Wally knew, until he had the bottle in his possession . . .

Tuesday night the telephone rang after he was in bed. He leaped out, tripped over one of his slippers in the dark, and fell against a chest of drawers. Dazed by the blow, he couldn't find the light switch in his haste and stumbled out to the hall. The telephone was urging him on insistently. His breath came in great gasps by the time he picked up the receiver.

"Steady," he counseled himself. "Your voice now . . ."

He brought out a falsetto "Hello?" but at the other end of the wire his sister Mary was too upset to find anything strange in it. She said, "Wally?"

"Yes."

"This is Mary speaking."

He groped for the chair beside the stand and sank into it.

"I don't know how to tell you—it's bad news." Her sobbing was a faint, attenuated sound across the distance between them. "Oh, Wally, Ginny died a little while ago!"

"What?"

"The doctor just left . . ." There was a pause during which he heard Mary blowing her nose and the thud of his own heart. "We told him about the at-

199

tack she had before. He said she'd had another . . .
Oh, Wally, I can't believe it! She was all right at
dinner and during the evening. It's so—sudden. I—"
Tears choked her voice.

He made no answer, and after a moment she
asked, "Are you there, Wally?"

Couldn't she hear his harsh breathing? He felt as
if he were strangling. He lowered the mouthpiece
before he said, "Yes, I'm here. But I don't know
what to say. The shock—"

"Yes. And you didn't see her as I did—apparently
in perfect health and then—right after she went to
bed—"

"Frightful," he said. "I can't even begin to grasp
it."

"N-neither can I," Mary wept.

Wally thought of the bottle. He would get hold of
it immediately. "I'll call Bob," he told her. "We'll
start up there at daylight."

"You'll come here? . . . Wait a minute, Anne
wants to speak to you."

"It was the girl's voice that he heard next. "Uncle
Wally, I think you'd better stay where you are.
There's nothing you can do here."

"Oh, but my place is with you, child. There'll be
so many things to take care of. They mustn't be left
to Mary and you."

"Uncle Wally, the Kierans from next door are
with us now. Mr. Kieran will make the arrangements
to have Aunt Ginny's body sent on, and we're coming home ourselves tomorrow. After all, the funeral
will be in Kinnelly and it's there that you can help
the most. We'll need an undertaker and—Yes, Aunt

Mary?" Anne's voice faded as she turned away from the telephone. It was clear again when she resumed, "Aunt Mary says to call the Sneath funeral home and get in touch with Lena's sister first thing in the morning to clean the house. And there'll be people to notify . . ."

She concluded, "So you see, Uncle Wally, there's lots to do. Aunt Martha will help you and we'll be home sometime tomorrow afternoon."

Her reasoning was sound and barred his way to the bottle. Nevertheless he made a last protest. "But you can't be equal to that long drive, child, after this."

"I'm perfectly all right, Uncle Wally. Do you mind if I hang up now? We'll see you tomorrow."

"No, don't hang up yet. You haven't told me what happened. All I know is that Sister had an attack and died. It's terrible for me, alone here and all."

Her voice softened. "I know, Uncle Wally. But there isn't much to tell. She wasn't ill, she seemed like herself when Aunt Mary and she went to bed about ten o'clock. I was reading in the living room, and a few minutes later I heard her call out. I went into her and she was clinging to the bedpost . . ."

For the first time Anne's self-control faltered. "She said—she felt numb—and that her eyes bothered her. I was terribly frightened. I called a doctor. He lives just down the beach and came right away. But—but there wasn't anything he could do. We told him about her other attack and he said she'd had a second one . . ."

Wally had had enough details. He had asked for them only because he wanted to be sure that no suspicion had been aroused. He said hastily, "Well, child, we'll have to make the best of it. Go to bed now and try to get some sleep. I'll take care of everything here. Good night and give my love to Mary."

There was no sleep for him that night. He prowled through the house, talking aloud to his dead: his mother and father; his four brothers; he even included the baby sister, that least substantial of all the wraiths from the past. He explained himself to them again; why he had been forced to do what he had done.

The empty house watched his progress. The walls and furniture looked on as he moved from room to room, leaving a trail of half-smoked cigarettes in each of them. The house didn't seem to understand the stress under which he had acted. He pleaded with it. "I never meant this to happen; I never wanted it. But what else could I do?

"I'm a good man. I go to church and read my Bible. I never willfully harmed anyone in my life. Is it my fault that both Henry and Sister pushed me too far?"

Wally flung himself into a chair and began to weep because none of them answered him. He was left alone in this awful silence. He had been alone in it all his life.

When dawn was lighting the sky he had borne it as long as he could. He telephoned Martha, and as soon as her sleepy voice spoke he told her Virginia was dead. "I didn't mean to call you until later . . . I've been here by myself, though, not able to sleep . . ."

"You should have called hours ago," Martha said. "I'll come right away."

Bob drove her over. She made coffee in the gray light of the kitchen, and her kind sympathetic presence drove out the hobgoblins of the night.

Wally put his head on the table. "Sister," he moaned. "Dear, dear Sister."

CHAPTER SIXTEEN —

He stood looking at Virginia, her body placed in front of the windows where so many dead Howards had lain. He wiped his eyes. "There were seven of us," he said to the discreetly hovering undertaker. "And now only Mary and I are left. We must bow to God's will, I know, but it's very hard. Sister and I were together always . . ."

The casket was an imposing one of gray metal. "Sister must have the best . . ." She lay on a special mattress. Wally had insisted on it. "She had such trouble with her back. I want to feel that she's resting comfortably . . ."

He had put the night of Virginia's death well behind him.

He was in his element greeting the people who came to pay their respects. "Dear Mrs. Gratton." He took an elderly woman's hand in both of his. "How kind of you to come when you go out so little nowadays. I know it would have meant so much to Sister to have you here."

Anne, keeping in the background, watched her uncle. How could he do it? He couldn't mean it. He was telling old Miss Whittlesey how close he and Aunt Ginny had been. Tears came readily to his eyes.

Aunt Ginny hadn't been very kind to her brother. She had never let him forget that he was financially dependent on her. She had shown her best side, what stock of warmth she had to offer, to her niece. Uncle Wally's display of grief was reasonless and excessive.

Anne shook hands with some new arrivals and saw them move on to Wally. She caught some of the things he said. ". . . Everything to me . . . Depended on her absolutely . . . Lost . . . Like a child . . . Learn to walk all over again by myself . . . I don't know where to turn. . . ."

A fresh handkerchief came out.

Aunt Ginny had ordered him around unflaggingly. He had had little affection or understanding from her.

By the time of the funeral Anne had decided that her uncle's behavior must be something peculiar to an older generation. In their respect for the dead they carried self-deception to inordinate lengths.

After Aunt Ginny was buried, however, and things returned to normal, Uncle Wally would feel free to face the truth. He could call his soul his own at last; he'd have money to spend as he pleased; he'd be the master of this house as long as he lived. . . .

In the meantime, Anne thought, let him hold the center of the stage. It was a new experience for poor Uncle Wally to have so much attention from everyone. She, Anne, wanted none of that kind of attention; nor did Aunt Mary, resting upstairs on Anne's bed, want it.

Aunt Mary, a widow for five years, went home with her daughter after the funeral. When all the relatives had gone, Martha and Bob stayed until the late evening. Bob was gentle with Anne, quiet in her grief, in a way that recalled the same kind of gentleness toward her when her father died.

It was Wally who talked on and on about the dead woman.

The girl was wakeful that night and knew that her uncle, in the next room, was wakeful too. She felt sorry for him when she heard him moving about. Aunt Ginny and he hadn't got along well together, but still they had lived under the one roof all their lives. They were brother and sister. It would take him a while to get used to her death.

Anne's thoughts went back to the night her aunt died. She lived it over. Aunt Mary, then Aunt Ginny, in bed. Across the narrow hall the latter's room faced the living room. The cry had come and she had gone to her. A light was turned on and Aunt Ginny was sitting up in bed clinging to the bedpost. She gasped, "An attack—doctor——"

Anne had run to the telephone and called the doctor who lived a few cottages away. Going back to her aunt, she remembered the capsules and brought them and a glass of water with her.

Aunt Ginny took a swallow of water but waved the capsules away. "I had one—tonight—Mary——"

Anne called Mary, already asleep. The two of them leaned over the bed, helpless, frantic, watching the losing battle for life go on.

Aunt Ginny gasped, "Can't breathe—can't see—legs—numb——"

Anne had rubbed her aunt's legs. "All pins—and needles——" her aunt cried, and she had rubbed harder.

It hadn't lasted long. She slumped forward. The sudden silence that ensued was more shocking than the rasping breath had been. Aunt Ginny died even as the doctor was coming into the cottage. . . .

Anne shifted from side to side in the bed. Her aunt had appeared perfectly well that last evening. She had talked about a drive to Truro the next day to visit an old friend who was summering there. She hadn't been thinking of death; she had looked forward confidently to the next day and many days thereafter. Death could come like that, swiftly. There was something about it in the Bible. Her grandmother used to read it; about the way man springeth up and is cut down. . . .

That was how Anne remembered Emma Howard best: reading the Bible. An episode long forgotten came back to her. Her father was teasing her grandmother. "Mother, you must be the foremost living authority on the Bible."

"It would do you some good to read it yourself," Emma Howard retorted.

"I did when I was a kid," Henry reminded her. "You gave each of us a dollar for every time we read it through. I earned only one dollar, though. Wally was the boy who read it most."

Uncle Wally must have been present. Anne couldn't place him on the scene, but he had been there and had said something about the Bible being his source of strength. And her father said that he looked for his strength inside himself. . . .

The scene faded as her disconnected thoughts moved on among family incidents. She had been in bed for what seemed to her like several hours before she fell asleep. The last thing she heard was her uncle's door opening and his footsteps on the stairs.

It was Anne who answered the telephone the next day when the real-estate agent called and asked to speak to Wally.

They were at lunch, the door to the hall standing open. Anne heard her uncle say, "Hello?" and, "Oh yes, Mr. Hollister." He listened, said, "Yes, I can understand that you'd want to know as soon as possible. Life goes on. No matter how deep one's sorrow, there are always these mundane claims . . ."

He listened again. Anne faced the door and could see him shake his head. "No, I shan't go through with the lease. I haven't, of course, even had time to think of how Sister's affairs stand, but I'm sure I shan't be renting the house . . . Yes, I know it places your client in an unfortunate position . . . I'm sorry, Mr. Hollister, but I'm afraid my mind is made up. . . ."

Uncle Wally hadn't wanted to give up the house. But if Aunt Ginny had lived, he would have had no choice. Her death had occurred in time to prevent the lease being signed. He must be thinking of that as he talked to the real-estate agent. He sounded almost triumphant.

That afternoon Wally walked to the cemetery and spent an hour there. He had it to himself, and it was quiet and peaceful in the sunshine. He talked to his mother.

When he returned home he found Anne on the porch. With gentlest melancholy he told her that it was time to turn their faces to the future.

Although Virginia's will hadn't yet been opened, they both knew its terms. The cottage had been left to Anne. "But I don't want to go back there this summer," she said. "I couldn't think of staying there—not so soon."

Wally nodded understandingly. "You'll have to take care of things, though," he pointed out. "You'll want the water and electricity shut off, the telephone disconnected. You said you'd left most of your clothes behind too. And"—eagerness underlay his offhand note—"Sister's things. They'll have to be seen to."

"I suppose so," the girl assented without interest. "In a week or two, perhaps."

"Should you let it go at all?" he asked. "The shutters, for instance. They ought to be put up right away in case there's a bad storm. And there are lots of other things. I don't think you should put them off, child. I'll be glad to go with you and help. It's really my duty to go and look over Sister's effects. Papers, you know. Letters, possibly, that need a reply . . ."

His voice trailed off. He wouldn't enjoy an easy moment until he had Virginia's medicine bottle in his hands. It must be at the cottage. Anne had brought only one suitcase to Kinnelly with her. He had looked through it when the girl was absent from her room and the bottle wasn't in it.

"I don't like loose ends," he thought fretfully. "Maybe I'm making too much of it, with Ginny dead and buried, but I have to get hold of that bottle before I can feel it's all over and done with."

He was again picturing a film of powder on its inner surface. After all, Bob had carried it in his pocket; it had got jostled around . . .

Anne started the glider swaying with her foot. "I'd much rather let it go for a while, Uncle Wally."

"Why don't I go alone, then, and take care of things for you?" he suggested.

The obstinate, maddening girl shook her head. "A man couldn't. There are too many things. I couldn't begin to list all of them for you."

His preoccupation with the bottle goaded him into indiscretion. "You didn't bring back any of Sister's belongings, did you?" he asked. "I don't suppose you even gave a thought to anything like—well, like Sister's medicine, say."

Anne looked so astonished that he continued quickly, "I couldn't sleep last night and I happened to recall that those capsules she took were a sedative. If it hadn't been that I didn't want to wake you, I'd have asked about them last night. Goodness, child, what a time I had getting to sleep."

"I heard you moving around . . . But I can't imagine your thinking of taking Aunt Ginny's medicine. It wouldn't be safe, would it? The prescription was made up specifically for her."

"It was seconal," he said, unnecessarily sharp. "It couldn't have done me the least harm. And I don't see anything extraordinary in my thinking of it. I had the prescription filled for her, and Bob——" He broke off. It was a mistake to remind his niece that he, Wally, had had the bottle in his possession. "You're making a mountain out of a molehill," he finished accusingly.

Anne saw his hand go to his forehead and come away wet. It must have been wet, for he wiped it on his light gray slacks and a few tiny dots of moisture darkened them.

All at once the girl was frightened. Fright squeezed her heart and tightened the grip her hands had got on each other. It was Uncle Wally who was making a mountain out of a molehill. He was lying about the capsules. He hadn't wanted them to take himself. His voice and manner, his forehead shining with sweat, proclaimed the lie.

Too late he achieved casualness. "Well, we won't labor such a trifling point," he remarked with a smile and turned the conversation to Virginia's funeral, how many had attended the service, what handsome flowers had been sent.

Anne nodded and made appropriate comment.

His glance came back to her again and again. It darted suspicion at her, she thought.

Uncle Wally had had the prescription filled. ". . . and Bob——" he had said and stopped. Bob what? Had he only intended to add that Bob had brought the bottle of medicine to Aunt Ginny? —or was there something else?

For the first of many times to come Anne's mind reverted to the weekend when Bob was at the cottage. They were going to bed when he remembered the capsules and took them out of his pocket. . . .

211

She looked at the little gray-haired man with fright and bewilderment growing in her.

They were invited to dinner at Martha's that evening. For Anne, however, there was no pleasure in Bob's company. She couldn't look at his angular face and big, substantial figure without a question in her eyes. Did Uncle Wally and he share some secret about Aunt Ginny's medicine?

The girl forced herself to wait two days before she said at breakfast, "After I went to bed last night, Uncle Wally, I started worrying about the windows at the cottage. I just couldn't remember closing the ones in my bedroom. And I forgot to leave the keys with Mrs. Kieran, you know, so she'd have no way of taking care of them."

"But, my dear child, a storm would soak everything in the room. Or someone might break in!"

"That's what I was worrying about. I suppose I could mail Mrs. Kieran the keys . . ." Anne's eyebrows, darker than her hair, were drawn into a troubled frown.

"Anne, you'll have to go up there sometime soon, anyway, so why not take care of the windows yourself?" Wally looked out at the sunlit lawn. "You couldn't ask for a better day for a trip. We could start now. I'd be glad to go with you."

He spoke urgently. But he couldn't, Anne reflected, be any more anxious than she was to get hold of the bottle.

They had lunch in Providence. Anne let her uncle keep conversation alive as the afternoon went by and they neared their destination.

She went through the whole affair again. Aunt

Ginny had written to her brother to have her prescription refilled. She had done that other summers. There was nothing about it that was worthy of note. He had taken care of it; but instead of mailing the medicine to her or bringing it himself on one of his occasional visits, he had given it to Bob. That was where the situation first deviated from the usual. It was Bob who had taken the bottle out of his pocket. . . .

The girl was back at visualizing the scene. Bob had been in the living room and had handed the medicine to Aunt Ginny, joking about nearly forgetting it. She would surely have noticed it if there had been anything out of the ordinary in his manner. . . .

Bob had spent the weekend with them and taken his mother home to Kinnelly. Another week had passed and Aunt Ginny had had that attack and died. . . .

She had waved the bottle away that night and said she'd already had one of the capsules. . . .

She took them quite often, however. How could there be anything harmful in the ones Bob had brought to her? Bob. . . .

It wasn't he who had asked about the bottle, in any case. It was Uncle Wally who made her spine creep with his eagerness to get hold of it.

She glanced at him, sitting beside her. He didn't look in the least the sort of person to fill her or anyone with undefinable fear.

Her plans were made during the drive. A few miles from the cottage she slowed the car almost to a full stop at a gas station and said, "I think I'll use

213

the rest room here . . . No, I'll wait till we get to the cottage."

The byplay made her first action on reaching it seem natural. Wally unlocked the front door, stepped aside with his accustomed courtesy to allow her to precede him, and Anne headed straight for the bathroom. That was where the bottle was. She herself had put it back in the medicine cabinet the night Virginia died.

There were eleven or twelve capsules in it and a faint film of white powder on the inside.

The girl shook the bottle, unscrewed the cap, and sniffed purposelessly at the contents. So far as she could see there was nothing about it that made it any different from its predecessors. Except for her uncle's concern over it, she would have thrown it out or left it there indefinitely without giving it a thought.

He was in his sister's room and she heard a drawer close as she went to join him. His next action was to go into the bathroom himself, and Anne was as certain as if she stood beside him that he was searching the medicine cabinet for the bottle that was hidden at the bottom of her handbag.

She entered her bedroom and called out to him that after all she had shut the windows. He came to the doorway and she saw his eyes take inventory of possible places where the bottle might be found.

He said, "If you don't mind, child, I think I'll spend a few minutes alone in Sister's room—where she died."

He closed the door after him, but Anne, listening from the hall, heard subdued sounds that indicated a search in progress.

She moved on to the living room and sat down, keeping a tight grip on her handbag. If Uncle Wally didn't ask for the bottle within the next few minutes, there would be no chance left that he wanted it for any innocent reason.

Half hopeful, half afraid, she waited and he didn't mention it.

They worked for a while storing away the porch furniture and other outdoor things and then had dinner at a near-by restaurant. The Kierans came in for a brief visit. After they were gone Anne and her uncle went on packing until bedtime.

Once she left him alone for a while, saying that she must take the box of foodstuffs she had assembled to the Kierans so that they wouldn't go to waste. She came back into the cottage on tiptoe, and Wally was searching her bedroom as she had expected him to do.

The girl slipped out to the kitchen to open and slam the screen door. She found her uncle in the living room after the warning of her approach. He was unhooking window screens.

Her tension mounted. She worked with him for another hour in almost complete silence. He was quiet too, lacking his fund of small talk.

Anne went to bed. Wally said, "I think I'll get the screens down in the guest room before I call it a night."

That gave him the opportunity to search in there, Anne told herself. And to make a thorough search of the living room and kitchen.

He continued his hunt, going farther and farther afield from the logical places. Midnight found him taking books from the shelves and looking behind them, and lifting pictures from the walls to assure himself that they didn't conceal the bottle. He removed every item from the cabinet under the kitchen sink, cleansers, soap powders, ammonia, bleach water, and all the rest, playing the beam of a flashlight on its darkest recesses. There was a half cellar under the cottage, and he looked there too, returning to the living room a little smudged and grimy and quite uneasy.

He sat down and took stock of the situation. The places to which he had carried his search were absurd. Why should anyone go to such lengths to hide the bottle? Why should it be hidden at all?

It hadn't been hidden, of course. He was letting his imagination get the better of him. The whole thing was nerves, nothing else.

Wally thought it over. There wasn't a genuine cause for uneasiness. The bottle could have been thrown out in the rubbish the day after Ginny died. Some tidying up must have taken place before Mary and Anne left the cottage. The bottle could have been scooped up with a pile of newspapers, with anything. It wasn't as if Ginny's death had stirred up suspicion. No one had given a thought to her medicine; no one had mentioned it.

No one except himself. He had, most unfortunately, spoken to Anne about it. But the child hadn't paid any heed to what he said; he had given her a good explanation for his inquiry. . . .

Wally was momentarily taut in the chair, remembering that Anne had gone directly to the bathroom on their arrival. He relaxed and lit a cigarette. It hadn't been the medicine cabinet; she'd wanted to stop at that gas station. . .

While he smoked he convinced himself that the last thought in Anne's mind was the bottle; that it had been thrown out in the confusion following his sister's death; that it didn't matter anyway since the capsules in it were all harmless and none of the aconitine could have leaked out of the lethal one. He went to bed satisfied with his conclusions. If a residue of uneasiness remained and a faint doubt of Anne, he wasn't conscious of such feelings.

After the girl was in bed she lay awake listening to her uncle moving around. He was still looking for the bottle, of course, but it was safe in her handbag.

Was it, though? Suppose he thought of that and after she was asleep slipped in and found it?

The mere idea of it sent her flying across the room in her bare feet to the dresser. She put the bottle under her pillow and lay thinking of it; of something about it that strained the matter-of-fact relationship existing heretofore between her and her uncle.

The cellar hatchway was outside her bedroom window. She heard Wally open it and saw the beam of the flashlight before it disappeared down the steps.

He was even looking in the cellar! It was as serious as that. . . .

"Don't keep trying to duck the thing," Anne told herself, upright in the bed. "You know why Aunt Ginny's medicine is important to him. He did something to it. He must have. He did it by himself, or he and Bob did it together."

It was nonsense to include Bob. Why should he,

away for five years, be involved in a plot against Aunt Ginny?

He had had the medicine, though. Again the moment when he handed the bottle to her aunt spread itself out for contemplation. She could see Virginia and him clearly and even hear their voices.

That picture was supplanted by another for which, at the moment, there was indeed no rhyme or reason. Her father was struggling in the lake; Uncle Wally was slow, stupidly slow, in going to his rescue. Bob and she were swimming out side by side, Bob ordering her to turn back . . .

Bob and Uncle Wally and her father who drowned . . . Aunt Ginny died suddenly, and Bob and her uncle were somehow connected with her death. . . .

The girl looked at another old memory: Uncle Wally was pouring a dribble of whisky from her father's flask into the kitchen sink. He was rinsing out the flask carefully . . . Bob wasn't present then, however. . . .

Anne lay back on the pillow. These were terrible thoughts to entertain, to nurture; yes, to nurture.

Outside the window quiet footsteps sounded on the cellar stairs. The search below was completed.

CHAPTER SEVENTEEN —

Home in Kinnelly, Anne looked up the address of a commercial laboratory in the telephone directory, selected half a dozen capsules at random from the bottle, and took them into town with her. She left them at the laboratory, explaining that she'd like to have them checked to be sure they contained seconal and that she would call back the next day for the report.

Driving back to Kinnelly, she discovered that mixed with dread of what the analysis might reveal there was relief in positive action. At least she'd know. She would put an end to the increasing fear of Uncle Wally that had her one moment avoiding his gaze, the next fastening her eyes, leechlike, on his face as though it must tell her what he had done.

Thank God she'd be returning to New London in two more weeks. She wouldn't have to try to be natural with Uncle Wally; she wouldn't have to feel her flesh crawl now and again when it seemed to her that

219

he was watching her and that there was something disturbing about his eyes.

Suppose there was poison in the capsules?

Her hands tightened on the wheel. She'd face that when she had to, she decided.

There was a telephone number for her to call, Lena said, when the girl came into the house by the back door. "A young man," the elderly woman added. "He asked for you to call him as soon as you were home."

Anne hurried to the telephone. But the number on the pad wasn't Martha's familiar one; it wasn't Bob who had called her. It had been a foolish hope to entertain anyway. Lena would have told her if it had been Bob.

It was Kurt Roser, Kinnelly's perennial dashing young man. "Hello, darling," he began. "I've just been saying to myself, 'What you need is the company of the most charming girl in Kinnelly.' "

Anne laughed and her mood lightened a little. Kurt, years older than she, lacking seriousness, would take her mind off her worries, she thought.

She agreed to have dinner with him and went upstairs to shower and change.

Wally was reading in the small room next to the bathroom. He looked up as she passed the open door. "Oh, hello, child," he said. "What did you do in town?"

"I looked for a suit."

"Well, did you find one you liked?" He took an interest in clothes. Usually the girl showed him everything she bought.

"No, nothing that seemed just right."

"Ah, an afternoon wasted then," he remarked and went back to his reading.

In the book-lined room, at ease in a deep chair, Uncle Wally personified innocuousness. Taking the capsules to the laboratory was practically a form of hysteria. . . .

Anne felt happier than she had since her aunt's death while she was deciding what dress to wear. She brushed her hair, counting one hundred strokes, and stopped thinking about her uncle entirely.

The lighter mood persisted. It carried her through Kurt Roser's arrival, out to his car, and along the highway to the inn where they were to have dinner.

Anne never did learn what Yolanda's last name was. Either Bob or Kurt must have mentioned it in the moment of introduction, but it passed the girl by.

It was Yolanda who saw them come into the dining room of the inn and hailed Kurt enthusiastically. When she discovered that Bob and Anne knew each other she insisted that the newcomers join them at their table. Kurt was the attraction, of course, Anne realized, even though Yolanda moved her chair closer to Bob's, reached for his hand, and called him "Honey boy."

Yolanda was blond. The younger girl was immediately convinced that she had given nature a lift with her hair. She had a wide-eyed look and a knowledgeable mouth. She threw Kurt languishing glances and, in all likelihood, Anne reflected, knew the impressive total of the Roser fortune. When she got up to dance with Bob her figure and legs turned out to be beautiful.

Anne looked after her and recalled Uncle Nick's summary of a lady of dubious virtue. "She's been around the corner," he had said.

Bob wasn't pleased with the foursome arrangement that had been forced upon him. He probably resented Yolanda's attentions to Kurt, Anne thought.

Yolanda had several drinks as the meal progressed. "Call me Yo-Yo," she urged the younger girl. "All my friends do."

Her refinement slipped a little. Kurt's laughter encouraged her in an off-color story. He was matching her drink for drink.

Anne, because her aunt was dead so recently, didn't dance. It was Yolanda whom Kurt led out to the floor.

As soon as they were away from the table Bob turned to look straight at her. "What in hell do you think you're doing, dating Roser?" he demanded.

She stiffened. "I don't know that it concerns you, but since you ask, I've been out with him two or three times before."

"Did your aunt Ginny know about it?"

The girl flushed. "She didn't happen to be home."

I guess not! Of course it's too much to expect that your uncle would come out of his dreamworld long enough to check on the people you go out with—and if he did, he'd probably say Kurt was a nice little fellow—but you ought to have more sense yourself!" He leaned toward her, his jaw thrust out. "God, that guy's been the town playboy as far back as when I was in high school. Some of the stories about him have been pretty bad, too, even if his old man's money did cover up the worst of them. It won't do

222

your reputation any good to be seen around with him!"

Anne, who had been flattered by having a worldling like Kurt notice her, defended herself. "Kurt has behaved perfectly the few times I've been out with him," she stated coldly.

"Oh, sure. The perfect little gent—so far. You expect it to last?" His angry blue eyes swept over her.

Anne became aloof. "It's the girl's behavior that sets the example for the man."

"Oh, my God!"

She resorted to attack. "And furthermore, who are you to talk? I wouldn't call 'Yo-Yo' the most edifying companion in the world. If you're so particular, what are you doing with her?"

"I——" He stopped short, not prepared to discuss his reasons for taking out Yolanda. "There's no comparison," he snapped. "I'm not Roser, and Yolanda is well able to look after herself."

"So am I. I didn't ask your advice."

The argument continued until the others came back to the table. It was doubly bitter because beneath it was a special awareness of each other and self-consciousness engendered by the amorphous family tie.

Bob came to see her the next evening after dinner, rationalizing his visit by telling himself that perhaps he had been a little hard on the girl. She had no parents, she'd been brought up by a spinster aunt, and now she had no one to turn to, really, except Wally Howard; and he was an erratic prop indeed. Not even inwardly was Bob acknowledging how much interest Anne aroused in him.

He was matter-of-fact when he arrived, ignoring last night's hot words. "There's a good movie downtown," he said. "I thought you might like to see it."

"Yes, I would."

When they were in the car Bob said, "Maybe I was a little rough on you at the inn. I'm sorry."

"Oh, but you were right," Anne asserted. "I thought it over afterward—about Kurt, I mean—and I don't think I will go out with him again."

"Good." He started the motor and gave her a sidewise smile. "You see the method I'm following, don't you? If I'm with you myself I needn't worry about the company you're keeping."

Her answering smile sent him into retreat from his own feelings. She was a swell kid; let it go at that; be wary of a thing like falling for a girl when it hit you suddenly after all these years.

At the movie Anne was relaxed and content. She could revel in being with Bob. She needn't be frightened to death any longer when she was with Uncle Wally. That afternoon she had gone to the laboratory and received the report on the capsules. One and all, they contained seconal. Whatever Uncle Wally's reasons were for hunting the bottle, there was nothing sinister in them. He was full of foibles. Why should she worry about this one?

The picture was a swift-moving melodrama. There came a scene where the hero was invited to drink from one of two glasses. One held poisoned wine; the other was harmless.

The girl sat up straighter. The hero didn't drink. In one of the ever-successful, low, lunging tackles that movie heroes make, he knocked the gun from the villain's hand. . . .

Anne scarcely followed the rest of the story. In the picture the poison was in a wineglass; but it could be in a capsule, in just one capsule out of a bottle in which all the others were what they were supposed to be.

They didn't stay for what was advertised as the "co-hit." Bob took her for a drive. When he asked if she would like coffee, Anne told him that what she would really like was a sundae with lots of nuts and whipped cream. He hunted up a drugstore.

Sitting opposite him in a booth, she found it an effort to smile and make conversation. But with the triumphant appetite of youth, she ate her sundae down to the last dripping spoonful while Bob drank a milk shake.

He lit a cigarette and asked, "What's gone wrong all of a sudden?"

"Why, not a thing."

"Don't give me any of that. Let's hear about it."

He smiled encouragingly as she looked at him. His tanned face was modeled on pleasant lines. He was Bob who had been part of her childhood and had taken the trouble to be kind to a little girl. Could he have changed into someone who shared an evil secret about a medicine bottle?

No, it wasn't possible. Anne said, "There was something in the picture that made me think of something else."

"Well, that's a clear explanation." He wasn't smiling now. Her troubled face told him it was serious.

"It was about Aunt Ginny, Bob. The way she died."

"Oh . . . It was an awful blow, of course, coming so quickly." He spoke sympathetically. "And you must miss her a lot. You'd always had her."

She shook her head. "It's not that. I mean, what you said is true, but it's not what I keep thinking about . . ." The girl paused and sighed. "I'm not very coherent, am I? What I'm trying to say is that Uncle Wally asked me what had become of her bottle of medicine. And when were on the Cape he hunted and hunted for it. . . . Why do you think he'd be doing that?"

Bob returned her anxious gaze blankly. "After your aunt was dead he asked where her medicine was and hunted for it?"

"Yes. He looked everywhere in the cottage, even down cellar. I had it, though, so he didn't find it."

"Jesus," Bob said to himself. "Oh, Jesus." Thought and motion hung suspended. He tried to hide the consternation he felt.

Presently he was telling himself that it couldn't mean a thing. It was nothing more than one of Wally Howard's eccentricities. How could he believe anything but the best of Wally, who had protected Martha and, inferentially, Bob, when Wally's own brother lay dead at the foot of the steps? Bob owed the older man a debt he could never repay. . . .

Anne couldn't miss the conflict revealed in his face.

Frowning, looking down at the table, he asked, "Well, what reason did he give for wanting the thing?"

"He didn't say a word about it at the cottage. He asked me where it was before that . . ." Misery cut the girl's voice to a low monotone. Bob wasn't being straightforward with her; he shared the secret of the bottle. "When he was hunting for it, it was done behind my back."

"He never does things like anyone else would." Bob's tone was careful, guarded. Anne wanted to get away; to leave him and shut herself in her room away from the whole wretched affair.

"You still haven't told me what reason he gave," Bob reminded her.

"He said the capsules contained a sedative and he wanted to take one."

"Well, then, good Lord!" Relief loosened his voice and facial muscles. He straightened himself and spoke with assurance. "Of course that was it. You know what a funny old bird your uncle is. He wanted to take the stuff and hunted for it on his own because you probably let him see you thought the thing was queer. . . . What'd you do with it, by the way?"

"I left the bottle at a laboratory in town," Anne told him, lying because she no longer trusted him. "They're going to keep it for me."

"Have they made any tests on the capsules yet?"

"Yes. There was seconal in them."

"Then what in the name of heaven are you worrying about? It's nothing more than what I said it was a minute ago. Your uncle just doesn't do things the way anyone else would. You've lived with the man long enough to know that. . . ."

He urged this opinion on her, enlarging on it and

227

shaking his head at the end. "I can't imagine what's got into you."

Anne wouldn't tell him how strained and eager Wally had been in asking if she had the bottle; nor of the furtive way in which he had looked at her; nor that he had talked too much in explaining himself; nor of how terrifyingly stealthy he had been in the middle of the night searching the cottage. Bob had brought the bottle to Aunt Ginny; his manner confirmed the girl's fear that he shared whatever knowledge there was to share concerning it. It didn't make sense—but what part of it did?

Her voice was flat as she said, "I guess you're right. I've been so upset that I've been thinking all kinds of things."

"It's time you stopped. Your uncle Wally is the most harmless old codger that ever lived."

Her glance flickered over him and away. He was harmless too, he meant to imply. The word poison would remain unsaid between them. It was a dreadful word.

Anne found herself looking at Bob's hands. They were as tanned as his face, wide and strong with square-tipped fingers. They had held her up when she was learning to swim. They had lifted her onto a horse's back when she was learning to ride. One of them was closed around the glass of milk shake. The other held a cigarette.

She had only to keep quiet in agreement with him. She stared at his hands.

Bob said slowly and emphatically, "You've got to forget the whole thing, Anne. There's nothing to it. Your aunt died of a heart attack. The lab tells you there was only seconal in the capsules she took. If you set out to raise a stink about it you'll be laughed at. But no matter how wrong you are, you'll be hurting your uncle. You'll have him living under a cloud the rest of his life."

"Yes," Anne agreed. "Yes, that's true."

"So," he concluded, "the best thing to do is to drop it entirely. Don't think about it. Don't talk about it."

"Yes, that's the best thing to do. It's the only thing to do. I can see that now." He was warning her, wasn't he?

He smiled at her approvingly. He was Bob again, loved, surely to be trusted. Anne brought a smile to her own lips and the constriction in her throat eased. Not a trace of the guarded look he had had was left on his face.

The thoughts that had beset her a moment ago were fantastic. She was like a pendulum swinging back and forth. She must steady herself into acceptance of the logical view that Bob was taking.

It was the only possible view. . . . She said, "You think I'm plain nuts, don't you?"

"No. I simply think that you haven't been allowing enough room for the kind of person your uncle is."

The end of next week she'd be in New London. When she got there she'd put the bottle away in a drawer and forget it. Why should she let herself be burdened with such a problem? Especially when it didn't exist; not anywhere except in her own agitated mind. . . .

Anne began to talk animatedly about the picture

they had seen. It was Bob who was abstracted. He was remembering that over-insistence of Wally Howard's that he be sure to give Virginia the medicine and the call he had made the following week to ask if it had been delivered.

He was annoyed with himself for dwelling on it. Wally had done his mother and him the greatest service a man could do; he had always been fond of Martha and kindness itself to Bob. Wally's odd behavior was his own affair. It didn't mean a thing in this instance. How could it mean a thing anyway? The capsules had been analyzed and there was nothing in them but seconal. . . .

Bob was able to convince himself finally and completely that none of it mattered before he slept that night.

Anne had no obligation of gratitude toward Wally Howard. When she was home and in bed, pendulumlike she swung the other way again. But this time she thought about Bob rather than her uncle.

He had been too quick in charging the entire affair off to the older man's temperament. He had showed confusion and dismay when she told the story. He had immediately begun to belittle its significance. He had ended by warning her, yes, warning her, to forget it.

Her mind dulled by the repetitiveness of what she did, the girl once more went through the sequence of events.

There was nothing new to be added. No fresh possibilities presented themselves.

Anne got out of bed and sat down at an open window. What had she expected Bob to say or do?

Well, at a minimum, the normal thing would have been to discuss it with her exhaustively until every angle, however improbable, had been explored. Even if he had no plan of action to suggest, he should have done that.

Instead he had cut her off and urged her to drop it. He had been impelled to take that stand, and he had had that confused look on his face because he knew what was behind the whole thing.

She tried to combat the unwanted conclusion. "Aunt Ginny was nothing to him. Why should he, as soon as he was out of the Army, get himself mixed up in some plot against her?"

She had resorted to that argument often enough from the first. It was Bob himself who had refuted its logic tonight.

CHAPTER EIGHTEEN — 1947

"I can't believe it." Martha shook her head. "Here you are planning to take a job in the fall. It seems no time ago that you were a little bit of a thing coming to visit us and following Bob around the place."

"Anne's given that up," Bob remarked. "There hasn't been a sign of following me around since I got home last year."

He was lounging on the porch glider and smiled at the girl in the old friendly fashion.

She met his gaze equably. "I'm past the age for that sort of thing."

"Certainly," Martha agreed. "Let the men do the following."

Not Bob, though, was Anne's thought. She couldn't let herself think of him as more than a family connection; not since Aunt Ginny died.

Martha wanted details about the job. Anne gave them to her, personnel work, Washington, looking at the older woman and yet seeing out of the corner of her eye the long figure on the glider.

She had seen Bob a few times during the past year on her infrequent visits home from New London. Her aunt's death hadn't been mentioned. Bob was content to keep it in the background. A clear conscience would have led to a question or two as to whether or not she had found out anything else or reached any new conclusions. He was being consistent, of course. He had warned her not to talk about it. The deeper it was buried the better satisfied he was. . . .

"I'm glad I'm leaving Kinnelly for good in the fall," she thought next. "I don't want to be anywhere near Bob or Uncle Wally."

Martha Howard was also considering the girl's departure. "We'll miss you, Anne," she said. "That's one thing I don't like about your job. It takes you away from Kinnelly."

Bob didn't say he would miss her too, Anne noticed. He didn't say anything.

It was Wally who spoke. "That's what I tell the child. On the other hand, what is there for her here? The town hasn't much to offer a young woman. Naturally, though"—he divided a beaming smile between the two women—"Anne knows she must look on this place as home. She'll always be welcome here."

Anne looked at him without expression. He had been saying that since she arrived yesterday and told him about the job in Washington. He meant to convey the exact opposite. The house, part of her whole life, wasn't home any longer. Uncle Wally was master. She was here on sufferance.

All at once tears burned against her eyelids. She blinked them back and felt forlorn. She had no home. Her education was completed, and Uncle Wally was eager to thrust her from the nest.

She looked at her uncle again. He didn't like her. He never had liked her. A hodgepodge of memories rushed in on her, little things that proved the sudden realization true. It was because of her mother; she had heard her elders drop a word or so about it. Uncle Wally had been in love with her mother, and her father had cut him out.

That was only half of it. He resented what her mother had done, but she was her father's daughter too. He hadn't liked her father either.

Anne let the others carry on the disconnected conversation of people who had known each other a long time and are content to let silences fall in the quiet of a June evening.

She was back in the past, the day in the orchard when she had been hidden behind the hedge. Her father had hit Uncle Wally and the hatred the latter showed had terrified her. She remembered it still and always would. She was how old then? She was six, because she was wearing the blue bathing suit Aunt Martha had given her on her sixth birthday. That was the summer her father was drowned. His death must have occurred only a few weeks later. . . .

Uncle Wally hadn't been quick enough in going to her father's assistance. Bob had been there too, swimming out beside her and slowing down because she was with him. He had told her to go back. But he needn't have waited for her. He was a fast swimmer and perhaps could have reached her father in time to save him. . . .

Was that fair to Bob, though? Wouldn't anyone hesitate to swim away from a child of six out beyond her depth? Wasn't it too late anyway, by then?

Anne closed her eyes, the better to visualize the never-to-be-forgotten scene. Her father had gone under by that time. But Bob could have been diving for him sooner if he had gone ahead. . . .

The girl sighed. All year in New London she had been able—most of the time—to keep this thing out of her thoughts. And here it was again, the moment she was home.

If only there were someone she could talk to about it; someone she could trust.

Wally was saying, "Yes, I think Alfred will be agreeable. His lease runs out in November. And with Anne gone for good, I'd be rattling around here by myself. It should work out nicely."

"With Anne gone for good . . ." He was indeed pushing her out. It needn't be just because he disliked her; it might be that he still had in mind the slip he had made to her about the bottle. . . .

When the girl was unpacking her trunk the next morning she came upon it. She held it in her hand and looked at it. "I ought to smash it to bits," she said to herself. "Then I'd be rid of it for good."

That wasn't the way to get rid of it, however; it would be worse than ever then. She locked it in a drawer. "I'll be taking it with me when I leave in the fall," she reflected. "Wherever I go the damn thing will be going with me . . . I wish it were September now."

Actually she didn't wish anything of the sort. She was renting the cottage on the Cape this summer and staying in Kinnelly. Why was she staying? She made no attempt to deceive herself. She was staying because Bob was here and this was the last summer she would be near him. Once she was living in Washington she would come less and less often to Kinnelly.

Wally offered to go to the Cape with her to open the cottage. Ginny had been dead nearly a year and nothing had ever come up about her death. He no longer worried about the bottle; still it was odd for it to have disappeared like that. . . .

So Wally accompanied his niece to the Cape. She watched him at the cottage. It wasn't like last year. He didn't make a systematic search, but he fidgeted about, going at random over ground already covered.

A half-formed purpose took shape and hardened in the girl. "I'm going to do something about it," she thought. "I'm going to find out, once and for all."

To whom, though, did you turn when you were inexperienced and needed help? Aunt Mary was too old, her health not good; Aunt Martha was Bob's mother. . . .

Anne considered various relatives and friends. No one seemed just right. She wished she could trust Bob. He was older, he'd fought in the war, he'd been to lots of places; he was intelligent; he'd know about ways and means that didn't occur to her.

She reminded herself that Bob was on the other side, on Wally's side. That was how it was. She'd loved him all her life, but he was on the other side, and if she went on with this she might learn something about him that would darken her whole future. . . .

No matter what she found out, however, it would be easier to bear than the present torment of doubt.

It was Dr. Harshbarger on whom she finally settled as a confidant.

When the cottage was ready for the tenants, Anne left the keys next door and started back to Kinnelly, her uncle beside her in the car.

They were both preoccupied during the drive home. The girl was rehearsing what she would say to the doctor; Wally was again a prey to last year's uneasiness. He studied his niece's profile as she drove. The medicine cabinet was the proper place for Ginny's medicine to have been kept, and Anne had been the first to go into the bathroom that other time. He had made the unlucky blunder of asking her about the capsules. . . .

What a nuisance the child had become! He had never wanted her around in the first place. It had been Ginny's and Henry's doing that he had had her on his hands all these years. . . .

There was no need to worry, really. In the autumn she'd be gone. Once she was in Washington he'd find ways enough to discourage visits from her and to make it plain that she must no longer look on his house as home. Then Alfred and he would settle down together. . . .

Wally let his mind turn to the future. Two months

more and he'd be free of his inconvenient niece, the last of them to complicate his life. He'd have Alfred's companionship. . . .

After all, Anne's courage failed her when she was in Dr. Harshbarger's office. She began with an imaginary sore throat. It had developed yesterday, she said, and was still bothering her today. The doctor examined her throat and found nothing the matter with it. He wrote out a prescription for a gargle that she was to use if it became sore again.

The girl sat back in the chair and answered the doctor's questions about her graduation and future plans. He had been the Howard family doctor since before the time when she was born; he had known her since her infancy. His dark eyes rested on her with kindly interest. There was a store of knowledge and experience inside his white head for her to draw on.

And yet she couldn't tap it. He had gone to school with Uncle Wally and Aunt Ginny. Face to face with him, she couldn't talk about the medicine bottle and her uncle's search for it. It was too grave a charge to present on such slight evidence.

Angry with herself, confused, Anne made the best start she could. She spoke of having been to the Cape and of renting the cottage. "Aunt Ginny left it to me, you know," she added.

That brought her aunt's name into the conversation. "I didn't feel like going there without her this summer. We always went together."

Dr. Harshbarger nodded. He hadn't liked Virginia Howard himself, but he was prepared to accept

Anne's affection for her since it was she who had reared the girl.

Anne continued haltingly, "It was so sudden—the way she died. I haven't got used to it yet. If—we'd been home—and she was sick for a while—and you were taking care of her—it would have been different." Her face felt hot. This was ghastly.

"You never know with coronary attacks. They can come without warning."

"But she took good care of herself . . . and that other attack wasn't severe." Anne's head was lowered. Without raising it, she looked at him from under her brows. "Weren't you surprised yourself that she went so quickly?"

The doctor ascribed her high color and hesitant manner to grief and was mildly surprised that a personality like Virginia's could have inspired so enduring an affection. He set about reassuring the girl that her aunt's death could have occurred just as it had anywhere, any time.

The bottle stayed in Anne's handbag.

Restlessness sent her to the river later in the afternoon. She was in a mood of despair. She had botched the whole thing with Dr. Harshbarger and couldn't go back to him again.

On the riverbank she was approximately where she had been the night her father drowned. The fireplace was at her left, crumbling into ruins. After Henry's death family picnics at this spot had been discontinued. But they still kept a rowboat, and the oars were hung from hooks on the underside of the dock. Anne went for a row, let the boat drift in midstream, and sat with her chin in her hands. It was all to be gone over another time.

She went back to the night of her father's death and looked again at Uncle Wally emptying the flask into the sink and rinsing it out. The impression of secretiveness and haste grew in her.

The flask became entangled with the bottle in her thoughts. Her father had drunk from the flask. He had come in from swimming, unscrewed the cap, and drunk . . .

Anne pressed her hands to her head. What was she started on now?

She looked up Dr. Trail's name and address in the telephone directory. She had heard of him in some association with a police case. He had made some sort of examination and analysis that led to the detection of a murderer.

His offices in town were handsome and imposing and bore the impersonal stamp of the interior decorator who had furnished them. They had nothing in common with the comfortable shabbiness of Dr. Harshbarger's quarters in a wing of his home.

Anne found the impersonal atmosphere reassuring. She was early for her appointment and sat in the waiting room reviewing her story. She wouldn't beat around the bush this time. She would come straight to the point.

Dr. Trail was a youngish man, as handsome in an impersonal way as his surroundings. He stood up when Anne entered his consulting room and indicated a chair.

She was placed across the wide desk from him. He sat down and said, "Well, Miss Howard?"

The bottle was already in her hand and she held it out to him. "I came about this."

"Yes?" Dr. Trail took the bottle and read the label.

He had never seen her before. He knew none of the principals involved. It wasn't at all difficult to give him the story. She talked slowly, wanting to bring out every detail in chronological order, because he wasn't, she sensed, a man who would be patient with verboseness or repetition. She told it well. Bob came into it and there was no hesitation or special inflection given to his role in it.

At the end Dr. Trail took off the cap of the bottle, shook out the capsules, and opened them. With the tip of his little finger he tasted the contents of each one.

His glance flicked over her. "They're all seconal."

"So were the ones I took to the laboratory," she said.

He was looking thoughtfully into the bottle. "You said your aunt had been perfectly well, that after she cried out and you went to her she refused her capsules. She said she'd taken one already?"

"Yes."

"How long did she live after you went to her?"

Anne was careful, going back in her mind to everything she had done that night: the call to the doctor, the trip to the bathroom for the medicine, the glass of water, waking her aunt Mary, rubbing her aunt's legs . . .

"Perhaps ten or twelve minutes," she said.

"Now, let's go through her symptoms again."

241

The girl recited them for the second time. The numbness, the complaint about pins and needles in her legs, the fact that she couldn't see, the sense of suffocation.

They seemed to suggest something to Dr. Trail. He went to a shelf, pulled out a book, and consulted a page of it.

Back at his desk, he sat looking at her. He must know that there were patients in his waiting room, but he was unhurried. Anne saw that she had gained his full attention. She could relax in the knowledge that she was no longer alone with the problem.

The doctor linked his hands on the desk. "Of course, Miss Howard, what we're considering is murder, done either by your uncle alone or in collaboration with the young man you mentioned. Perhaps you'd better tell me a little more about the family background. It doesn't seem that your suspicions would have sprung full-grown from what you've told me; in other words, you were prepared to believe the worst. Wasn't there something that happened before your aunt's death?"

Anne found herself going back to the quarrel in the orchard; then, before that, to the hearsay of her uncle's courtship of her mother. Less careful now of chronological order, she went on to further hearsay that indicated bad feeling between the two brothers. She returned to the orchard, including Bob in the scene. Her eyes closed once, briefly, against the memory of his anger at her father. The flare-up of the boy he had been had merged into the hatred her uncle had shown. Then she told about the picnic at the river, Henry drinking from the flask and all the rest of it.

The doctor was silent for a space, turning the bottle over in his hands, his look measuring her. "How old are you, Miss Howard?"

"Twenty-two."

"You're young to be mixed up in a thing like this. If there's anything in it and any way of proving that there is, it's a police affair, you know. And your own uncle."

Anne returned his look steadily. "Yes, I know. But nothing could be worse than not being sure." She hadn't meant to tell him, a stranger with a dispassionate air, about her love for Bob; but unexpectedly she did, concluding, "Above all, I've got to find out where Bob stands in this. He means much more to me than my uncle."

Dr. Trail nodded. He held the bottle up and studied the film of powder inside it. "Your aunt's symptoms, the numbness and tingling, suggest aconite—if anything. It's a very slim chance, but we can have the bottle tested for a bit of it having filtered out of the capsule she took that night. If the test is negative, I can't see what else you can do."

"I have to find out," Anne said. "One way or another."

Dr. Trail was contemplative. "Does your uncle have any idea of what you're doing, do you think?"

"Oh no. There's no way he could learn about it."

Her confidence didn't communicate itself to the doctor. "You talked to the young man you're interested in," he reminded her. "If he's in it too, why wouldn't he have told your uncle what you said?"

A vision of Bob and Uncle Wally with their heads together conspiring against her—it was unthinkable. "No," she said decisively. "It's out of the question. Bob wouldn't. Besides"—Anne found firmer ground for her objections—"Bob told me to forget about it, and I said I would. That was nearly a year ago, and I haven't mentioned it or done anything about it since. Why should either of them expect me to revive it after all this time?"

"Well . . ." Dr. Trail nodded acceptance of the premise. "I guess you'll be all right then." He rose. "I'll have the tests made as soon as I can arrange it. It may be a day or so. If you'll leave your telephone number, I'll call you when I hear anything."

He was frowning a little as he watched her walk out of his office. Couldn't her position be dangerous? Of course the time she had let go by without making any move negated that angle to some extent. . . .

The thing was, she hadn't much of a case. It had impressed him to the point of taking action, but that was because of the way the girl carried conviction. Her facts were flimsy enough.

Dr. Trail decided that discretion was the proper course. Without more to go on, he couldn't have stirred up a hornet's nest by advising a young woman like her to leave her uncle's roof immediately.

Anne hadn't told him about her talk with Dr. Harshbarger. Nothing had come of it. It seemed irrelevant to her.

CHAPTER NINETEEN —

"You've been in town?" Wally inquired at dinner.

"Yes. I looked for a bathing suit but I didn't get one." Last year it had been a street suit she invented to account for an afternoon in town, Anne remembered. "I couldn't make up my mind whether I wanted a one-piece or a two-piece." She didn't look at her uncle. "Don't be so edgy," she admonished herself. "Dr. Trail's name isn't written on your face."

Lena brought in the roast and said, "Betty Jensen called you, Anne. She said to tell you a crowd of them is driving to the shore tomorrow for the day and did you want to go."

Wally commented, "That will make a nice trip for you, child."

She wouldn't go. Dr. Trail had said a day or so, but suppose he needed to reach her? She met her uncle's eyes. "I don't think I'm interested. I'd have to wear that old bathing suit of mine and Betty's such a fashion plate."

Lena, at the door to the kitchen, contributed, "You look better in that old suit of yours than Betty Jensen'd look if she spent a fortune on hers."

She went on to the kitchen. "The bread, please," Wally requested. "Indeed, I think you should go tomorrow. You've been home two weeks and you're not seeing your friends. . . . Lena calls it moping."

"But I don't feel like going!" Anne was too emphatic. She added in a quieter tone, "I've been working quite hard these last few months. I feel like moping around—if that's the way Lena and you want to describe it."

"You must suit yourself, child." Wally spoke amiably. There was no reason for the girl's uncomfortable thought that he was looking at her in any unusual way.

Sunlight shone through the windows at the west. But the room was long and narrow and the table was out of its range. They faced each other in comparative dimness across the dark wood, a small gray man and a girl with burnished hair.

He was watching her. For a moment Anne wondered if he could have followed her to Dr. Trail's office that day. He couldn't have, though; she had had the car.

Yet whenever she raised her eyes she found his resting on her. Lena went back and forth. Anne could look out the windows at the sunlit summer evening. It was absurd that her heartbeat should quicken.

Then she discovered that, like her, Wally was

making only a pretense of eating. Bringing in dessert, Lena scolded, "What's the matter with the pair of you? My good dinner gone to waste."

Anne said lightly, "It's the hot weather, Lena. It spoils our appetites."

That was the wrong thing to say. It wasn't hot. The thermometer's highest reading had been seventy-five and there was a pleasant breeze.

Lena's sniff expressed incredulity. "Where do you want coffee?"

"Shall we have it right here at the table, Uncle Wally?"

Anne was glad he nodded. She wanted to escape his scrutiny, not to prolong the time she must spend with him while they drank coffee on the porch.

There was strawberry shortcake for dessert. It was easier to get it past the knot of nervousness in her throat than the main dishes had been. She poured coffee, and as she was pouring it Wally said casually, "I happened to run into Dr. Harshbarger at the Center today. We had a little chat— Be careful, child!"

The coffee spilled over the side of the cup at Anne's involuntary start. She sat looking at him, the color running out of her face.

"Sorry. I'll get a clean saucer." She got up and went to the china cabinet. By the time she was back at the table she had regained self-control. She would accept the challenge—if that was what it was—he offered.

Anne handed her uncle's cup to him and said, "I saw Dr. Harshbarger the other day about the sore throat I had. We were discussing Aunt Ginny."

"So he told me." Wally's high, thin voice was without inflection.

Anne couldn't seem to keep the conversation on the unstrained level she wanted to maintain as she added, "We talked about her death; how sudden it was."

She must do better than that. She waited until she was sure of a more even tone before she said, "Haven't you always found it strange that she died like that, Uncle Wally?"

He repeated the doctor. "That's the way coronary attacks are." He sighed softly. "One moment Sister enjoyed the fullness of health; the next moment she was cut down."

A slight smile touched his mouth. Then she saw the cup shake a little in his hand as he raised it to drink. The smile left his mouth. It was pinched with the knowledge of her purpose.

The girl had been trying to give her uncle the benefit of the doubt, but certainly supplanted it as they looked at each other. He had killed Aunt Ginny . . . Her father too. There was something out of kilter in him, the way he looked at her. . . .

She pushed back the chair and stood up.

"You haven't finished your coffee, child," Wally reminded her. His soft dark eyes went over her without seeming to see her. They were empty. He might have been sightless.

"I don't want any more." Anne left the table.

In the safety of her own room she gradually became calmer. The feelings of dealing with an insane man surrounded by an aura of malignancy dissipated somewhat. There was still a residue of the uncle she had always known left in him.

Dr. Trail had asked her if her uncle had any suspicion of what she was doing. He meant, of course, that it could be dangerous. . . . Well, Uncle Wally knew now that she was doing something, but he had no way of knowing what action she intended to take. What had she said? Quiet at last, Anne went through the exchange at the table. She hadn't, after all, said very much. Nothing conclusive. It was all right for the time being. She had Lena here in the house with her and she would lock her bedroom door at night. . . .

The girl hadn't seen Bob since the day after her return from New London. When he stopped by with his mother after dinner that night she went downstairs. Her behavior, she thought, was perfectly normal as the four of them sat talking on the porch.

Apparently it wasn't so normal, however; Bob kept eying her, and the girl's taut nerves turned his speculative gaze into a repetition of what had gone on with her uncle.

Wally took Bob across the lawn to show him, he said, what the Japanese beetles were doing to the rose bushes. Anne watched the two men. They stood close together, so that to her their attitude was confidential; and once Bob looked toward the porch.

When they were back he said, "Want to take a little drive, Anne? I'm low on cigarettes and I want to get some."

Go for a drive with him? At its best it could only mean that Uncle Wally was sending him out to question her; at its worst it could mean . . . anything.

They were counting on the fact that he was her long-time idol. Anne's cheeks burned and her "No!" was explosive. They glanced at her in surprise. She amended the refusal hastily. "No, thank you. I'm rather tired. I'd just as soon stay here."

Bob's eyebrows appeared to be permanently elevated as he looked at her.

"Aunt Martha, wouldn't you like a cold drink? Some ginger ale, perhaps?" Anne sent a smile to the older woman.

"Why, yes, I would, thank you."

Bob followed the girl to the kitchen. He sat on the edge of the table and watched her take ice cubes and ginger ale from the refrigerator. She collected a tray and glasses, asking him if he would have water or soda with liquor. Her cheeks were still scarlet; dilated pupils made her eyes seem darker than they were. Bob thought she was especially attractive in her agitated state. "What's troubling you, Anne?" he asked gently.

"Nothing." She filled the last of the glasses on the tray. "There, it's ready. Will you take it out to the porch for me, please?"

"Yes." He came to her. "Anne . . ."

She couldn't immediately try to pull herself free. She couldn't help responding a little to the first kiss she had ever had from him. He held her close, kissing her lips and face. "Anne . . ." he said again.

The dream was over a year ago. How could she think it had come true tonight? Uncle Wally must have said, "Play up to her, boy. You can do anything with her. You know how she's always felt about you."

Anne pushed hard against him with the flat of her hands and broke away. "You think—but I'm not—it isn't going to be that simple——"

Bob stood back, looking at her with narrowed gaze. "I don't know what you're talking about!"

"Oh, yes, you do! You—ever since last year—— Oh, what's the use?" Tears filled her eyes. She ran from him.

He remained where he was for a moment. He said slowly and with bewilderment, "For Christ's sake," and picked up the tray.

Several minutes passed before Anne came downstairs and joined them on the porch. She sat down beside Martha, as far away from Bob as she could get.

He made no effort to take part in the conversation carried on by Wally and his mother. He was dwelling on the scene in the kitchen. It would have been pleasant to linger over how good it had been to have Anne in his arms; but it was her abrupt withdrawal, the accusation and anger in what she had said, that must be straightened out first.

He smoked, looking at her averted face and at Wally. The older man's glance kept going to his niece. It was a probing glance, and Anne had said something about last year. . . .

But Bob refused to connect the glance with what the girl had said. The sense of obligation to Wally was too fixed in him. It couldn't be that business about the medicine bottle, he told himself. Anne had never mentioned it except that one time. She had accepted his verdict that it was no more than one of her uncle's foibles. . . .

He measured Wally, rocking in Emma Howard's chair, feel close together and set precisely in front of him. Like an old maid, Bob thought. The man undoubtedly was a queer little jerk. But he was kindhearted and well-meaning.

A whole year later Anne couldn't have come upon anything new associated with the bottle. The issue was as dead and buried as the aunt who had inspired it. . . .

Wally Howard sat at a window of his room. He was in pajamas and had put out the light. From the window he had a view of the orchard, a wedge of the back yard, and part of the barn. The moon had risen, and in the foreground, off from the rear of the house, a round, dark shape loomed. It was the old well that hadn't been used since early in the century.

He lit a cigarette. The flame of the lighter showed melancholy on his face.

Anne would have to go. Before she brought ruin on him or even black suspicion, he would have to kill her.

All her life she had been a child who had to notice everything. And she had been conscientious, as she was in this case when she should have let well enough alone.

Dr. Harshbarger, that afternoon, had commented on the girl's devotion to Ginny. Fool! That was the interpretation he put on her questions about the suddenness of Ginny's death. The doctor had called her conscientious too, assuming that Anne was worrying that they had left something undone that might have saved Ginny.

He himself had still been worrying a year later about the medicine bottle. Quite rightly, it seemed. The chance meeting with the doctor had been providential.

Thinking it over, Wally felt safe in believing that the girl had done nothing yet. The questions she had asked Dr. Harshbarger indicated that she wasn't sure of what she knew. But the minx had the bottle. The slyness of her, darting into the cottage ahead of him and taking it! And afterward, with that innocent look on her face, acting as if she hadn't done a thing. She must have understood that he was hunting for it. . . .

Ever since she had been mulling over her knowledge, reluctant to take any steps, perhaps, because she had so little to go on; and because of the close blood tie between them.

He should have been able to rely on the latter factor alone. He couldn't, though, he reflected bitterly. It would slow her down, but it wouldn't stop her in the end. He had tolerated her presence in the house; he had tried to be kind to her; and this was his reward. . . .

It was pointless to sit pondering the depths of the child's ingratitude. He must think of a plan.

It was a difficult assignment. Anne was young, healthy, and on her guard. This last was the hardest element of all to overcome. It was much simpler, he brooded, to kill when there was no suspicion.

His cigarette was smoked and he put it out in the ash tray on the window sill. Hands clasped around his knees, Wally looked out at the dark shape of the well. It went down—a hundred feet, wasn't it? It was very deep, anyway.

If he could push Anne into it late at night and lead the search for her the next day . . .

It began to be more than a random possibility. Wally's mind grew busy with it. He'd have to catch the girl unawares, hit her with something so that she'd be unconscious when he threw her in . . . Head injuries would later appear to be the result of the fall . . .

He was brought up short by the realization that there was no plausible way to account for the well being open. In the old days it had merely had boards laid across it. But during Anne's childhood Ginny had had the top permanently sealed, for fear the child might fall into it. That was nonsense. The well had once been the family's sole water supply and none of them had ever fallen into it.

It was just like Sister to have had it sealed. She had always made an unnecessary fuss over Anne.

The well was ruled out, then. Wally's thoughts turned unwillingly to his father's gun. Since he had known the bottle was missing the gun had been in the back of his mind. He shivered. All these years it had been waiting for another victim.

God, how he hated the sight of blood! How could he bring himself to use it?

The method of using it was there. The outlines of it were filling in even as he was fighting off the memory of what it had done to his father.

Wally shrank deeper into the chair. He couldn't face a shooting. He couldn't. That was all there was to it.

But an hour later no other likely method of getting rid of Anne had presented itself. He dared not risk poison again. It wasn't as if his niece were ever ill or in the habit of taking medicine. . . .

Wally ended up by being exasperated with the girl. Sly, persistent, interfering creature that she was, she ought to die! But it wasn't right that she should be putting him under such a frightful strain in accomplishing her death.

Before he got into bed he went downstairs and out on the porch. Tonight again there was mist rising from the pasture. Not so thick as it had been the other times, but wispy, like trails of smoke curling above a vast cooking pot.

CHAPTER TWENTY —

After an uneasy night Anne was awake early. The cool air of yesterday was gone, the morning hot and still. She unlocked her bedroom door when she heard Lena going down the stairs. Uncle Wally hadn't left his room during the night. Her sleep had been so light and broken that Anne knew she would have heard him if he had.

At breakfast he was matter-of-fact. The girl was disconcerted by the absence of undercurrents and the blandness of his smile. The contrast to the atmosphere at dinner last night was so great that she was at a loss to account for it.

When breakfast was over Anne looked at her watch and thought of calling Betty Jensen to say that she had changed her mind and would go to the shore. She didn't do it, however, because she wasn't quite that far removed from last night.

The day had to be filled in with some activity. She considered a visit to her aunt Mary and then remembered that the latter was away on a vacation in Canada. What she finally did was to telephone a girl with whom she had gone to high school and get herself invited to lunch.

That would take her out of the house for a few hours, and it wasn't, she reflected, like being absent for a long day at the shore. She'd be back by the time Dr. Trail's office hours began, in case—just in case—he did call her today.

After lunch, in the hottest part of the day, Anne drove home. Bob was there when she arrived. He had on swimming trunks, and his chest and shoulders were tanned and broad and solid looking. Finding him on the porch with a drink in his hand, Anne wanted nothing so much as to lean against that solidity and leave her cares upon it.

The next moment the girl was annoyed with herself for having such a thought. It was a form of emotional weakness that she had to control. She had to get over the feeling she had for this man whose eyes, very blue against his tan, were seeking hers and trying to find out what she was thinking. He was on the other side. The boy he had been years ago had disappeared—if he had ever existed, when you considered the day in the orchard and her father's drowning.

Anne said, "Hello, Bob . . . Uncle Wally," her voice flat.

"Hello." Bob finished the drink and set the glass down. "I'm playing hooky this afternoon. I came over to see if you'd go swimming with me."

Her father had gone swimming with Uncle Wally and him. . . .

She wouldn't do it. Not ever. But she was careful

to make her refusal sound unconcerned. "No, thanks. I've got a lot of things to do. You and Uncle Wally will have your swim without me."

Bob hadn't asked the other man to accompany him. He wanted to get the girl away by herself, where he could have a talk with her and get to the bottom of whatever it was that she had on her mind. "You can't do anything in this heat." He was pleasantly insistent. "Forget about it and come for a swim."

The more he insisted the more positive Anne's refusal became. Her gaze went from one to the other of the two men, banded against her. She left them and went upstairs, and saw them going toward the river together after Wally had got into his trunks.

Her room was hot with afternoon sunshine pouring into it. She lowered the blinds and took a shower. After that, going to a drawer for fresh underwear, she discovered that her room had been searched. Neatness and care had been used, but still her belongings weren't quite as she had left them.

Anne sat down on the bed slowly. The bottle was safely out of the house, of course. Uncle Wally—she could see him, swift, silent, thorough, making the search—had been put to all that trouble for nothing.

She remembered that Bob had been here at the house, too, and covered her face with her hands. . . .

Later that afternoon, immovable on the bed, the girl contemplated flight. She could get away now, while they were both at the river. She need never come back.

She wouldn't be routed like that, however. That was probably what Uncle Wally wanted. She wasn't afraid of him. Lena was in the house. As long as she

258

kept her door locked at night, when she was defenseless in sleep, she was a physical match for her slight, elderly relative.

The other reason for staying—Bob, whom she loved—went unacknowledged. There was the faint but obstinate hope that he wasn't her uncle's partner, no matter how guilty he seemed; there was, equally unacknowledged, the bleak sense that stay she must because away from Bob nothing counted. Washington and the job she would have were a dreary, lonely prospect.

Dr. Trail didn't call her. Anne heard the men return from their swim and Bob drive away. She heard her uncle in his room getting dressed. Then a car came into the yard and she heard Bob's voice again. It was time for dinner. She dressed and went downstairs.

Wally had invited the younger man to have dinner with them. He sat between the girl and her uncle in Aunt Ginny's old place at the head of the table.

It was like last night. But Anne talked a lot on this occasion. She told long pointless anecdotes about the girls at college and laughed too frequently and too excitedly; and tonight there were two men to watch her instead of one.

Wally was benign while he studied Anne and decided that she was near the breaking point. Her nerves weren't equal to the stress. Once his nerves had been like that. Now he could do anything. He had learned to protect himself and had faced unpleasant situations in doing it. The girl would have to learn too.

Wally remembered that she wouldn't live to learn.

The telephone rang during dinner and Anne hurried to answer it. It wasn't Dr. Trail. It was a young man asking for a date. She accepted immediately. It would get her out of the house.

"Then shall I stop by for you at about eight-thirty?" he inquired.

"Eight would be better," Anne told him. That meant half an hour less to be with Bob and her uncle.

"Fine. I'll be there."

The girl hung up and went back to the table. To Wally's question about who had called she replied brightly that it was someone for her and that she was going out. A sidewise glance at Bob showed her that he was scowling. It indicated that her plans for the evening didn't coincide with whatever he had in mind for her.

She was quite right. After dinner Bob had intended to separate her from Wally. "If I have to drag her off by the hair," he had thought grimly, more and more disturbed by her overwrought gaiety and laughter.

They had coffee on the porch, as they usually did in summer. Anne's tongue still ran on uncontrollably. At quarter to eight she terminated an involved tale about a friend who was trying to find an apartment in Washington and went upstairs. She was at her dressing table putting on lipstick when she looked up and saw Bob in the doorway. He had come quietly. She hadn't heard him.

"What do you want?" she demanded.

"I want to talk with you. My God, you'd think I

was a leper the way you're avoiding me. I had to follow you up here."

The girl's hands shook, closing the lipstick and replacing it in her handbag. Bob advanced into the room.

"Don't you dare come in here! I'll scream if you do!" Lena was downstairs; Lena would hear her.

Anne was on her feet, sliding quickly along the wall toward the open door. "I'll scream if you come another foot nearer to me." She was no physical match for Bob. It was he whom she must fear, not Uncle Wally.

Bob's face showed outrage and went red under the tan. "You little fool, what do you think I came up here for?"

She was backing out through the doorway, sending a glance over her shoulder to make sure that her uncle wasn't there to help him.

Bob was putting on an act, of course, now that she had shown him she wasn't such easy prey after all. Still, the interpretation of her behavior that the act included gave Anne pause. She went on less forcefully, "I know why you came. Don't try to pretend. But I can take care of myself. I——" She broke off at the sound of a car stopping outside. It was her date arriving. She was safe. She ran for the stairs.

Bob was gone when she returned home that night. It was after midnight and the house was in darkness. Anne gave the young man her latchkey and waited for him to press the light switch just inside before she stepped over the threshold. The hall was empty; Wally Howard wasn't waiting there with a club.

She smiled and shook hands. "I've had an awfully nice evening," she said. "Thanks a lot."

The young man hadn't had a nice evening. The girl had been silent and distrait the whole time. He had reason to feel injured; she could at least kiss him good night.

But she evaded his embrace and hurried toward the stairs. "Don't go yet." She looked back at him with an air of helpless femininity. "I hate going upstairs late at night by myself," she confessed. "Would you mind waiting here until I turn the light on in my room? It's silly of me, isn't it?"

The young man's sense of injury ebbed. She made him feel strong-minded. "Not at all," he said indulgently. "Go ahead . . . No, wait a second." He came to the foot of the stairs. This time, out of gratitude for his presence, Anne let him kiss her. The kiss was meaningless; he wasn't Bob. She went upstairs, and when she had her light on came back to smile and wave at him. He let himself out of the house.

Anne looked under the bed and in the closet and locked the door. She undressed and was putting on pajamas when someone rapped lightly on the door. Her heart achieved the impossible: it turned over completely. "Yes?" she said.

"It's I, child." Wally sounded excited. "We've had a prowler! I was at my window with the light out when I saw a man slip across the yard. I called to him and he ran away through the orchard. I don't know what to make of it."

Neither did the girl. She stood with one hand on the bedpost. Ordinarily the thing to do would be to open the door and discuss the affair. She didn't move. It was a ruse designed to get her out into the hall.

"Did you call the police?" she asked.

"No. It happened only a few minutes before you came in. By the time I'd got over my surprise the fellow was away through the orchard."

Perhaps it wasn't a ruse. He didn't ask her to open the door. He said, "Well, I thought I'd tell you. Tomorrow we'll have a look around for traces of our visitor. Good night."

"Good night, Uncle Wally."

The light out, Anne stood at a window. The moonlit night was clear; yard and orchard showed no lurking figure. After a few minutes she went to bed, frowning in thought. There hadn't been a prowler about the place as far back as her memory could take her. . . .

In the morning, after breakfast, Wally brought Lena and his niece outside to show them a blurred impression in loose soil at the edge of the orchard. "That must be the fellow's footprint," he said. "He ran through the gap in the hedge here."

Lena shook her head. "You'd better call the police . . . although I don't know what good it will do. Ab Whitehead would come out and look around and scratch his head. He'd say, 'Well, you see any more of him, let me know right away.' " She imitated the Kinnelly police chief's nasal drawl.

Anne and Wally laughed. The latter protested, "At that, I don't know what else he could do."

"You can bet your bottom dollar he couldn't catch a prowler if the man ran right under his nose." Lena turned back to the house and Anne followed her.

Dr. Trail didn't call. After lunch, with her uncle safely downstairs in his cellar workshop, the girl called the doctor's office.

It was a Wednesday afternoon. The doctor's nurse informed her that he had no office hours that day and could be reached only in case of an emergency.

Her vague, persistent uneasiness couldn't be called an emergency, Anne thought. She left her name and hung up.

It wasn't as hot as it had been yesterday. She took the car out. She might as well go for a drive, visit someone, do something.

There wasn't anyone she wanted to see, however; she wasn't in a social mood. She took the road past Wolf Creek and drove miles out into the country. A right fork brought her back to Kinnelly late in the afternoon. Still the girl didn't want to go home, and decided to pay her aunt Martha a visit. The older woman was a restful and undemanding companion.

"Stop lying to yourself," Anne said aloud, turning the car toward Martha's. "It's Bob you want to see."

No woman had ever been as abject as she, was her next thought. No matter what Bob did or had done, there it was: she loved him.

Martha was alone, reading on the front porch. "I'm so glad you came," she said cordially. "And I'm going to insist on keeping you for dinner." She laughed. "Having Bob back has spoiled me. I don't like eating by myself."

"He's away?" Anne tried to sound as if Bob's presence or absence was of no consequence.

"All day. There's the dairy farmers' conference in town, you know."

The girl, who hadn't known, said "Oh yes."

"They're going to discuss another rise in milk prices," Martha continued. "It's simply scandalous the way operating costs have gone up."

She stood up. "Let me get you a cold drink. While I'm inside I'll call Wally and tell him I'm keeping you for dinner. You will stay, won't you?"

"Yes, I'd like to."

"There's root beer and ginger ale. Which will you have?"

"What I'd really like is a highball," Anne stated. "And quite a large one, too, please."

"Why, yes," Martha said. "Of course."

They had salad and rolls and iced tea, the kind of a meal that women enjoy on a warm summer evening. Anne dried the dishes for her aunt, and afterward they sat on the porch watching the sun slide below the horizon and the purpling fall of night.

Martha said, "Just think, it's nearly a year since Ginny died. It's gone so fast." She spoke of how unexpected Virginia's death had been; of how unbelievable it had seemed when Wally called at dawn to tell her about it.

Suddenly Anne was sobbing with an abandonment that was too wild, Martha knew, for grief a year old. She had cried like that herself long ago because of the way Douglas had died. It was an outlet for pressure grown too acute to bear.

She went to the girl and dropped down on the arm of the chair, stroking the auburn hair. "It can't be as bad as all that," she said sympathetically when Anne's sobbing lessened. "Tell me about it. Perhaps I can help."

Anne leaned against her and then drew away, mopping at her eyes with a handkerchief. Aunt Martha was kind, but she was Bob's mother first of all.

"I'm just tired." She sat up straight. "And talking about Aunt Ginny brought it all back."

The telephone rang while the older woman sat in silence wondering what she could say that would lead the girl to unburden herself. She felt sorry for Anne, who had no one to turn to, actually, but Wally Howard.

"And he isn't so close to her," Martha thought, rising and going into the house to answer the ring. "He lacks something . . ."

It was good red blood Wally lacked, she was deciding as she picked up the receiver. He always had lacked it; she'd never thought of it in quite that way before.

"Hello?" she said.

The subject of her reflections was at the other end of the wire. "Hello, Martha," he greeted her. "Is Anne still with you?"

"Yes."

"Well, will you tell her the Curtises are here? I know she wouldn't want to miss seeing them, and Eve says they're leaving the end of the week for Lake Louise."

"I'll tell her."

Martha returned to the porch and delivered Wally's message. "But if you don't feel like seeing the Curtises, you can make some excuse," she added.

Anne, her tears dried, stood up. "I'll go," she said.

She wanted to go. If she stayed here, Aunt Martha

would start asking questions; and Eve, she thought, could be persuaded to spend the night with her. They would drive Mrs. Curtis home, and Eve would come back with her and she'd feel quite comfortable in her mind with the other girl across the hall.

She thanked Martha, went out to the car, and drove home.

Only one light was burning. Anne saw, driving around in back of the house. That was in the kitchen, where Lena was sitting with her newspaper. The Curtises must be on the porch with her uncle.

Apparently the two women had walked over, since there was no car in the driveway. Thinking that they had, Anne didn't go on to the garage but left the car in back of the house. She would be using it to take Mrs. Curtis home if Eve was to stay.

She went into the living room through the french doors at the side, calling out, "Hello!" rather more loudly than was necessary because she found it disquieting to go into the dark stillness of the room.

Instead of a gay response from Eve Curtis, it was her uncle who spoke out of the dark quite near at hand. "Hello, child," he said.

Anne cried out in panic and backed toward the doors. The light switch clicked and the ceiling lights went on. She blinked at Wally in the sudden brightness and explained, "You—startled me."

"Did I? I'm sorry."

"Where are the Curtises?"

"They couldn't wait. Eve said she'd call you to-morrow." He didn't add that the Curtises had come and gone before he used their visit as an excuse to bring Anne home.

The french doors were just behind her. But the girl stifled an impulse to flee. Panic died. After all, Lena was within call in the kitchen. The situation wasn't changed from what it had been all along merely because the Curtises weren't here. Her glance rested on the heavy carved book ends on a table. If her uncle moved toward her, she would pick one of them up.

Wally showed no sign of any action. He stood in the doorway, one hand still on the light switch, the other in his pocket.

Anne sat down and turned on the lamp beside the chair. She picked up the evening newspaper and looked at the front page. In a few minutes she'd say good night to her uncle and Lena and go upstairs to her room. Tomorrow she'd put an end to the affair; if Dr. Trail didn't call her in the morning, she would go to his office in the afternoon.

"We don't need the overhead lights, do we?"

"No." Wally pressed the switch and went to a chair.

The girl pretended to read. Her uncle sat, knees together, his hands resting on them lightly, palms down.

His attitude reminded Anne of something. She commented on a news item so as to have a reason for glancing at him. He looked alert, shoulders and back straight. He looked . . . on guard. That was it. Ready to spring on the instant.

The house seemed to grow quieter. The one lamp she had turned on cast a glow of light around the chair, but outside the glow it only pushed the dark back toward the corners of the room.

Wally sat outside it. What light there was on him caught his glasses, making them round shining blanks above his drawn-in mouth.

Anne turned a page, folding the paper over with care, unhurriedly. Lena would be going to bed soon, the girl thought. She was sitting in the kitchen rocker at present, reading her own copy of the paper. That was why the house seemed so still. It was a large house and there were only three of them in it.

Anne forced her mind away from the idea that the house watched and waited as silently as its master. She concentrated on its size. No wonder Aunt Ginny had wanted to rent it and take a smaller one. That was good sense. Why, the three of them left were lost in all the space.

She remembered that her uncle hadn't wanted to leave it. He clung to the house. He had argued and pleaded with Aunt Ginny not to lease it . . . And then Aunt Ginny had died. In time not to sign the lease. That was the whole story, of course.

It was a curious mental lapse on her part not to have given any thought before this to Uncle Wally's reason for killing his sister. She had been too obsessed, perhaps, by the deed itself to look for the cause. . . .

The newspaper made a small rustle in the stillness. It rustled because her hands weren't steady. Uncle Wally must hear it too.

Anne laid it on the table, stood up, and simulated a yawn. "I'm dead," she announced. "I think I'll go to bed." Her voice, at least, was under good control. She added. "After I've had a drink of water."

Lena was in the kitchen. The girl wanted a glimpse

of that stout, shapeless figure; its commonplaceness would abolish fear. Once she saw Lena she would be able to breathe again, shedding the notion that the very air was oppressive.

"I guess I'll have a drink of water too." Wally rose and followed her into the hall.

Faintly, light from the kitchen revealed the stairs, the low chest, the chairs flanking it. Anne's scalp tightened with the consciousness of her uncle behind her, close on her defenseless back. It was the essence of horror. She would never be able to reach the light shining into the dining room through the open kitchen door.

Lena was there. The reminder strengthened her. She crossed the dining room and stopped short at the threshold of the kitchen. It was empty. Lena's unread newspaper lay folded on the table. The elderly servant had gone to bed, apparently, without reading it. She was in her attic room two flights up and might as well not be in the house for all the use she was to Anne at the moment.

The bright light, however, and the immaculate order of the familiar room lifted the girl's courage a notch. She walked to the sink with a firm tread. Next to it was the door to the back porch, closed and locked. While she let the water run to get cold, Anne looked at the bolt. There wouldn't be time to throw it back and escape into the shelter of the night before Wally could reach her. He was standing right at hand by the table.

She went to the pantry for a glass, filled it, and turned sidewise to face her uncle. "Lena went to bed early."

"Lena?" She could see his eyes now, wide and staring behind the glasses. His pale face showed a little color. "Oh, didn't I tell you about Lena?"

"No." The syllable came from lips gone dry. Anne moistened them with a swallow of water.

"Well, her sister called this afternoon. It seems she had a fall. The doctor thinks her ankle is broken. So I gave Lena permission to spend the night with her."

The glass slipped from the girl's hand and crashed in the sink. She jumped at the sound and took a step toward the back door.

"Don't do it, child," Wally advised her gently. "I've got a gun."

CHAPTER TWENTY-ONE —

Anne leaned against the sink. She tried to speak and couldn't. The gun was in her uncle's hand, a heavy-looking, old-fashioned weapon. All the while it had been in his pocket; she had been trapped from the moment she stepped through the french doors. She, who had been so sure she was a match for him, never thinking of a gun.

Anne tried again to speak, and her voice came squeakily. "Uncle Wally, put that away."

"Oh no. I have a use for it. You thought you were being very clever and discreet, didn't you, while you were poking that long nose of yours into my affairs?"

"What affairs? What do you mean?"

"You know quite well what I mean. It's high time we had a talk, child." He gestured with the gun. "Walk ahead of me to the living room."

He wasn't going to kill her; not immediately, anyway. The thought made it possible for Anne to go through the dining room and hall. Wally turned off the kitchen light behind him and was close at her heels. The front door invited her to make a run for it. It was closed and sure to be locked, though. In her terror she might fumble the lock. And outside, with her uncle right behind her, there was no one to hear her scream. The McArdle house was all the way around the bend of the road, and along the road itself there was scarcely any travel at this hour.

Anne walked ahead of Wally to the living room. There were windows on the three sides of it.

"Shut the windows," he directed. "No, you can leave the back ones open. We'll be here awhile and we'll need air."

She shut the other windows. The back pair left open brought a glimmer of hope that instantly faded. They faced the orchard and river. You could scream your lungs out either of them and only the night birds and fishes would hear you.

"Sit down," Wally said next, motioning her to the far end of the room away from the open windows. He pulled a chair over to the spot where he wanted it and raised the window blinds behind it. When the girl was seated moonlight shone in on her.

Her uncle turned out the lamp she had lighted half an hour ago. "That's better," he observed with satisfaction. "Now there's no chance of interruption from late callers."

He sat down, drawing up a chair to face hers a few feet away. "This is fine," he said. "Put your hands on the chair arms, child . . . Good. I can see you perfectly. You'll not be able to get away with any tricks."

The moonlight reached him, gleaming dully on the

gun as he laid it across his knees. He was relieved to get it out of his hands. The touch of it unnerved him, and its weight would steady his trembling legs. The whole thing was most unpleasant. It was a pity he couldn't shoot the girl at once and get it over with.

Anne fixed her gaze on the gleam of metal. It did her good to tell herself it couldn't be happening. He wouldn't pick up the gun and shoot her. He was her own uncle who had known her since her babyhood. . . .

She mustn't think of Aunt Ginny who had been his sister . . .

"I'll have to keep calm," she thought. "I can try to talk him out of it."

"Uncle Wally," she began. "I'm all at sea. Why are you doing this?"

"What have you done with Sister's medicine bottle?"

Oh, that blessed bottle! Anne relaxed all over, her head against the chair back, her hands loosening their grip on the arms. The bottle would save her.

She discarded pretense. "Uncle Wally, I took the bottle in town with me the other day. I left it with a doctor who is having tests made. I told him what Aunt Ginny's symptoms were and he said she might have been given aconite . . ." Terror was vanquished. Words poured from her. ". . . and he's to call me when he has the report. I told him the whole story about you, your name, everything!" Anne's voice hit stridency. She stopped for a moment and added in triumph, "If anything happened to me, you wouldn't be able to explain it away, you see. The doctor would know."

Wally was silent, going over what he had just heard. It presented a dismaying complication. He hadn't thought she had gone so far. Perhaps she was lying? No, her words had the ring of truth. The mention of aconite, for example; she couldn't have made that up.

He said flatly. "I don't believe you. Who is this doctor?"

"It's Dr. Trail. In town. He has offices on Queen Street."

Well, he knew the doctor's name. Confidence swelled again. Hadn't everything worked out to his advantage when Henry and Ginny died? He would go to see Dr. Trail tomorrow. He would cry and look old and broken by the tragedy that had befallen his niece. He would say that before she died she gave him a message to be delivered to the doctor without the least delay; she said, "Tell Dr. Trail I was mistaken." He would profess bewilderment as to the meaning of the message.

There was the bottle, of course, in the doctor's possession. But providence favored his enterprises. The tests wouldn't show any aconitine.

If providence deserted him? He would still profess bewilderment. After all, he hadn't put up the prescription. For that matter, Ginny could have killed herself, inserting aconitine in one of the capsules herself. . . .

And what proof would the doctor have? None. There'd be only hearsay evidence with Anne dead, and that would be inadmissible in a court of law.

The thing could become highly disagreeable, though, thanks to her troublemaking. If she'd had an ounce of decency in her she never would have gone to a stranger with such a nasty tale about her uncle, her own flesh and blood. But in the end all she had accomplished by her disloyalty was to make the need of killing her stronger. . . .

Rage thrust out the other considerations as Wally dwelt on his niece's behavior. One should be able to count on one's family standing by one in any tribulation. Anne's criminal betrayal of this principle—as old as the human race, he reminded himself—removed the taint of murder from what lay ahead. He was no more than her executioner.

His hand went of its own volition to the gun. Her punishment ought to overtake her at once.

The feel of the metal made him draw back. The wiser course was to follow the original plan. His rage against his niece rose still higher because there was relief in postponing action.

"The time, child?" he shrilled.

Anne lifted her arm so that moonlight shone on her watch. "It's twenty minutes to eleven."

"Ah. Then you have something over an hour left."

"What?"

"Around twelve o'clock I shall shoot you; that's late enough to wait." He savored the explanation, extracting revenge from every word. "I shall shoot you and call the police. I'll tell them you woke me and said there was a man moving around downstairs; that I took the gun and went down in the dark to surprise him; and that you went the other way by the back stairs. I was keyed up, I'll say, and shot you, thinking you were the prowler. I'd almost as soon Lena was in the house, so that I could get her on the scene immediately. But as it is, I have her believing that there was someone around the premises last night."

She couldn't die like this at the hands of a madman. Her voice was bodiless: "You can't get away with it, Uncle Wally. You'll go to the chair."

"Of course not!" he snapped. "How can you even speak of such a thing? It will go off without a hitch, I tell you."

"Dr. Trail . . ."

"I'll take care of him." Wally told the girl what he meant to say to the doctor.

Anne recalled the keen intelligence of the doctor's face and knew her uncle would never put the story over with him. What good would that do her, though? "I'll be dead," she thought despairingly. "It won't help me if he's charged with my murder."

"Uncle Wally . . ." She flung out her hands beseechingly. "Please don't do it. Please! I'll go away. I'll leave tomorrow for Washington, and I promise you I'll never come back, I'll never say a word to anyone."

He shook his head. "I couldn't trust you. I wouldn't know an easy minute." He added severely, "You have only yourself to thank for the fix you're in. Ever since you were a little thing you've shown a stubborn streak, a tedious persistence about having your own way. You've brought it all on your own head, child."

The sense of unreality heightened in Anne. She sat here and discussed her murder with her uncle.

No, he wasn't Uncle Wally any longer. As soon as he knew she suspected him of killing Aunt Ginny he had changed utterly. The madness in him had risen; its hideousness was out in the open. And he was right; she had done it herself. If she had let Aunt Ginny's death alone, the delicate mental balance he was able to maintain wouldn't have been put to any strain. . . .

He was going to kill her. He meant to do it; he waited here, his face a white oval in the moonlight, until the hour was late enough to make plausible the story he would offer. She was young but she was to die.

Anne thought about Bob. She said, "Aunt Martha won't believe you—nor Bob," and waited. At least she would find out about the man she loved; the uncertainty about where he stood in the affair would be resolved.

Wally laughed a little. "Martha and Bob? They'll feel sorry for me. They won't suspect anything. If they did, I have my hold over them . . ." he told her in detail about Douglas Howard's death.

The account of it set Anne free. It fitted in perfectly with Bob's strange behavior. She could love him as much as she pleased.

For a moment joy surmounted the desperateness of her position. Then the thought came that it made no difference to her now that Bob wasn't implicated in her aunt's death. She was going to share Aunt Ginny's fate. . . .

But she wouldn't die like this! She wouldn't sit here meekly and wait for a madman to choose the moment of her dying.

The girl eased herself forward. Wally's hand went to the gun. He was reading her mind, for he said, "Don't move, child. If you force me to, I'll shoot now." He was in deadly earnest. Anne huddled back in the chair.

Her uncle smiled. "That's better. Life is sweet, isn't it? You can't really believe it's almost over. You're hoping that something will turn up to save you in the next hour. Well, keep on hoping."

The white clear light fell on them as they watched each other. He was too far away to lift her foot suddenly, kick the gun from his knees, and run screaming out into the summer night; run all the way to the McArdles, to sanity and the prospect of a long life.

Wally found the silence trying. The minx had no business to sit there, her eyes dark in her white face, staring at him. It was a trick of light, of course, but she had never resembled Henry more closely than she did at the moment. She was just like her father—her abominable father who had hounded him until he was compelled to take steps against him.

There had always been someone to hound him. Sister too, with her bossy ways . . . And when at last he was rid of both of them, Henry's child, whom he had never harmed, had, by sly, underhanded means, set about destroying the peace he had achieved. She was Janice's daughter as well as Henry's, and for her mother's sake he would have let her go her way if she hadn't interfered with him. After all, he had forgiven her mother long ago when she lay dead.

Wally felt driven to tell the girl what his thoughts were. Too many ghosts were crowding the silence. He said, "I didn't want this to happen, child. I loved your mother. For her sake I wished you well even though you aren't like her. You're entirely your father's daughter."

"And you killed him." It was a statement Anne regretted as soon as it left her lips. The more knowledge she revealed the more dangerous he must find her.

She regretted it more when she saw how infuriated he became. He pounded the chair arm. "Damn your father," he cried. "Damn him to hell, where he surely is! He ruined my life, child, that fine father of yours. I hated him for the things he did to me. I couldn't fix a flower for the table, I couldn't take a sign of interest in how Mother did the cooking, I couldn't show fear of anything without him poking fun at me! And he was so big—you don't remember the size of his fists—you don't know . . ."

He grew more and more incoherent; about her father; about Sister; about Mother, who had been so blind she loved Henry best. Henry was responsible for her death because of the way he treated Wally and drove him into protecting himself. . . .

He was raving. Anne closed her eyes to shut out the sight of him, his mouth working with the vehemence of his speech. His forefinger pointed at her. Somehow she was to blame for everything that had happened to people long dead and thronging back to the dark house. The tomblike quiet of it conjured them up. Any moment they would begin to tell their side of it. . . .

Ancient terrors shattered the girl's hold on reason and fortitude. Her grandmother's frail ghost, her father struggling in the river, her aunt fighting for

280

breath—Wally brought them back into the room. He was talking to them, not to her.

"Sister, before you were in your teens Mother used to warn you about your arrogant ways. She told you they'd bring you to grief, didn't she? Mother knew . . ."

His babble was an icy wind stirring her hair at the roots, raising goose flesh on her body.

He wasn't talking to Aunt Ginny when Anne could bear to listen again. It was another sister, the baby sister, dead for nearly sixty years. He had killed her, he said; and then there was something about power and God that was too irrational to understand.

He came back to the present and to her long enough to say that she had no right to upset him like this. He looked at her and seemed to see her. Anne was emboldened to suggest that too much blood had been shed already; if he would let her go she would never tell anyone about him.

The mention of blood sent him off again. But now he lowered his voice to a whisper. "They knew that the sight of blood turned me sick . . . They thought they knew why . . . They never suspected the truth about Father."

He had seen his father die, Anne remembered. Grandfather Howard had cleaned and loaded his gun and it had gone off and killed him right before his son's eyes . . . It was the gun that lay on her uncle's knees. . . .

Wally's gaze followed hers to the metal with its dull glint. He touched it tentatively. "I never dared to tell them the truth. My dear mother worshiped him. If I'd told her she would have held it against me—but,

281

child, you don't know how I wanted to tell! I used to feel I would burst with keeping it to myself."

Uncle Wally had been only a small boy at the time of the tragedy. Anything, however, was possible in the boy who had become this kind of man. Anne said slowly, "You killed him, you mean. It wasn't an accident after all."

"Oh yes, it was! I never meant——" His tone went heavy with suspicion. "What do you know about it? It was long before your time."

"I guessed it." She spoke soothingly. "Or, rather, you told me yourself just now."

"I don't care if I did!" He shrieked defiance that ended in a sob. "You'll never be able to tell, and I've kept it to myself too long; far too long, child. But it was an accident. Father used to laugh at me too, for being afraid. And the gun was on the dresser. I picked it up to show him that I wasn't too cowardly to handle it . . ." He reached out a hand. "It went off itself! A boy, nine years old . . ."

Tears ran down his face. He brushed them away. "Even if he hated someone, a boy of nine wouldn't shoot deliberately. Even if he hated—as I hated Father . . ."

Hypnotically, the girl's eyes were fastened on him. He added softly. "I was well brought up, child. Mother was a wonderful woman. A real Christian. She taught us our prayers as soon as we could talk. . . ."

Bob Vanderbrouk got home that night a few minutes before eleven. He put the car in the garage and crossed the yard to the house. He yawned when he was letting himself in through the back door. It had been a strenuous day, and after dinner he had got into an interminable conversation with a group in the hotel lobby. He yawned again. He'd get to bed right away.

Martha changed his mind for him. She put down her book when he entered the living room and told him about Anne's distraught weeping when Virginia Howard's death was mentioned. "I almost called her a little while ago," Martha concluded. "She's been in my thoughts ever since she left. But I decided it was too late to disturb them."

Bob stood frowning into space for an interval before he said, "I guess I'll take a run over there."

"They're probably in bed!"

"Not if the Curtises are with them. You said that was why her uncle wanted her to come home."

"Yes, but that was nearly two hours ago."

He was out in the hall before Martha could voice any further protest. He rushed through the house and across the yard to the garage. He didn't ask himself what need there was for haste as he backed out the car. That thing about Ginny Howard's medicine—he'd let it ride and ride—he'd been a damned fool, he reflected, swinging out into the road.

"I'll get Anne out of bed if I have to," he resolved, the car gaining speed until the needle hovered around fifty. "I'm going to find out what it's all about." He took the road that paralleled the river, the road that had been a dirt track when Wally used to ride on it.

Moonlight glistened on the roof of the Howard

house. Its windows were dark. It had dignity and orderliness, set back from the road behind a white-painted fence.

They were all in bed. Bob slowed down, but the sense of urgency in his mission evaporated. He'd look an awful fool hammering on the knocker to rouse the household.

He drove past. The man and the girl inside watched the headlights disappear. Hope flamed and died in Anne, and her uncle let out suspended breath hissingly.

When the McArdle farm was behind him Bob pulled over to the side of the road. He sat wrapped in thought. Anne—undoubtedly asleep in the house back there—meant a lot to him. She meant everything that a woman could mean to a man. He'd been slow to admit it, nor had he had any encouragement from Anne. She kept out of his way. He'd had other problems to consider, too, after five years in the Army. So, although he'd known something had gone wrong between them—he must even have known, subconsciously, what it was—he'd let it go. He'd thought that as soon as Anne was home for good they'd get it straightened out.

Had he let it go too long?

Too long for what?

He backed the car around. The way Anne had looked the other night when he kissed her . . . Only for a moment, though . . . Then she had run from him. . . .

Bob parked the car at the bend. Failing the sensible course of going home, the next best one was to make no disturbance by knocking at the door but to slip around to the back of the house and call to the girl under her windows.

Her car was behind the house. Trained by Virginia to put things in their places, it was unusual that Anne should have left it there. Bob opened the door and glanced inside quite as if he expected her to be sitting in it.

Her bedroom windows were open. He called to her again and again. Wally's room was beyond hers. He'd be awake, wanting to know what was going on. Older people slept less soundly than the young, Bob remembered, and lowered his voice. But there was no response from either bedroom.

He walked around the kitchen ell to the opposite side of the house, his footsteps noiseless on the grass, the sense of something wrong nagging at him.

He heard the sound of talking in the living room and stopped short at the open windows, standing close to them to look inside. It was Wally who was speaking, and that was Anne facing him, moonlight on her hair, her face shadowed.

Bob let out a breath of relief and called out cheerfully, "Hello! What are you two doing sitting there in the dark?"

Wally leaped to his feet and spun around to face the windows. Anne cried, "Look out, he's got a gun!" and ran for the hall.

She had the door unlocked and was pulling it open by the time her uncle fired, not aiming, just pulling the trigger. Bob was flat on the ground when the bullet broke through the screen and was up instantly, crouching low, close to the protecting walls of the house, as he raced toward the front where the door slammed behind Anne.

The room rocked around Wally Howard. Fifty-two years ago he had last heard the explosive, deafening noise of a gun close at hand. Fifty-two years ago he had fired it and his father had sagged to the floor, blood streaming down his face.

Wally's hands went up, threshing the air. Someone was screaming and wouldn't stop. It was he who was screaming, and in a moment Mother would come running as she had before.

She came and dropped to her knees, cradling that awful, bloody head in her arms. "He's dead!" she cried. "Oh, Lord above!"

The gun lay on the floor beside his father. It had been jerked out of the boy's hand when it went off. . . .

The boy was he. Wally screamed, "Mother! Mother!" She didn't answer; she didn't even glance at him.

And then his father did a monstrous thing. He got to his feet and developed a multitude of faces. Blood streamed down each of them and the room was no longer dark. Brilliant lights flashed around them. They were looking at him from the walls and ceiling.

He couldn't, he wouldn't stand for such a horror as this! No one could be asked to stand for it. It had to be blotted out. Wally raised the gun to his head and fired.

Outside in the comforting shadows of a large maple tree Anne was crying in Bob's arms, holding tighter and tighter to him, when the second shot blasted the stillness of the night.

MYSTERIES TO KEEP YOU GUESSING
by John Dickson Carr

CASTLE SKULL   (1974, $3.50)

The hand may be quicker than the eye, but ghost stories didn't hoodwink Henri Bencolin. A very real murderer was afoot in Castle Skull—a murderer who must be found before he strikes again.

IT WALKS BY NIGHT   (1931, $3.50)

The police burst in and found the Duc's severed head staring at them from the center of the room. Both the doors had been guarded, yet the murderer had gone in and out *without having been seen*!

THE EIGHT OF SWORDS   (1881, $3.50)

The evidence showed that while waiting to kill Mr. Depping, the murderer had calmly eaten his victim's dinner. But before famed crime-solver Dr. Gideon Fell could serve up the killer to Scotland Yard, there would be another course of murder.

THE MAN WHO COULD NOT SHUDDER (1703, $3.50)

Three guests at Martin Clarke's weekend party swore they saw the pistol lifted from the wall, levelled, and shot. *Yet no hand held it*. It couldn't have happened—but there was a dead body on the floor to prove that it had.